High school superstar meets old-school baller...

He watched the guy walk to the far edge of the concrete, as far away from the basket as he could get, take a deep breath, let it out, then glide toward the hoop, long legs eating up the distance.

Then he was in air, somehow exploding in slow motion, like it wasn't just the kicks he was wearing, like he was Air Jordan himself, the ball high in his right hand until he threw it down from so far above the rim it was as if he had fallen out of the sky.

Catching the ball with his left on his way down before it even hit the ground.

He wasn't done.

He bounced the ball to himself, high as he could, elevated, caught the ball as he started to come down. Only he didn't throw it down right away. Instead he tucked it into his belly like he was a running back in football, somehow stayed in the air as he went underneath the iron, then reverse-slammed it home.

Ten, Drew thought.

Perfect dag-gone ten.

BOOKS BY MIKE LUPICA

Travel Team

Heat

Miracle on 49th Street

Summer Ball

The Big Field

Million-Dollar Throw

The Batboy

Hero

The Underdogs

True Legend

QB 1

THE COMEBACK KIDS SERIES

Hot Hand

Two-Minute Drill

Long Shot

Safe at Home

Shoot-Out

TRUE LEGEND

MIKE LUPICA

TRUE LEGEND

PUFFIN BOOKS
An Imprint of Penguin Group (USA) Inc.

PUFFIN BOOKS
An imprint of Penguin Young Readers Group
Published by the Penguin Group
Penguin Group (USA) Inc.
375 Hudson Street
New York, New York 10014, U.S.A.

USA / Canada / UK / Ireland / Australia / New Zealand / India / South Africa / China
Penguin Books Ltd, Registered Offices: 80 Strand, London WC2R 0RL, England

For more information about the Penguin Group visit www.penguin.com

First published in the United States of America by Philomel Books,
a division of Penguin Young Readers Group, 2012
Published by Puffin Books, an imprint of Penguin Young Readers Group, 2013

THE LIBRARY OF CONGRESS HAS CATALOGED THE PHILOMEL EDITION AS FOLLOWS:
Lupica, Mike. True legend / Mike Lupica. p. cm.
Summary: Fifteen-year-old Drew "True" Robinson loves being the best point-guard prospect in high school basketball, but learns the consequences of fame through a former player, as well as through the man who expects to be his manager when True reaches the NBA.
[1. Basketball—Fiction. 2. Teamwork (Sports)—Fiction. 3. Conduct of life—Fiction.
4. High schools—Fiction. 5. Schools—Fiction. 6. African Americans—Fiction.]
I. Title PZ7.L97914Ts 2012 [Fic]—dc23 2011047155
ISBN (hardcover) 978-0-399-25227-3

Puffin Books ISBN 978-0-14-242650-0

Edited by Michael Green. Designed by Amy Wu.

Printed in the United States of America

9 10

For my wife, Taylor, again. And our amazing children:
Chris and Alex and Zach and Hannah.
This is the work I always dreamed about doing,
and the life I dreamed about having.

ONE

It started with him thinking he'd seen a ghost.

A basketball ghost.

A ghost in a gray hooded sweatshirt, no writing on the front or back, one that seemed way too warm even for a Southern California night, and almost two sizes too big for his long, skinny body. The guy was six three or six four, easy.

He was wearing baggy blue jeans, the carpenter kind with pockets, faded nearly to white. They seemed to hang on him, too, like they were about to fall down around his ankles.

He had old Air Jordans on him, old-school classics, high-top red-and-blacks.

Drew Robinson recognized the shoes right away because he always did. Nobody knew old-time basketball kicks better than he did. He knew these shoes because he'd just bought a pair for himself off Classickicks.com, where he went for sneaks out of the past you couldn't find anywhere else.

The ghost also had a beat-up Lakers cap pulled down low over his eyes, so Drew couldn't get a good look at his face. But he could see just enough to tell he was a light-skinned brother—not as light as *me,* Drew thought—out here on the half-court that nobody ever used at Morrison Park, not during the day, certainly not at night, not when there was a lighted full court for you to use at Morrison. This one here was lit only by the moon, up high in the sky tonight.

Usually Drew Robinson—known as *True* Robinson by now to everybody who followed basketball—didn't see anybody using either of Morrison's courts when he arrived after midnight. Whether the courts were lighted up or not.

There was nothing fancy about this park. If you were a good player looking for a game, you went to Shoup Park over in Woodland Hills. Drew just liked the full court at Morrison, liked being able to walk the couple of blocks here from home, knowing he could work out in peace, work on his game, without everybody watching every move he made.

Watching him the way they had been for a while now, even before he and his mom moved out to Southern California, from the time back in New York, when they'd first started calling him the best point-guard prospect since—pick a name—Chris Paul or Derrick Rose or John Wall. All the new ones that had come along since they used to say Jason Kidd was the best pure point to ever come along.

Even Stephen Curry, one of Drew's favorites, who came out of Davidson as a shooter and then showed the NBA the way he could pass the ball.

LeBron Junior, some people even called Drew that, not because of the way he played or looked—he was half a foot shorter than the real LeBron—but because he'd made that kind of name for himself before he was even a junior in high school.

Truth was, he played more like Steph Curry, and looked like him even more.

Drew (True) Robinson and his mom lived here in Agoura Hills, just over the line from Westlake Village, where his school—Oakley Academy—was. Quiet town, at least as far as he was concerned, with this quiet playground in it. He could come here when Morrison had emptied out and remember, every single time, why he'd loved playing ball so much in the first place.

Before it became a ticket to dreams he didn't even know he had.

A basketball friend of his from New York, from 182nd and Crotona in the Bronx, Shamel Williams, a boy with no parents and no money, barely getting by on his grandma's welfare check, had told Drew once that the best thing about basketball, the thing he loved about it the most, was that it could even make him forget he was hungry sometimes.

"Playing ball just fills me up in another way," Shamel said. "You know what I mean?"

Drew had never gone hungry. His mom had always been a professional woman; her last job in New York was working as a secretary at a real-estate company in Forest Hills. There'd always been food on the table.

Still, Drew knew what Shamel was saying to him.

Basketball had always filled him up, too.

Morrison gave him that feeling when he had the place to himself. Only tonight he was sharing the place with this ghost player, the ghost doing things on this bad court that made Drew think he was in some kind of dream.

Dribbling the ball like a Harlem Globetrotter, like Curly Neal, who Drew had met at Madison Square Garden one time, like the ball was on some kind of string. High dribbles to low, both hands—Drew wasn't even sure at first whether he was righty or lefty—behind his back, through his legs. He was making it look easy, like he wasn't even paying attention, like he could've been doing something else at the same time, checking his phone or texting on it.

Then off the dribble came the spin moves and shots, the guy working the outside, draining shots that would have been three-pointers easy if there had been a three-point line on this old used-up court instead of just potholes and weeds.

And the guy—ghost—hardly ever missed, even though there were these moves he made, ones that started with his back to the basket, moves like a blur that should have made it impossible for him to pick up where the rim was when he came out of them.

Here under the light of the moon.

Unreal, Drew thought.

Because how could it be anything else?

Drew saw all this without being seen himself. He was hidden by a palm tree, his own ball resting on his hip.

He watched the guy walk to the far edge of the concrete, as far away from the basket as he could get, take a deep breath, let it out, then glide toward the hoop, long legs eating up the distance.

Then he was in the air, somehow exploding in slow motion, like it wasn't just the kicks he was wearing, like he was Air Jordan himself, the ball high in his right hand until he threw it down from so far above the rim it was as if he had fallen out of the sky.

Catching the ball with his left on his way down before it even hit the ground.

He wasn't done.

He bounced the ball to himself, high as he could, elevated, caught the ball as he started to come down. Only he didn't throw it down right away. Instead he tucked it into his belly like he was a running back in football, somehow stayed in the air as he went underneath the iron, *then* reverse-slammed it home.

Ten, Drew thought.

Perfect dag-gone ten.

Who *was* he?

This ghost who seemed as happy to have Morrison to himself as Drew always did.

Only tonight neither one of them was alone.

And even though Drew knew he should be moving on, *getting* on with his own business, he couldn't stop watching the show.

Drew thought, *I'm watching him do things with a ball that only I'm supposed to do around here.*

Not so much the dunking things, even though Drew could definitely throw down with flair when he wanted to. No. It was the shooting, the ballhandling, like the ball was one more *part* of this guy, same as his arms and legs.

Drew watched now as the guy dribbled away from the basket,

like he was on his way into the trees himself. Then he gave one quick look over his shoulder before casually tossing the ball up over his head, a crazy no-look shot that floated through the night and hit nothing but net. Even the forgotten courts at Morrison had nets.

Drew couldn't help himself, couldn't restrain himself any longer.

He started clapping, like he was at some kind of outdoor concert.

"Man," Drew said, laughing, "I got to get some of *this*."

Then he said, "You want some company?"

Half thinking to himself that if the guy turned around as Drew stepped out from behind the tree, an old hooper like this, he might recognize Drew, might see that the voice calling out to him belonged to True Robinson.

Himself.

The guy didn't turn around.

He just ran.

Didn't want to know who was talking to him, didn't care, just ran and picked up his ball like it was the most valuable possession he had in the world and disappeared into the night.

"Wait!" Drew yelled after him. His voice sounded as loud as thunder.

But just like that, the guy was gone.

As if he'd never been there at all.

Drew walked onto the empty court, out to where the guy had just made that last shot. He was replaying it all in his head, as a way of telling himself it hadn't been a dream, that he hadn't imagined it all: the moves the guy had made. Flying through the air, almost floating, jamming the ball down so hard and yet somehow making it hit the string so soft.

What was that ghost movie he used to watch over and over when he was little? He'd made his mom buy it after she rented it for him one time when he stayed home sick from school . . . *The 6th Man*. That was the one. About this kid who died and then came back later in the movie to help out his little brother. Both of them basketball players.

Or maybe this was something that happened to you when you moved this close to Hollywood, and were one more person thinking your whole life was a movie just waiting to happen.

Enough of that, he told himself, all these night thoughts running through his head. The guy was probably just another Southern California homeless.

But what homeless guy could hoop like *that*?

Enough, Drew told himself again. *Just play.*

He had realized a long time ago that there was no problem in his life that couldn't be fixed by playing.

Drew made up his mind then, just like that, like one of his snap decisions on the court, that he wasn't going to go over to the good court and play under the lights tonight, wave to the cops when they made one of their drive-through checks of Morrison. The cops knew who he was by now, even looked out for him and got out of the car sometimes to watch him play.

But before he played, he got down on the ground to do his stretches. Another thing that made him hear Darlene Robinson's voice inside his head, his mom telling him all the time he'd thank her someday for making him do his stretches now.

Drew knew how he was going to thank her someday, the big house he was going to buy for her, one he'd already built inside his head, before he bought one for himself.

In the quiet of Morrison now, he got up and went through his basketball drills. First came dribbling, one hand and then the other. He didn't need any bright lights for those—he could make a basketball do exactly what he wanted it to do in the dark.

Before long, Drew was the one making threes from where the ghost had just made his, and Drew was the one trying to make the no-look, over-the-shoulder shot, staying with it until he did.

Harder than it looked, even though the ghost had made it seem as easy as a layup.

No dunking the ball for him tonight, even though he wanted to, after watching the guy.

He wished he could have shown the guy at least one of his best dunks, even if he was only six one for real, not the six two the Oakley Academy program said, what the newspaper and online stories about him said when he Googled himself, something he did more and more of these days.

But with the ghost guy gone, there was no one to show off for, and he didn't want to risk coming out of the sky himself and landing in some hole on the bad court at Morrison.

So he just ran from spot to spot and started making jump shots, getting hot right away, lights or no lights, feeling it, imagining himself in game situations, knowing that in half of them he wouldn't be shooting—he'd be passing, setting up his teammates, his buddy Lee and the rest of the guys.

Passing them the ball, even if they all knew he was just passing through here.

Drew was the youngest junior at Oakley, not even sixteen yet. Not even taking driver's ed. But he felt older in basketball, like he was ready for college. Already starting to narrow his choices, even though he hadn't told anybody. Kentucky maybe. UCLA if he wanted to stay home, even though Southern California still didn't feel like home. Duke or Carolina or UConn if he wanted to go back East.

The only reason he was even thinking about college, having to go through all that, was because they'd passed that rule a while back saying you couldn't go straight to the pros from high school anymore, that you had to spend one year in college. The "one-and-done year," as it had come to be called.

One reporter wrote that if Drew really was LeBron Junior—though he didn't like that nickname, didn't want to be anybody's *junior*—he should be able to go straight to the league after high school the way the real LeBron had.

Whatever.

He thought he heard something in the trees, in the dark, so he held the ball and looked around. Wondered if the ghost guy was out there somewhere right now, watching Drew like Drew had watched him.

Watching every move he made, the way the scouts did—and the college coaches and the writers and his teammates and the players on the other teams, who sometimes couldn't play their own games because they were too busy watching Drew play *his.*

And the cameras; don't forget the cameras.

It was funny, Drew thought. It had gotten to where he felt eyes on him even when there weren't any around.

THREE

He knew exactly when it had all changed for him, when people had started talking him up and wanting to watch him play.

When Drew Robinson had turned into True Robinson.

And everybody knew that, in sports, when they put a nickname on you, that's when you've really arrived.

It was when he'd played that AAU all-star game, East versus West—back when he was still East, just thirteen years old—with a bunch of other guys from his New Heights team.

The game was on ESPN, first time on national TV for all of them. Huge deal.

People in New York, in high school ball and AAU ball, had started to notice Drew that year, his freshman year at Archbishop Molloy in Queens, playing for Jack Curran, a New York City basketball legend who'd been at Molloy long enough to win more games than any high school coach the city ever had.

Then came that all-star game and the two passes Drew made that ended up as SportsCenter's number one and number two plays in their Top 10, ahead of everything else that happened in college and the pros that night.

Two passes he threw that were still getting hits on YouTube, even now.

And the funny thing was, there were at least four other passes in that game they could have gone with, if they'd wanted.

The first was one he'd been working on from the time his hands got big enough to control a regulation-size ball, one he knew he'd invented before other guys started showing up on YouTube with their own versions.

The one off his elbow.

What happened: Drew came down on the break, three on two, the defense backing up because they just *knew* something bad was about to happen to them, Drew on the fly, completely in charge of the action in front of him and all around him.

He had a Brooklyn kid from another AAU team, the Riverside Hawks, a stone-cold shooter named Ray Pope, in the right-hand corner, wide open, ahead of the play, all spotted up to make a three, waving for the ball.

Drew also had his own big dog from New Heights, DeMarcus Nelson, busting it from the left wing.

Drew knew the ball was *supposed* to go to the corner. Ray was on fire shooting the ball. He'd made his last three bombs in a row to break the game wide open.

And they'd left Ray wide open again.

Only Drew had a better idea.

He wanted to get the ball to DeMarcus as soon as he cleared traffic, let him throw one down, just because he'd earned the right, the way he'd been dominating the boards on both ends.

So what Drew did, he went behind his back with his left hand, like he was going to style the ball to Ray Pope that way.

Only as the ball came behind him, Drew pulled his right arm back just enough, used his right *elbow* to deflect the ball in the opposite direction. To DeMarcus. Whose dunk almost brought down the whole backboard, like he was trying to make ESPN's Top 10 his own bad self.

That was Drew's second-best pass of the night, at least according to SportsCenter.

Number one really *was* the one, the pass people still asked him about, just because they wanted to know how he saw everything he did and *did* everything he did on the last play of the first half.

It started simple enough. Drew was just trying to save the ball from going out of bounds, jumping in the air to save it in front of his own bench. Maybe in a real game he would've tried to call time-out from the air, because that was before they'd changed the rules. But it was an all-star game. It was on TV. Was supposed to be fun.

So why not have some?

As he got his hands on the ball, he was able to turn his body just enough to pick up the clock behind the basket, pick up where all the other players were at the same time.

Drew could always do that, from the time he was the smallest kid on Crotona Avenue, before he and his mom moved to Forest Hills. When John Calipari, the Kentucky coach, first saw him play in person, he told Drew, "Got an expression, kid. 'The great coaches can see all ten.' Meaning all ten players on the court at once. No matter where you *think* they're looking. You? You always see the other nine, no matter where you are."

What Drew saw in that moment, four seconds left in the half, was DeMarcus's man in a switch, running to cover up on Corey Miles, another big kid on the East team, who was all alone on the right side of the basket, like Brandon was a dunk or layup waiting to happen.

It left DeMarcus open just enough on the other side.

But Drew had angled his body as much as he could. So the only way for him to make the pass to DeMarcus was to fire it off the shoulder of the defender who'd switched off him to chase Corey.

Like a bank shot in pool.

A *kiss,* like the announcers said, only not off the backboard—off somebody's back instead.

The ball caught the kid just right, bounced straight into DeMarcus's hands. Another dunk. Horn sounded. Halftime at Madison Square Garden, where the game was being played, the first time Drew had been there as anything except a fan.

Like they say: crowd went wild.

So did the announcers.

"I've heard of guys having to call backboard in H-O-R-S-E!" the play-by-play guy yelled. "But I never saw anybody bank one on purpose off the other team!"

His partner said it then.

"True *that*!"

The nickname stuck.

He was True Robinson after that. Just like that, the little kid from the Bronx was big. "Almost as big as your own *head*," his mom liked to say.

Every time she did, she'd say it smiling, letting him know she was playing, the way he did with her, wanting him to know she didn't really think his head had gotten too big for him.

Drew knew better. True knowing the real truth on *that*.

Darlene Robinson was watching him closer than anybody else was. Just not seeing the same things they were. She was always getting in her points—and digs—about the son she used to have and the star she was raising now.

It was why sometimes Drew had to get away from even her.

Her eyes.

Get himself his alone time.

His phone said it was one in the morning when he was ready to walk home. Before he left, he saw the patrol car pull up. That always happened at least once at this time of night.

The car usually came by more than once.

Tonight it was the two officers Drew knew best, Archey and Delano. Archey, who was behind the wheel, rolled down the window on his side, grinning at Drew as he stopped the car.

"There a reason we should know about why you're perfecting your skills in the dark tonight?"

Delano was already out of the car, arms leaning on the roof. "You want to make sure you've got an edge if the lights ever go out in the gym?"

"Just sharpening my shooting eye," Drew said.

"Gets any sharper," Officer Archey said, "you'll be able to slice up bread with it and make a sandwich."

"No worries," Drew said. "Done for the night."

He tried to make one more over-the-shoulder shot, like the ghost guy had. Showing off for the cops.

Missed by a mile.

Drew retrieved his ball, walked toward the cop car. "Thanks for looking in on me," he said. "Like always."

Hearing his mom's voice inside his head again—he'd never admit to her how much that happened, didn't want to give her the satisfaction—the voice telling him to mind his manners with adults.

Officer Delano said, "We're just looking to work security for you once you make the league."

Drew smiled. The smile he used to save for the cameras, but was using more and more, trying to come across as nicer than he really was. "Oh, so that's it?" he said. "Not doing your civic duty, just lookin' for a piece of the boy?"

Officer Archey asked if Drew wanted a lift home.

Drew laughed. "Are you buggin'?" he said. "Next thing we all know, there'd be a picture of me on somebody's cell, getting into the back of a police car."

"But there's nobody else around," Archey said.

Drew said, "You sure?"

Delano said, "You see somebody?"

Maybe it was the way Drew had said it. Maybe cops were trained to hear things when nobody else did, even when you hadn't said anything. But Delano stepped away from the car now, looked around.

Just doing his job.

"No, sir," Drew said.

Not feeling like he was lying to the police—he still wasn't positive that he *had* seen anything more than a ghost tonight at Morrison.

FOUR

The next day, he was going to take the bus over to Mr. Gilbert's house in Thousand Oaks, just to hang before practice.

Mr. Gilbert said he never had to call first, just show up, bring friends if he wanted to, but they both knew that just meant the friend Drew needed to drive him there.

But Drew *always* called first, minding his manners the way his mom told him to. She never came out and said it, but she especially meant grown-ups who could help him.

Or maybe Drew just wanted to make sure Mr. Gilbert *thought* he was minding his manners. Even with people he liked, and he liked Mr. Gilbert, it was just part of being True Robinson. Putting moves on people out of force of habit.

So when he woke up he called and asked if he could come over later, watch a movie in the screening room or just play video games on the big screen in there, a kind of screen Drew had never seen outside a movie theater. You killed aliens on that sucker, you felt like you were in an action movie yourself.

"Mi casa es su casa," Mr. Gilbert said on the phone.

"Gotta tell you about something weird I saw last night that sketched me out," Drew said.

"Tell me when you get here," Mr. Gilbert said. That meant he was on another call—Drew could always tell. "I'm in the middle of some deep commerce here."

Meaning business. In Mr. Gilbert-speak.

Before he hung up, Mr. Gilbert said, "How you getting here? Lee bringing you?"

"He's at the dentist's today," Drew said. "I was gonna take the bus."

"Bus?" Seth Gilbert said. "My man True on a bus? I'll have Eddie come get you."

Eddie was Mr. Gilbert's all-around guy, who lived in his gatehouse, drove him when he didn't feel like driving, sometimes acted like a bodyguard.

"You don't have to," Drew said.

"I know," Mr. Gilbert said.

Then he hung up.

Drew wasn't clear how Seth Gilbert had made all his money. Just that he'd made the kind of money in his life that Drew hoped to make off playing ball eventually.

Seth Gilbert had made so much money that he and a couple of other rich-guy friends had put up the money to start Oakley Academy on about twenty acres of land in Westlake Village. The other guys, Drew had learned from Mr. Gilbert, wanted to build a high-end, college-prep-type school their kids could go to. Seth Gilbert was sending his son, Robbie, there, too, but he didn't care as much about education, Robbie's or anybody else's, as much as this:

He wanted to build one of the best basketball programs in the state.

The gym at Oakley was even called the Henry Gilbert Athletic Center. It had been paid for by Mr. Gilbert alone and was named after his father.

As far as Drew could tell, Mr. Gilbert was obsessed with two things: making more money than he already had and basketball. He bragged all the time about the kids he'd sent to big colleges from some of the AAU teams he used to run. Only these days, he had nothing to do with AAU teams, just the players of Oakley Academy.

Mostly his focus was on one Oakley player: Drew.

"He says it's about helping you get to where you need to go," Darlene Robinson had said to Drew when they first moved to California. "The way I see it, it's more about where *he* wants to go."

"*Here* we go," Drew said.

"I'm just sayin'," she said.

"Mom," Drew said, "he *is* your boss, right?"

"A good one, too. Best I ever had. But I'm not talking about the Mr. Gilbert of business. I'm talking about the *basketball* Mr. Gilbert."

She did run his office for him, as his office manager, more like his assistant. Gilbert Consulting, it was called. She and Drew had first met him at the all-star game when Drew had made his TV passes, made a name—and a nickname—for himself just like that.

Mr. Gilbert had introduced himself in the locker room, and they had gotten to talking, and it was there that Darlene Robinson had mentioned that she was thinking about making what she called a "life change" for her and her son.

Before long, Seth Gilbert had taken charge of that change, offering her a better job and a better life in California, helping them move, even cosigning for a mortgage so they could have a nicer house in Agoura Hills than they would have been able to get on their own.

Just like that, they had a new life on the West Coast. They moved in the summer after Drew's sophomore year at Molloy.

Darlene Robinson had what she wanted, and thought Drew needed, a basketball career away from the guys known as "street agents" in basketball, guys who worked for real agents and college coaches and even sneaker companies, trying to get their hooks into kids like Drew, future stars, as early as they could.

Drew knew there were street agents pretty much wherever there was a court and a game going on. But his mom had made up her mind—and once she did, you had about as much chance of changing it as of changing your Social Security number—that the worst street guys were in New York City, giving stuff to kids who had nothing, filling their heads with lies. They were nothing more than leeches and bloodsuckers, she kept telling Drew, with boxes of new sneakers in their arms and money that didn't stay in their pockets very long because they were passing it around to kids who didn't have any and whose eyes grew wide at the sight of easy money and free stuff.

Mr. Gilbert had made it all happen for them, as easy as if he'd snapped his fingers.

"Tell me again how all this helps him?" Drew said to his mom. "A hundred percent, he doesn't need anything from me."

Darlene Robinson said, "You think he's joking when he says he wants to be your manager someday?"

"What if he did?" Drew said. "It wouldn't be for *my* money. The man's already got his."

Darlene Robinson shook her head, smiling, like she was trying to be patient with a little boy. Sometimes she told Drew the only place where he could see clearly was on the basketball court. The rest of the time, he missed things that were right in front of his nose.

"You provide something more valuable to him than money," she said.

"What's that?"

"Access."

"To who?"

"Whom?"

"Okay, whom?"

"To *you*," she said. "What he wants more than anything is to be the man *next* to the man."

"Me," Drew said.

"Gives him a kind of power he could never have, no matter how much beach property he buys and sells from here to Malibu."

"He's already been real good to us, Mom."

"I'm not saying he hasn't," she said. "I just want to make sure we always know *why*. Because it's been my experience that nobody in this world ever does something for nothing."

"Yes, ma'am," he'd said at the time, because sometimes that was the only way to break free of a conversation like this, act all sweet and ma'am her, like he was breaking out of a double-team in the corner.

Now he was getting out of the Maserati Eddie had driven him over in, walking into Mr. Gilbert's house, the idea of that word—*house*—always making him laugh, because this was a lot more than a house, it was more like Gilbert World.

The first time he brought Lee here, Lee had said, "Where's the gift shop?"

That coming from somebody whose family lived in this part of Thousand Oaks, too.

There was the big main house, what Mr. Gilbert had told Drew was built "hacienda style." There was the gatehouse where Eddie lived. There was a pool house that would have been big enough for Drew and his mom to live in. And an Olympic-sized swimming pool. And a full basketball court, lighted. Mr. Gilbert had always told Drew that he could use the court anytime, day or night, whether anybody was home or not.

For some reason, Drew still preferred Morrison, maybe because it reminded him more of where he came from, not where he was going.

Mr. Gilbert was at the pool, finished with his morning swim, a

BlackBerry on the table in front of him, along with a landline phone, a pot of coffee, and a big fruit plate. He had slicked-back gray hair, Pat Riley hair, still wet from the pool. He was wearing a *Family Guy* T-shirt.

Robbie Gilbert, his only child, was sitting across the table from him, eating scrambled eggs with one hand while he texted with the other, his iPhone almost on his plate.

Drew said, “Morning, Mr. G. Morning, Robbie.”

Robbie was frowning, like whatever text he was sending or receiving was some math problem he needed to solve.

Mr. Gilbert said, “Robbie, Drew said good morning.”

Robbie sighed, his fingers still on the iPhone. “Yo,” he said, not looking up.

Then his phone, on vibrate, made a buzzing sound and he had it in his hand with blinding speed.

His dad said, “You want to have a conversation with us or with . . . ?”

“I’m just setting up something for later with the guys in the band,” Robbie said. “You know I’m in a band, right? Even during basketball season?”

Drew poured himself some ice water, not wanting to be a part of this.

“You’re referring to the band I help finance?” his dad said.

“Here we go.”

It could start with the two of them, that fast, Drew knew from experience.

Just as fast, Robbie was up, cell phone in hand. “I’m out of here," he said. He looked at his father, then Drew, and said, "I'm sure you two have a lot to talk about."

Drew said, "I didn't mean to interrupt your breakfast."

Robbie Gilbert laughed. But the sound made Drew wonder, as always, how a laugh could sound that mean. Maybe because it came out of him so loud. Robbie talked loudly, laughed loudly, and his band played loud, tuneless, heavy-metal music. Drew had heard them one time at school.

One time was enough.

"You?" Robbie said. "Interrupt us? Dude, you're family. Like the brother I never asked for."

He walked back to the main house, shaking his head, talking on his phone now, not looking back. Seth Gilbert watched him go, shaking *his* head, not saying anything.

By the time Eddie appeared to clear Robbie's plate, it was almost as if Seth Gilbert's son hadn't been there at all.

"You want me to have Eddie get you some breakfast?" It was almost like he was telling Drew more than asking.

"I'm good," Drew said.

"I gotta get some healthy food in you," Mr. Gilbert said. "You can't go through life eating your Lucky Charms and Froot Loops."

"You left out Cap'n Crunch," Drew said. "Ended up eating a whole box this morning after my mom left for the office."

"You need a nutritionist."

"I got everything I need in my cereal boxes," Drew said. "Breakfast and a great snack all at once."

He'd read one time that Derrick Rose, another one of his point-guard heroes, liked the same kinds of cereals he did.

Mr. Gilbert wanted to know why Drew had gotten up so early when there was no school, and Drew told him that not only couldn't he get to sleep last night, he couldn't *stay* asleep this morning. Then he told him about the ghost guy and how he couldn't get him out of his mind now.

"You sure it just wasn't some kid from town who looked older?"

"No, it was an old guy for sure. Not as old as you—"

Drew clamped a hand over his mouth as soon as he said it, but it was too late. "Wait, I can explain what I meant," he said.

"Please don't," Mr. Gilbert said, grinning. "It can only get worse for me."

"He was a man, is all I'm saying," Drew said. "But a man who played some big ball sometime in his life."

Seth Gilbert said, "Well, maybe you'll run into him again on one of your midnight runs." And just like that, Drew could tell he was already bored with the subject.

Drew liked Mr. Gilbert a lot, but the man had the attention span of a TV remote.

"How's the ankle?" Mr. Gilbert said now, moving on to the next thing.

Drew had tweaked his ankle at practice a couple of days ago, no big thing. He'd just been putting extra tape on it. Hadn't even felt it last night in the park.

"Better," Drew said. "When I got out there last night, made all my cuts, put my weight on it, no problem."

"I could have my orthopedic guy take a look," Mr. Gilbert said. "You've got time today."

"It wasn't even a sprain," Drew said. "I'll be good to go for all the big games after the break."

Mr. Gilbert smiled now—he had the whitest teeth Drew had ever seen.

"Kid, the next big game for you is your first one in college," he said.

"I know that," Drew said. "But Lee and all the other seniors on the team are counting on me to get them their title. And help get a couple of them scholarships, too. *And* finally beat Park along the way."

Park Prep, over in Oak Park, had always been the big powerhouse in their league. Oakley had come a long way in the six years the school had been in existence, had built a winning program and sent some kids off to college scholarships. But the Wolves still had never beaten the Park Prep Eagles.

"You keep telling them that it's just as important to you," Mr. Gilbert said, "and they'll believe you. You know why? Because they want to, that's why."

"But I do want to win as much as they do," Drew said.

Mr. Gilbert turned halfway around in his chair now, as if Drew were talking to somebody behind him. "This is me you're talking to, kid. Not some guy interviewing you that you've got to say all the right things to."

"But I *do* want to win. Same as you."

"And you keep selling that to anybody who'll listen. It'll be one more reason for people to call you a leader and a winner. Just understand that there are other priorities here, and they don't change. Stay healthy. Stay out of trouble. And what else?"

Drew smiled. "And stay close to you," he said.

"Your mom's looking out for her baby boy, too. But I'm looking out for his brand."

Drew said, "I'm a brand already?"

"Yeah, but that's not anything for you to worry about," Mr. Gilbert said. "That's my job."

Drew didn't say this next thing, but thought it:

Mr. Gilbert's talking like he's the man next to the man already.

Like the two of them already had a contract, even if nothing was written down on paper.

FIVE

Practice was held in the late afternoon, even during Christmas break.

Their coach, Billy DiGregorio, was big on being a creature of habit, even when he didn't really need to be. It was just another way for him to be the boss. In front of the other players, anyway.

He and Drew both knew it was different between them. They were more like partners.

So of course Coach ran the practice schedule for the holidays past Drew, the way he did pretty much everything else having to do with the Oakley Wolves.

Billy DiGregorio was a no-nonsense guy. Hundred percent. He had been a tough little point guard at Santa Clara in his day, way before Steve Nash went to Santa Clara. And he knew more about basketball than a lot of guys Drew had played for—most of the guys he'd played for, to be honest—but even with that, he knew the team ran through Drew, not him.

Nobody would say it, there was no point, but they both knew Drew was as much the coach of the Wolves as Billy DiGregorio was.

"You care whether or not we stay on our normal schedule over break?" Coach said to Drew the day before classes let out.

Drew had grinned. "Not nearly as much as you would if we started changing things all around, Coach. I know how you lose your mind when things get moved out of their proper place."

"The only days we'll have off will be Christmas Eve, Christmas Day, New Year's Eve, New Year's Day."

"We can go on those days, too," Drew had said to him. "There's no holidays with me, not from basketball."

"But you still remember what your mom and I tell you," Coach DiGregorio said. "There has to be more to your life than putting a ball through a hoop."

"Whatever you say, Coach."

The truth was, Drew did just enough to get by in school, keep his grades respectable. Keep up appearances. His mom would push him to do better when he'd start to slip in something, the way he was with English right now, and then he'd have to step on it.

He'd done well enough on his PSATs to know he'd be able to handle the real SATs fine when the time came. And Drew knew something else: there wasn't a college he was interested in that was going to care too much what kind of SAT scores he had, or ACT scores, what grade point average he ended up with before he left Oakley.

They just wanted Drew Robinson to come to their school for a year and fill out a stat sheet, not the college application form known as the "Common App."

Drew remembered a story he'd heard from one of his AAU coaches back in New York, about an old-time hooper named David (Big Daddy D) Lattin. Lattin had finally ended up at Texas Western, played on the NCAA champion team they did the movie *Glory Road* about, the mostly all-black team that beat all-white Kentucky in what some people said was the most important college basketball game ever played.

But before Big Daddy D ended up in El Paso, at the school called UTEP now, he was recruited by some schools up north. One day he was sitting with the athletic director at Boston College.

And the AD guy finally said to him, "What about the boards?"

Meaning college boards.

Big Daddy D, according to the story, smiled wide and said, "I sweep 'em clean at both ends!"

Big Daddy D, even fifty years ago, wasn't looking for a college education, he was just stopping at college on his way to the pros. Same as Drew, even though he would never say that to his mother, knowing she would give him a gentle whack to the back of his head.

Drew's body was still in high school, classrooms and gyms. His mind? Truth be told, it was already in the NBA, no matter how much Darlene Robinson pushed back on him about hitting the books, the value of an education. Same as his adviser at school, Mr. Shockey, did.

Drew would joke sometimes with Mr. Shockey, “My main interest in books is that my accountant keeps ’em straight once the money starts to roll in a few years from now.”

Mr. Shockey would give him that look that was part bored and part disgusted and say, “Make sure you tell your mom that. I’m sure she’ll think you’re a riot.”

Mr. Shockey was a good guy, and he really cared about Drew, just wanted him to be the best student he could be while he still *was* a high school student. That was why Drew let Mr. Shockey think that he could get as much out of him in school as Coach DiGregorio did on the court.

But it was just one more role for Drew to play.

One more head fake to put on somebody.

After practice the next day, Drew talked Lee into driving him to Morrison that night to see if the ghost guy might come back.

“But, dude,” Lee said, “can’t we go earlier than you usually go? I’m not like you. I don’t keep vampire hours.”

As soon as Drew asked, both of them had known Lee would go. It was like when Drew would tell Lee to go sit on the wing when he was bringing the ball up the court—they both knew he would, no matter what play Coach had called.

All part of being Drew’s number two.

Funny thing was, Lee Atkins couldn’t have been any more different from Drew, and not just because one of them was black and the other one was white. It was *everything*. Drew was New York, born and bred. Lee had been born in Thousand Oaks, grew up there, only moved one time when his parents wanted a better neighborhood than they were already in. His dad was a doctor, his mom sold real estate, and the two of them had made sure that Lee had never wanted for anything his whole life.

One more thing that made him different from Drew: Lee never had to dream himself into a big house in a rich neighborhood. He was already there.

Lee never had to want for a dad, either, the way Drew did.

He was just the kind who had a good life going for him and seemed sure he always would. He liked basketball fine, and was the second-best shooter on the team after Drew, but he knew this last year of high school ball—he was one of the four seniors on the team starting along with Drew—was going to be the end of the line for him in hoops.

So this season was everything for him, this shot at the league title, maybe the state title after that.

This chance to be on the same court with somebody as good as Drew (True) Robinson.

The first day of school, in the cafeteria, everybody having known all summer that Drew was coming to Oakley Academy, Lee had searched him out, sat down next to him with his tray without being asked.

"You're going to need a wingman," he'd said, "and not just on the court. I'm it."

Drew couldn't help but smile at Lee's confidence that somebody he didn't know was going to like him. This blond, spiky-haired kid, maybe an inch shorter than Drew. Somehow being sure of himself, just in a laid-back California way, almost like one of the surfer dudes they'd see at the beach.

"I don't even get a vote?" Drew had said.

"Course you do. This is a democracy," Lee had said. "But it wouldn't change anything."

It hadn't. The only things Lee wanted off of Drew were championships and the ball when he was open.

And what Drew wanted from Lee, even though he'd never said it out loud to him, maybe because he was too proud, was Lee's friendship.

Drew had had guys he thought of as friends in his life, guys he *called* friends. But they hadn't really been. He hadn't ever had a real friend until Lee, and their friendship had started almost the moment Lee sat down with him in the cafeteria. Hadn't known what he'd been *missing* until Lee just showed up like that.

He kept telling himself he'd explain that to Lee one of these days, let him know he was something more than an assist to him, a ride somewhere when he needed one. He just hadn't gotten around to it yet.

"Why are you so fixed on this guy?" Lee said on their way to Morrison, his hands on the wheel of his BMW.

"If you see him, you'll understand," Drew said. "It was like watching some homeless dude turn himself into Kobe or LeBron."

"You don't get excited when you watch the real Kobe and LeBron."

"They're *supposed* to do the stuff this guy was doing."

Lee shook his head.

"One o'clock in the morning, when we could be watching a movie or playing video games at Mr. Gilbert's," he said. "And I'm on my way to the playground."

"There's just something about this guy, you'll see," Drew said. "I *got* to check him out again."

Just with a witness this time.

Lee knew more about old-time basketball players than anybody Drew knew. He was talking about old dunkers now as they passed the kids' playground at Morrison, with its swings and slides and monkey bars. Drew had told him again about the way the ghost had dunked the ball.

"Doctor J, Julius Erving, was the first guy who made people think he could fly before he threw it down," Lee said. "Made it mad cool to throw it down. There were plenty of other guys who dunked before him, just not with his kind of style."

"Then came Michael Jordan, right?" Drew said.

Lee shook his head.

"No, before him, and sort of at the same time as Doc, came David Thompson. He was supposed to be everything that Michael was in the pros, but he got down with drugs and partying and then *fell* down a flight of stairs in some New York club. Wrecked up his knee and was never the same."

"I think I knew that," Drew said. "People talked a lot about it after Jordan invited him to the Hall of Fame when he was inducted."

"Michael knew what everybody knew about David, what he *should* have been," Lee said. "Before he messed everything up."

Lee knew that Drew wasn't a big party guy, had never even touched a beer. But Lee talked all the time about guys who had messed things up for themselves in one way or another, how they'd lost their way. Trying to get the message across that he didn't want that to ever happen to Drew.

Lee always tried to find ways to tell Drew not to let himself get too spoiled by what he had already, what he was going to have, because sometimes it wasn't drinking or drugs that could get you sideways, make you lose your way—

It was just being spoiled.

Drew was worried that he was going to have to hear that speech again tonight, have to find a way to change the subject or just tell Lee all over again that *he* was worrying about something that was never going to happen.

But they were coming up on the bad court at Morrison now, and both of them could see, even in the dark, that the ghost guy was back.

Drew put a finger to his lips.

"What, you think he can hear us?" Lee said.

Drew's voice wasn't much more than a whisper. "I just don't want to spook the man this time is all."

They stayed close to the tree line, trying to hide themselves from the lights of the pool, like two kids sneaking through the night in a game of hide-and-seek.

It was him, no doubt.

Same clothes, same cap, hoodie, jeans, old ball. Deciding that it was safe for him to come back, have the park to himself again. Or maybe he'd been here last night even if Drew hadn't.

The first thing they saw when they snuck closer: the high-flyer, one-hand high dunk Drew had seen the first night. Even higher this time. Drew looked at Lee, wanting to see his reaction, saw his mouth drop open. He knew Lee was about to say something, and that—Lee being Lee—he might not be able to control his excitement. Might yell out like he did in a game sometimes when he drained a three.

Drew reached over and clamped a hand over his mouth.

Drew mouthed, *"Be quiet."*

Lee nodded.

They both watched as the guy bounced the ball to himself, not going underneath for a reverse slam this time, grabbing the ball out of the air and then doing a full 360 before throwing down another one.

Lee's eyes were as wide as his mouth now. He whispered, "You ever see that movie *The Soloist*?"

Drew shook his head. Put a finger to his lips, reminding him to keep his voice down.

"It's about this reporter finding a homeless guy playing this amazing music on his crummy violin," Lee said. "Jamie Foxx and Robert Downey. The guy isn't right in the head."

"Jamie Foxx or Robert Downey?"

"Jamie Foxx—he's the one who plays the violin."

Drew nodded at the court, "This guy doesn't look crazy to me. He can just flat *play*."

They hung behind a tree and watched for at least fifteen minutes, maybe more. For Drew the show was better the second time around, under a moon even brighter tonight. Or maybe it was the guy's game shining brighter. Now he turned the cap around on his head, drove down the lane, put the ball behind his back, laid it in with his left hand.

Cake.

He started to make his long-range shots, and the light from tonight's moon let Drew and Lee see him smiling. Like the guy was smiling *at* himself, enjoying his own show as much as Drew and Lee were.

Then he was dunking again, left-handed this time, making it look so easy you would have thought he *was* lefty if you didn't know better.

Finally he helicoptered around again, covered his eyes with his left hand, and dunked one so hard with his right hand that the ball bounced away from him, toward where Drew and Lee were hiding in the trees.

He walked toward them.

The cap was still turned around on his head, so for the first time Drew was able to notice a thin, wispy beard, a lot of gray in it.

He picked up his ball, rolled it up his arm and across his shoulders and then down the other arm. More Globetrotter stuff.

Finally he walked away, done for the night, whistling a tune Drew didn't recognize, but that sounded like the jazz his mom liked to listen to.

"Wow, one more," Lee said, shaking his head, watching the man leave.

"One more what?" Drew said.

"One more playground legend," Lee said.

"You don't even know who he is," Drew said.

"Doesn't matter," Lee said. "He's all of them. All the guys who never made it out of parks like this, or finally ended up back here."

The guy was just about out of sight now, limping noticeably, stopping finally to lean over and rub his left knee. Acting his age a little bit, even if Drew had no idea how old the guy really was.

"You want to follow him?" Lee said.

"No," Drew said. "Leave him go."

Drew couldn't explain it to Lee, wasn't sure he could even explain it to himself. But as much as he had wanted to come back here tonight, he felt like he was intruding now that he'd seen the man again.

There was something about him that made Drew think that if you took this court away from him, this part of the park and this part of the night, you might be taking away all he had.

"There's so many stories about guys who never made it out of the park," Lee said. "Like in that book I gave you. One you actually read."

Lee meant *The City Game*, by this guy Pete Axthelm who Lee

said was dead now. About the old Knicks, but about playground basketball in New York City, too. It really was the first nonschool book Drew had ever read all the way through.

"Like that guy they called 'the Goat,'" Drew said. "I knew about him even before I read the book. My coach at Molloy used to talk about him, when he was giving us another speech about staying on the straight and narrow."

"He got himself all messed up big-time," Lee said. "Another guy all spoiled by his talent."

"Don't start."

"Just sayin'."

The ghost guy had disappeared now, like the night had swallowed him up.

"Wonder what the ghost's story is," Drew said. "How he ended up here."

But he wasn't sure he wanted to know, really. This park had always made him happy, at peace with himself. The idea of somebody as good as the ghost guy ending up here—something about that was nagging on him.

Making him sad.

Maybe that was why when Lee asked if he wanted to shoot around, Drew said, no, he wanted to go home.

"But you always want to play, day or night," Lee said.

"Not tonight."

When Lee dropped him off at home a few minutes later, Drew did something he never did before he went to sleep: he read.

Got *The City Game* back down off his bookshelf, read back on

Earl "the Goat" Manigault, the guy he'd been talking about with Lee. And Joe Hammond and Herman (Helicopter) Knowings and other guys in the book who never made it past being playground legends, for this reason or that.

So maybe that's all this ghost was, Drew finally decided.

Another one of those hoopers who couldn't keep it together, who took their eyes off the prize. He knew these stories were sad, tragic even. He read all those parts of the book tonight and wanted them to turn out differently, for the guys not to take the wrong path.

But they didn't.

Drew closed the book finally, shut out the light, got into bed, told himself to stop worrying about some old Goat at Morrison and go back to worrying about his own game.

Because no matter how much or how often Lee worried about him, there was nothing in this world that was going to stop him like it did the guys in that book. Whatever his grades were, Drew Robinson was way too smart to be one of those guys who threw it all away.

And yet . . .

The last thing he thought about, right before he closed his eyes for good, was the image of David Thompson, tripping and falling down the steps of that club that night, like he was the one who'd come crashing down out of the sky.

The Monday after Christmas break, first thing in the morning, he found a note from Mr. Shockey, his English teacher and adviser, taped to his locker.

"See me after first period," it read. "Checked your schedule, know you have a free."

Drew wondered if Mr. Shockey knew everybody else's schedule this well.

And today of all days, he didn't want to let school get in his way, didn't want to think about *any*thing except the game against Park tomorrow night.

Not just because it was his first-ever game against Park, but also because the Park Eagles had the next best player in the Valley League and maybe in all of southern California, a point guard of their own named King Gadsen.

He was a couple of inches taller than Drew, a legit six three, and was averaging thirty-five a game this season. It was why the newspapers were going crazy with all the LeBron stuff: LeBron Junior going up against a guy named King, which was LeBron's nickname.

And there'd been plenty of Facebook trash talk going back and forth between kids from both schools. Nobody was sure if King Gadsen had actually posted the line "Only one guy gets to be King." Lee was following it all closer than Drew was, but it was still enough to get Drew's attention.

Only now he had to shift his attention to Mr. Shockey.

So after Drew barely managed to stay awake through anthropology, he walked downstairs to Mr. Shockey's office. He had actually thought about skipping anthro, but decided it would look bad if he skipped his very first class after vacation.

Appearances, Drew reminded himself.

Sometimes it felt like as much of a full-time job as basketball.

"Come on in and shut the door," Mr. Shockey said when he saw Drew slouched against the door frame.

Mr. Shockey was smiling, but telling Drew to close the door meant they were—tragically—going to be here awhile.

Mr. Shockey started off with some small talk.

"Good Christmas?"

"Yes, sir. You?"

"A week back in Chicago with my in-laws. Snowed the whole time. My father-in-law still wants to know why Mrs. Shockey didn't marry a lawyer. That sound good to you?"

"Missed us, didn't you?" Drew said.

"You have no idea."

Mr. Shockey was an assistant coach on the basketball team, even though he didn't do any coaching. It's like he was some kind of adviser there, too. Billy DiGregorio took care of the *X*'s and *O*'s and strategy; Mr. Shockey kept the stats, helped out any way Coach DiGregorio wanted him to at practice, and made himself available to the players anytime they wanted to talk, about basketball or anything else.

More a life coach than a basketball coach.

The players on the team knew that Mr. Shockey cared a lot more about them than he did about wins and losses. Drew cared about him, too. Liked the man a lot, liked the easy way he had about him, the no-pressure way he tried to push schooling on you. Even knowing that with Drew, he was playing a losing game.

Usually Drew cared about anything where you kept score. Just not school. To his way of thinking, grades didn't matter in the long run. The short run, even. LeBron never even made it to college, and so what? When he became a free agent, he had some of the richest, most powerful men in the world, ones who owned NBA teams, on their knees, practically begging him to take their money.

Saying, "Please, please, come play for my team."

And LeBron's grades in high school had nothing to do with that. Ball did. Playing ball the way he could. Being the best player he could be. The intelligence that Drew had—what he told himself were his street smarts—he wasn't going to sharpen it in a classroom, like he was trying to sharpen up his left-hand dribble.

Nothing against his teachers. Nothing against Mr. Shockey, a total dude. But they were just speed bumps, was all. That's why he didn't think he was doing anything wrong when he had Lee do most of the work on a paper for him. Or when he cut a class with a made-up excuse, either to sleep in or just go shoot around in the gym.

When Drew waited until the last minute to do a paper or study for a test, he'd just look at it as having to make another Hail Mary shot as the clock ran out.

He didn't see himself acting spoiled, no matter what anybody said. Didn't see himself cheating anybody. He was just keeping his own priorities lined up in a nice, neat way. Sometimes he thought of school as being like playing with four fouls.

He just had to make sure not to foul out.

Nothing more, nothing less.

If he got out of bed late and showed up late for his first class, it wasn't like he was showing up late for a *game*, was it? When LeBron was passing through St. Vincent–St. Mary High School back home, was he there to light it up in class, or on the basketball court?

As Drew liked to say, "figure it out"—it came out sounding like *figgeritout*.

Like when Lee and him would be in town for pizza or a burger or breakfast, and they'd finish and there'd be no check. It was all part of it. The guy or girl at the register would just wave and smile. Letting him know it was on the house. Drew knew and Lee knew and the people picking up the checks, they knew, too: the real classroom for Drew, the real education, was learning how to be famous.

How to be a star.

"So what's up?" Drew said, wanting to get down to it, not waste his whole free period here.

"What's up is this," Mr. Shockey said. "I've gotten evaluation reports from every one of your teachers, and every one of them says the same thing: you're not coming close to giving your full effort. And before I send those reports along to your mom, I want to talk to you about it."

He leaned forward, hands clasped in front of him.

"Quite frankly, Drew," he said, "I'd write up the same evaluation myself."

"I'm pulling my weight with you."

"You act more like you're having *teeth* pulled," Mr. Shockey said. "English is a second language for two kids in our class, and they're making A's. There's nobody in the class with lower than a B. Except you. You're a low C and not that far from a D."

"I'll pick it up the rest of the semester, watch and see," he said.

"You said you'd pick it up before Christmas the last time we had this talk."

Drew crossed his legs now, looked down at one of his favorite pairs of old kicks, high-top Adidas Superstars, blue stripes on white, like some of the old Knicks used to wear way back in the day.

"I don't have to tell you that if your grade gets any lower, you can't play."

"C'mon, you and I both know I won't let that happen."

It wasn't a school rule or even a league rule about earning D's in school. But it happened to be Coach DiGregorio's rule. He let everybody know, especially the media, that the academic standards for his team were higher than anybody else's. Same as his basketball standards were. He said he'd learned that from Bob Knight when Knight was still coaching.

Drew was just glad that he hadn't learned how to throw chairs and grab players by their necks, too.

Drew said to Mr. Shockey, "You wouldn't sit me down. Mr. S, you're my boy." Grinning.

"I can always feel us getting closer when you need a grade from me," Mr. Shockey said. "But then I imagine teachers have been letting you slide from the time you were the best basketball player in every school you ever went to."

Drew couldn't help himself, even now, hearing about academic trouble the day before the Park game, hitting on something Mr. Shockey always hit on in class.

"Ending a sentence with a preposition there, Mr. S?" he said.

Mr. Shockey slapped his desk, not in a mad way, looking excited, happy almost. "I know you're busting on me, but you're really proving my point at the same time," he said. "You're smart, Drew. You know it, and I know it, but the problem is that I'm the only one who cares. Wasting a mind like yours would be the same as wasting the talent you have for basketball."

Drew tried not to roll his eyes, listening to the same talk he'd been hearing from Mr. Shockey ever since they got to know each other.

"I'm trying, a hundred percent," Drew said.

"No, you're trying thirty percent, tops."

"Not true. Maybe I have been letting things slide, just wanting to get the basketball season off to a good start for me and my teammates."

"Baloney."

Drew really didn't want this to go on all day. "Tell me what I have to do," he said.

"You have to do your best work on the paper you've got coming up, because that *is* going to be thirty percent. Of your final grade."

The theme of the paper was "A Life Worth Knowing" and had been assigned before Christmas break. They had to find someone nobody else in the class knew about, had ever heard about, and write a paper making people care about him or her.

"Who'd you pick, by the way?" Mr. Shockey said. "You told me you were going to come up with an idea and start working on it over break."

Drew Robinson had always prided himself on being able to think fast, whether it was basketball coming at him or just life.

The way life was coming at him now.

"I do got somebody, as a matter of fact."

"You *have* somebody, Mr. Grammar. So who is it?"

"A guy I saw playing ball one night at Morrison Park," Drew said.

Then it was like he was writing the paper out loud as he leaned forward in his chair, telling Mr. Shockey about the guy, how amazed he was at the basketball things he could do, how he scared the man off, bringing Lee back with him, almost as a way of proving to himself that the guy was real.

Even as he talked his way through his paper, Drew realized he was actually going to have to find out what the guy's story *was*. But he'd worry about that later.

For now, he just needed to get Mr. Shockey off him, like he did when somebody guarded him too close.

Get out of this room.

"Why do you care about this man?" Mr. Shockey said.

Drew was still thinking fast.

"I think one of the themes of my paper ought to be that, even though I feel like I know this guy, I don't want to *be* him."

Mr. Shockey slapped the desk again, even harder than before. "See, *that's* what I'm talking about! This is a subject you're passionate about!"

"*Oh,* yeah," Drew said, trying to make himself sound as fired up as Mr. S was. "I feel like I've been watching guys like this from the first time my mom thought I was old enough to start going to playgrounds by myself back in New York."

One more time, he was letting somebody, Mr. Shockey in this case, hear what they wanted to hear.

It was easy, once you got the hang of it. Another way of getting somebody to do something for you.

If there were grades for learning how to do that, Drew Robinson knew he would be getting straight A's all the way through.

He didn't think he was being phony or playing a role. If anything, he told himself, he was playing the role of himself. People always said he made the game of basketball look easy, but Drew knew how hard you had to work to get to there, making it look that easy. It was the same with the things he had to say and do, the poses he needed, to make his life easier for him.

"I know you can come through," Mr. Shockey said, "just like you do when a game is on the line."

"I'm gonna prove to you I can do this."

"Prove it to your*self*," Mr. Shockey said. "I have a feeling this is going to be your best work yet."

Well, Drew thought, *mine and Lee's.*

As soon as he was out of Mr. Shockey's office, he went straight for the gym. He had a class after his free, history, but his history teacher, Mr. Williams, was the biggest basketball fan of all his teachers. Had played high school ball himself—a story he never got tired of telling Drew—and had never gotten over it.

Drew knew he could skip history as much or as often as he wanted, that Mr. Williams really was his boy and would take care of him.

The gym would be empty this time of day. So he went to his locker, got into a Kentucky T-shirt that John Wall had sent him before he went to Washington to play in the pros, got into his favorite baggy white practice shorts, went and found himself a game ball.

Then he was out there on the court at Henry Gilbert, not talking some talk about English or some paper he had to do and nodding his head to a teacher, even one he liked, about a game being on the line.

Not pretending he was all invested in some old playground player.

Not having to pretend, period.

Out there, Drew never did.

EIGHT

There was no practice on Thursday, because Coach DiGregorio had to attend a once-a-year coaches' conference in San Diego. So Lee and Drew had made a plan to hang out after school. Nothing solid—Lee told Drew he'd have to wait until around four thirty because he had a conference of his own with his Spanish teacher, Mrs. Conte.

"My name in class is Paco," Lee had said. "She thinks Paco should be pulling a higher grade."

"Welcome to my world."

"Only the classroom world."

"Well, then, *vamos, Paco*!" Drew said.

"You know Spanish, dude?"

Drew grinned. "*Vamos* and *hola* are pretty much all I got."

Then Drew said he'd meet him in the parking lot at four thirty.

"Paco" finished early with Mrs. Conte, and when he tried to get Drew on his cell, the call went straight to voice mail. So Lee went looking for Drew, checking the locker room first.

Then he poked his head into the gym, not really expecting to find him there, knowing the girls' team had practice in there today, with no competition from the guys' team.

And yet, there was Drew.

Lee didn't spot him right away, didn't even think to look up to the top level of Henry Gilbert—their gym was the only one in the league with two levels of stands, almost like a college arena. But somehow his eyes went up there, all the way to the last row of seats.

And that's where Drew was. As if he was hiding.

Lee backed up into the runway, walked up the back stairs to the second level, past a closed concession stand, and carefully poked his head through one of the entrances.

Hiding a little bit himself.

Maybe because Drew made fun of girls' basketball as much as he did. Except, watching him now, getting a look at his face, Lee realized his friend wasn't watching *girls'* basketball.

He was watching *girl's* basketball.

Singular.

That meant the singular Miss Callie Mason.

To use one of Drew's favorite words, Lee could see him watching every dag-gone move Callie made.

Some of the boys called her "Halle" Mason, because they thought she was as pretty as Halle Berry. Callie was the star of the Oakley girls' basketball team, a five-eight point guard, already drawing interest from colleges, even though she was only a junior.

From the start of the school year, Lee had noticed how quiet, even nervous, Drew would get when they passed Callie in the hall or saw her in the cafeteria. Or when they were coming out of the gym after practice and she and her teammates were on their way in.

But when Lee asked Drew if he wanted to go to one of the girls' games, he'd say no, almost like he was too proud, or maybe because he spent so much time busting on the idea of women's basketball.

"Why don't you at least try talking to her?" Lee had said a few days ago.

"We talk."

"Yeah," Lee had said. "That's some major conversating—'Hey, Callie.' 'Hey, Drew.'"

"I ever *need* to say something to her, I will," Drew had said.

"Sure you will."

"You're an idiot sometimes. You know that, right?"

"Yeah, I'm the dumb one."

Only now, not knowing he was being watched, tucked against a back wall, Drew looked completely happy watching Callie play. Like he'd be content to sit up here all day.

As if he could watch her dish and shoot and run the court—

pretty much be the True Robinson of the girls' team—until her coach blew the whistle and sent everybody home.

Lee thought about giving him a hard time, just for the fun of it.

But he couldn't.

Couldn't make himself walk down the row and call him out. Just because of the look on Drew's face. Almost like a kid looking through a window at a store at something inside that he couldn't have.

Interesting, Lee thought.

He loved the guy like a brother, but maybe it wasn't the worst thing in the world for there to be something he couldn't have.

So he went back outside, past the concession stand again, down the stairs, out to the parking lot to wait. When Drew showed up about twenty minutes later, neither one of them mentioned anything about girls' practice. They just talked about where they wanted to eat.

Park Prep had more kids than any other school in their league.

Park was loaded every single year, had won the league nine of the last eleven seasons, won it before Oakley joined the Valley in basketball, and kept on winning it after that. It was one of the most famous basketball programs in the state of California. Its coach, old John Mabry, was a California legend, having coached Park for forty years and won over seven hundred games.

And Mabry's team had beaten the Oakley Academy Wolves every single time they'd played.

It was, Drew knew, the single best reason why Mr. Gilbert had brought in Billy DiGregorio two years ago, hired him away from the powerhouse program Billy had built in Sacramento. He had been brought to Oakley to beat Park Prep—as much as he'd been brought there to win a league title, and maybe a Southern District title after that—for the first time in school history.

"I was at the press conference when he took the job," Lee had told Drew. "He said he wasn't taking on a job as much as a challenge. He didn't know the challenge would get a lot less challenging when *you* fell into his lap. And ours."

Drew hadn't fallen, of course. It was more like Mr. Gilbert had *placed* him there. From the time Mr. Gilbert started talking to Drew's mom about them moving to the West Coast, there had never been any question about where Drew was going to school, any more than there was a question about where Darlene Robinson was going to work or where they were going to live.

Maybe Mr. Gilbert had even picked out their street in Agoura Hills before he talked to Darlene Robinson after the all-star game that time.

"I'm gonna paraphrase an old line from sports," Mr. Gilbert had said to Drew once. "Your coach's good luck is the result of *my* design."

Mr. Gilbert always told Drew and his mom it was their decision, he could get Drew into some other fancy private school if she wanted. Chaminade over in Woodland Hills was a great school. But it didn't take too long for them to figure out that everything went a lot smoother when what they wanted was what he wanted.

Meaning Mr. Gilbert.

Like it was just one more part of the deal.

Everybody called games between Oakley and Park "rivalry games," but Drew could never see it as much of a rivalry when one team did all the winning.

Still, this was the first of two regular season games between them, and the Oakley kids—because they had Drew now—were treating it like some kind of high-school-basketball Super Bowl. There had been a pep rally in the gym after practice on Monday, handmade posters all over the corridors, a huge "Beat Park" banner hanging across the top of the main building of their campus, from one corner to the other.

"I've been waiting my whole life to beat these guys," Lee said in the locker room, maybe forty-five minutes from the tip. "At least it feels like my whole life."

"Dude," Drew said, "chill yourself out. We're playing Park tonight, not Kobe and the Lakers."

"But if you grew up in this town the way I did, they *are* the Lakers," Lee said. "Or the old Celtics. Or those UCLA teams from back in the day that used to win every year in college basketball."

"They're not winning tonight," Drew said, on the carpet now in front of his locker, doing his back stretches.

"It would be so great for our school," Lee said. "Finally getting those guys."

Drew nodded, meaning, Yeah, let's do it for our school. But he *wasn't* trying to do it for his school, or to make school history, or even for his buddy Lee.

Tonight was about him against King Gadsen.

That was the rivalry he was thinking on, even though he and King had never played against each other before.

The rivalry that was starting tonight.

No *way* Drew was losing to him.

He didn't usually think of basketball that way, thought of it as his five against the other five.

Not tonight.

Let's see who's king when the horn blows tonight.

Local TV and the LA papers had started to cover Oakley's games regularly now, the sportswriters always wanting to know which way Drew might be leaning on college.

When they came right out and asked, Drew would just say, "Let me enjoy being in high school. My mom keeps telling me it's all right to run the court fast. She just doesn't want me growing up too fast."

They ate that with a spoon.

So the media crowd had been big since the start of the season, and so had the home crowds, people wanting to see Drew play, see with their own eyes if he and the hype were both for real.

Nothing like tonight.

This huge sound hit Drew when he led his teammates out of the tunnel, biggest sound he'd heard yet in the Gilbert Athletic Center.

Even Drew Robinson, who could block out everything except the game he was playing, the pass or shot or steal he was about to make—put on what his mom called his "blinders"—felt like he'd gotten gut-punched by the force of the place in those first moments when he was on the court.

The sound told him how much they wanted him to beat Park, the way Lee Atkins had told him in the locker room.

Drew saw his mom across from the Wolves' bench, in the second row where she always was, with Seth Gilbert. They were standing along with everybody else, pointing at him as he got in the layup line. Drew just nodded. It was one of the things the media had picked up on about him, how he never changed expression on the court, how you never knew whether he'd just made a good play or a bad one, whether his team was up twenty or down twenty.

They said with True Robinson, you could never tell whether he'd just made one of his highlight-reel passes or missed an open jumper. Not that *that* happened very often.

Behind him in the layup line, Lee yelled, "You better be your *True* self tonight, you hear me?"

Drew yelled back, "Loud and clear."

Drew didn't let anybody notice, not the crowd or the cameras, but every chance he got, he snuck looks down the court to check out King Gadsen, showboating it up in his own layup line, waving his arms at the Park cheering section to pump his fans up, all the Park kids wearing their black "Sixth Man" T-shirts.

Every once in a while, King would pull out the front of his black jersey, making the Park kids go even crazier. He was wearing number 23, of course. LeBron's number. The real King.

Drew wore number 1. Had since New Heights. His coach there,

Coach Adams, had smiled when he handed it to him, not even giving him a choice as he pulled it off the top of the pile.

"Just because you *are* the one, kid," Coach Adams had said.

"One what?"

"The one every coach wants to walk into his gym."

Now he was about to show this hot dog King Gadsen that he wasn't the one around here anymore, wasn't the one in this league or this rivalry or on this coast or anywhere.

Before they left the huddle for the tip, Coach DiGregorio leaned over and said into Drew's ear, "Let it come to you."

Meaning the game. They talked about it all the time, how the game would go through Drew eventually, but he couldn't force himself on it early.

Not that Drew had to be told.

"I got this, Coach," he said.

"Don't let that guy turn this into some kind of playground dumbfest," Coach DiGregorio said.

"You know I'm not about that."

"But you know he wants to show you up."

Drew allowed himself a smile, in here, surrounded by his teammates. "Easier said than done," he said.

King made a show of coming over to shake Drew's hand, give him one of those fake, lean-in half hugs. Like they were bros.

"They afraid to have you guard me, Junior?" King said.

Leaving out the "LeBron" part of the nickname.

Drew didn't smile now, just gave King his blank stare and said, "Do I know you?"

King Gadsen didn't play the point for Park; another kid—Steve McCrae—did. But Coach Mabry didn't worry about that on defense, he had King guarding Drew. Not that it helped much at the start of the game. Lee made threes the first two times Drew threw him the ball, and the gym got even more insanely loud.

Coach Mabry immediately switched King over to Lee, but it didn't matter—he came around another screen the third time the Wolves had the ball and buried another bomb from the wing. Then Tyler Brandt, their power forward—his twin brother, Jake, was his backup—grabbed the rebound, threw a long pass to the streaking Brandon Yarborough, their skinny small forward, and as soon as he laid the ball up to make it 11–2, Coach John Mabry was standing up, hands over his head, signaling for a time-out.

Coach Mabry looked annoyed that he had to keep up out of his seat due to the way his team had started the game.

The Wolves ran to their own bench, jumping around like they'd already won the game. Drew didn't even wait for Coach to tell them they hadn't won anything.

"Settle down!" he snapped at them. "You think they're gonna run to the bus 'cause we played a couple of good minutes?"

"Drew's right," Coach D said, sticking his chair in the middle of them and sitting down. "Just keep doing what we're doing. And be ready when they make their run, because you know they're going to."

They did. Coming right out of the time-out. King Gadsen was still talking, both ends of the court, but now he began to back it up, scoring ten straight points. After he made a three-pointer from what looked like NBA distance to Drew, King ran past and yelled, "You know who I am now, Junior?"

From then until the end of the half, it was just a great high school basketball game. Everybody playing in it knew that, the way everybody in the stands did. Most of the Wolves' wins up to now had been blowouts, but this was different.

This was, as Lee liked to say, *all that*.

Only Drew couldn't get his shot to fall. It didn't matter, because Lee stayed hot, hot as Drew'd ever seen him. Still, Drew was pressing, whether he was open or coming off a screen, even missing a layup when he had gotten all the way to iron after blowing past everybody.

Coach had said let the game come to him, only now he couldn't find it anywhere in the gym, the way he couldn't find his shot.

The shoot-out that everybody had expected—that *he'd* expected—between him and King, wasn't happening. It was between King and Lee Atkins. King already had twenty-five for the game, and Lee had twenty.

Drew did get loose a few times for layups he made, and he managed to knock down a couple of teardrop floaters in the lane. But mostly he was getting his assists, content to feed Lee. That is, until the last shot of the half, when Drew hit a long, fadeaway three of his own from in front of the Wolves' bench. The shot broke a tie and put Oakley up by three, 49–46, going to the locker room.

Finally he heard the crowd chanting, "Truuuuuuuuuuue," the way it usually did when he was making everything he looked at, against King Gadsen or anybody else.

Seth Gilbert was waiting for him in the tunnel.

He put his hand out, and for a second, Drew thought he was going to give him some kind of halfhearted high-five. But what he did instead was pull him aside.

"Nice shot," he said. *"Finally."*

"Can't find my rhythm," Drew said.

"Well, you better." Mr. Gilbert spoke in a tone Drew knew by now, one with some teeth to it.

He had his hands on Drew's shoulders, and anybody watching the two of them would have thought he was giving him some kind of halftime pep talk.

"Trying," Drew said, wondering where this was going. He was against a wall, could see the rest of his teammates filing past him toward the locker room.

"Try harder," Mr. Gilbert said. "Everybody's supposed to be talking about you tonight, and all they're talking about is the other kid. The media guys are, the college scouts are. Our own *fans* are. You're supposed to be carrying your team, not your buddy."

"Don't worry," Drew said. "We'll win."

"Win what?" Mr. Gilbert said. "A game?"

Then he turned and walked back into the gym that he'd built.

NINE

They decided to go man-to-man defense to start the second half, that it was the only way to slow down King Gadsen. They needed to get a body on him, or he might end up going for fifty tonight.

In the past, Lee would take the other team's big scorer, even if he was a point guard, because Coach D didn't want Drew to gas himself out playing defense. But tonight was different, and they all knew it, so Drew took the pressure off Coach before he ever had to make a call.

"I'll take him," Drew said, everybody in the room knowing who he meant. "He's still gonna get his, but I'll shut him down enough for us to win the game."

Under his breath he said, "And I'm gonna start getting mine."

Coach D gave him a look. "Hey," he said, "we're winning the game, right?"

"Right," Drew said.

But Mr. Gilbert's words were still in his head, like winning the game wasn't going to be enough tonight, that even with Oakley up those three points, he was losing the game within the game he was playing against Gadsen.

And Drew, despite his tough talk about guarding King in the huddle, wasn't so sure he could shut him down. He knew that sometimes the hardest thing in sports was stopping somebody great when he was being great. In King's case, that meant *shooting* great. He didn't have nearly the all-around game that Drew did, the feel for the game, the vision or the passing or any of the rest of it.

But he could, in the words of Dick Vitale, shoot the rock.

He could fill it up.

"Yeah," Drew said again. "I got this."

Mr. Gilbert's words weren't just inside his head. They were stinging him. Maybe that was why he'd said he'd take King. People had come to see him versus King Gadsen tonight. Might as well give them what they wanted.

Park got the ball to start the second half. When King saw Drew picking him up in the backcourt, he barked out a laugh. The hot dog just sounding like a dog now.

"I forget," he said. "Is your real nickname True or False?"

Drew didn't shut him down from there. But he slowed him just enough. By the time there were four minutes left, the game was tied at 70, and Drew saw from the stats on the scoreboard that King had thirty-nine points for the game. But the ones he'd gotten in the second half, Drew had made him work for each one.

Lee, who'd stayed hot, had thirty.

Drew had scratched his way to twenty-two, but knew his shooting was way under fifty percent, which was never him.

Neither team had led by more than three points the whole second half. It didn't seem possible to Drew, but the noise inside the gym seemed to keep building, to the point where Drew imagined the walls and the roof just blowing away.

And no matter how much noise there was, King Gadsen kept talking, like he was broadcasting the game and playing it at the same time.

Drew had done his best to ignore him, not let him get inside his head. Or get mad. Or get more frustrated than he already was with his poor shooting. Coach DiGregorio always said, you get mad at the guy, he owns you. But Drew finally beat King off the dribble, drove down the baseline with his left hand, just over three minutes left, and somehow made this blind reverse layup, kissed high off the top of the backboard as King fouled him, hard, knocking him to the floor.

King didn't offer to help Drew up, and Drew didn't wait for him to extend his hand. But as he picked himself up, he walked close enough to King to say, "I *guess* that was a good shot."

"After the way you shot tonight," King said to him, smiling at him, "you're gonna start talking smack now? Go make your free throw, dog, so I can have the ball back."

Drew made the free throw.

Game tied again, 75 all.

King came right back, backed up his own smack—Drew had to

give him that. He stepped back and made a three with Drew hanging all over him, banging him hard as he went into the air, nearly fouling and turning it into a four-point play.

Park 78, Oakley 75.

Two minutes left.

Drew came down, saw Lee open on the right wing—Park had been dumb enough to double Drew, despite the way Lee had been shooting. Even with the double, Drew still thought about taking the ball to the basket, but Lee was way too open and way too hot.

Lee buried the shot.

He raised his arms like he'd made another three, which would have tied the game, but the refs waved it off, saying he had a foot on the line. It was only a two.

Oakley was now down a point, a minute and fifteen to play.

King Gadsen, who hadn't needed any luck all night long, got some now, banking in a ridiculous three of his own from the right side.

Park 81, Oakley 77.

But Brandon got open on a backdoor move, and Drew hit him with a perfect bounce pass for the assist. Then Tyler Brandt came flying out of nowhere to steal the inbounds pass and lay the ball in.

Game tied, 81 all.

Fifty seconds left. Park called its last time-out.

There were certain rules Drew followed with Coach, and one of them was that when it got down to crunch time like this, when it was what Drew had always thought of as *game* time, he let Coach do most of the talking.

"King will want to take a hero shot, that's his DNA," Coach said. "So give Drew as much help on defense as he needs. If by some chance he passes the ball and somebody else makes the shot, we just say, Too tough. Either way, miss or make, we take the first good shot we get, make the sucker, then see if we can get another stop and then walk off the court feeling the love."

Billy DiGregorio put his hand out. Drew and the other guys put theirs on top of his.

"Boys," he said, "these are the good parts."

But King came right down, no hesitation, split Drew and Lee, somehow elevated over the outstretched arms of both Brandon and Tyler Brandt, and hit a fifteen-footer like he was shooting by himself at Morrison.

Park back up by a basket, 83–81.

King gave Drew a blank stare, trash-talking him now without saying a word.

Drew ignored him and got out of a double-team as soon as he crossed half-court. Tyler Brandt threw a killer screen on the weak side, clearing Lee. Drew waited for it to develop, then threw him the ball. No hesitation. Lee made one more three like it was a layup. Oakley now up a point, 84–83.

Drew gave a quick look at the scoreboard, even knowing inside his head that Lee had thirty-eight points now. Boy was totally off the grid, had been all night.

Back in New York, they used to talk about the Monster of Madison Square Garden. Drew thought this high-school gym sounded like that now.

Oakley still needed one stop for the win. They just wouldn't get it against King Gadsen, not tonight. He ran some time, got himself into the lane even with Drew still in front of him, even with no room, and somehow made a crazy teardrop shot.

Park back up a point.

Fourteen seconds left.

Win the game, win the night, Drew told himself.

Billy DiGregorio just stood in front of their bench, arms folded, nodding at Drew. No time-out, that's what he was telling him. Just play.

Drew knew that was Coach's style in moments like this. The rest of the guys knew enough to spread the court, give Drew one chance to break the defense down off the dribble and get to the basket. If he couldn't, they all knew he'd find a way to pass to Lee.

Drew looked past King, to the clock behind the basket, and made his move with ten seconds left.

He crossed over on King, got past him with a left-handed dribble, then crossed *back* over to a right-handed dribble and got a step on the other defender. But King got a hand on the ball from behind Drew. Not enough to knock it away, just enough to knock off his timing, make him waste a couple of seconds getting the ball back under control.

Drew was a step inside the free-throw line.

True or False? King had said.

True, he thought to himself.

True Robinson.

It didn't matter that they'd been talking about King Gadsen all night. They'd be talking about Drew on their way home, the shot he was going to make to win it for his team.

But more for himself.

Next game he'd be a nice team player.

The entire Park defense seemed to be collapsing on him. Drew could hear Lee—having the night of his life, in the game he said he'd been waiting his whole life to win—yell, *"True!"*

Lee Atkins, trying to make himself heard over the roar that the end of a game like this makes.

"I'm open!" Lee yelled.

Drew knew he was. He had been all night and had to be now. But this time Drew wasn't passing. This time Drew was shooting, even in all that traffic, going as high as he could, as high as he did when he wanted to dunk the ball, still having to shoot *around* the stupidly long arms of the Park center, right before the horn sounded.

It was such an awkward shot, an awkward midair move, that Drew went down without being touched after he released the ball. He was sitting on the court when the quiet of the crowd, the worst kind of quiet in sports for the home team, told him the shot had missed.

Park 85, Oakley 84.

Drew stayed where he was for a moment. Before he got up, he saw King Gadsen standing over him. Still not offering him a hand.

"Just so you know," King said, "your buddy, he's still open over there on the wing. He just stopped calling for the ball."

King left him there.

Drew didn't move, just turned his head. And Lee hadn't moved from the wing. *Was* still standing there.

Staring at Drew like he was a stranger.

For some reason, Drew's eyes moved past Lee, past the Park kids celebrating on the court—*his* court—went up through the stands, up to the top of the gym, the far corner of the place, away from the basket where Drew had attempted his hero shot.

Up there, all alone, was a guy in a Lakers cap and a hoodie.

The ghost guy.

Eyeballing Drew has hard as Drew had eyeballed him at Morrison.

Shaking his head in disgust before he disappeared again.

TEN

Drew knew he should have passed Lee the ball for the last shot, knew his pride and his ego had gotten in the way of his basketball sense.

But he couldn't bring himself to admit that after the game.

Instead he told the reporters that he was going to kick it over to Lee but then he thought he could get all the way to the basket before the Park defense forced him into a tough shot.

"I want the ball in my hands at the end of the game," he said. "I want to take that shot. Tonight it wouldn't go down for me, but I had to try to make something happen."

Yeah, he thought, even as he told his locker room lies to the reporters. *I made something happen, all right.*

Made us lose by a bucket.

And then Drew heard Lee from the next locker, saying how many shots Drew had made tonight, that you could never go wrong with the ball in True's hands. Lee smiling as he nodded at

Drew and said, "How can I be the man when that guy right there is the man?"

Somehow it made Drew feel worse, Lee giving him a pass on the way the game had ended on the night when Drew *didn't* pass.

Before the reporters left Drew, they kept trying to get him to talk up King and the forty-eight points he'd scored. Nobody came right out and said that King had won the personal battle between him and Drew, in addition to the game, but Drew could hear it implied in every question.

He just kept saying, over and over, "Glad I got to finally see him in person. Glad I'm going to see him again before the season is over."

Before he added this: "Next time I'll be at my best."

He went to the shower finally, stayed in there a long time under the hot water, trying to wash the game away. He'd ended up with his twenty-two points, sixteen assists, and even pulled down eight boards. Yet it still felt as if he'd played the worst game of basketball since his first games as a freshman back at Archbishop Molloy.

The reporters were gone when he came out of the shower. Only Lee and Brandon and the Brandt twins were left in the locker room. Lee told Drew that the rest of the guys were already on their way to his house, to hang out and have pizza.

"Win as a team, lose as a team," Lee said.

Brandon said, "Next time will be different."

Tyler said, "You missed shots tonight you usually make in your sleep, and we *still* almost beat that guy."

Not Park. That guy. King Gadsen had won, Drew had lost. It

wasn't what Tyler was trying to say—he was just trying to make Drew feel better. But that's what Drew heard.

Drew looked at Lee and said, "I really thought I could take it all the way."

"Dude," Lee said, "you don't have to explain anything to me. I was making shots before you ever got here, and we never got a sniff of a league title or a state title."

Then he sighed and shook his head and said, "But, man, we nearly beat those guys finally."

It was then that Drew could see how much this game had hurt his friend, coming so close to beating Park. Drew was hurting, too. But not for the same reason. He felt bad because he'd *looked* bad.

Oakley had lost the game.

But Drew had lost face to King Gadsen.

In that way, it didn't matter to him that the loss had come against his school's big rival. It could have come against anybody. This wasn't about school spirit, because Drew knew he didn't have any.

Another hard truth about True Robinson.

Lee asked if he was ready to go, and Drew said yeah. They both knew, without it even coming up, that Lee would drive him home when the team party—if you could call it a party—was over. It was like that was one more part of the deal with them, something that was just understood.

"Let's do this, then," Lee said, "before the other guys eat up all the pizza."

They walked out of the locker room and into the tunnel.

Seth Gilbert was waiting across from the locker room door, texting somebody, looking impatient, which he could in the best of times.

He looked up at Drew and said, "Let's go."

"Go where?" Drew said.

"I've got some people over at the house," he said. "I want you to meet them, even though the night didn't turn out the way I'd hoped."

Drew wanted to tell him it hadn't exactly turned out the way he wanted, either. Instead he did something he did a lot with Mr. Gilbert: he swallowed the words.

It was then that Gilbert seemed to notice Lee standing there.

"Tough loss, kid," he said. "You played good."

Good? Drew wanted to say. He made threes like Kevin Durant tonight, and you thought he played . . . *good*?

Drew didn't say that, either.

Lee thanked Mr. Gilbert, who at least added, "You shot it tonight the way this guy was supposed to," giving his head a little jerk in Drew's direction.

Drew said, "Lee's having the team over to his house. Just to chill. I was gonna ride over with him."

"You can catch up with them later," Mr. Gilbert said. "I'll get Eddie to drive you over there."

It was his normal way when he wanted something, Drew knew, telling him what he was going to do, not asking.

Drew wasn't getting a vote on it, and neither did Lee, who'd been a better friend than ever to Drew tonight, letting him off the hook in the locker room the way he had. "Win as a team, lose as a team," he'd said.

Mr. Gilbert didn't even make a show of inviting Lee along, not that Lee would have wanted to go.

"Come on, we better get going," Mr. Gilbert said.

"These people you want me to meet," Drew said, "who are they?" He didn't mean anything by it, he was just asking.

Mr. Gilbert gave him a look, then answered as if Drew had just talked back to him. Giving him a fake smile.

"People . . . you . . . need . . . to . . . meet," he repeated.

Seth Gilbert started toward the exit that led to the parking lot. Walking away from Drew for the second time tonight. But expecting him to follow this time.

"You coming?" he said, giving a quick look over his shoulder, checking his BlackBerry again, as he did about every ten seconds.

Drew said to Lee, "I better do this. He is my mom's boss and all."

"Yours, too, sometimes."

"What's that mean?"

"No worries," Lee said. "Just kidding, dude."

"I'll catch you later, I promise."

"Sure," Lee said.

Drew walked fast to catch up with Mr. Gilbert. When he was the one looking back over his shoulder, he saw that Lee Atkins hadn't moved, he was standing exactly where Drew had left him.

Like he was still waiting for the ball.

Drew felt a little bad, leaving him. But it was like Mr. Gilbert said sometimes: where he was going, his buddies couldn't come.

ELEVEN

Mr. Gilbert made it clear, as the two of them walked through the front door, that there was nothing for him to worry about. Nothing that was going to happen at the party was a violation of NCAA rules, even if there were a couple of what he called "Nike guys" in the house.

"But I'm not even in college yet," Drew said.

"You're the most famous high school basketball player in the country. In the eyes of the NCAA suits, you might as well be playing by their rules already."

"Wish I'd played better tonight."

"Tell me about it," Mr. Gilbert said, but even as he did, he pulled Drew closer to him and said, "Who's got your back?"

"You do."

"Who's like your personal GPS, keeping us pointed where we want to go?"

"You are," Drew said.

It was always like that, almost from the first night they met back at the AAU tournament in New York. We. Us. Mr. Gilbert wanted the team at Oakley to do well. Obviously he had a lot invested in the school and the coach. And Mr. Gilbert was the one who'd picked the school out for Drew before his mom even made it official that they were moving.

All part of the *mi casa es su casa* deal, the house in this case being a high school.

But in the end, the only team Mr. Gilbert really cared about—even more than the college team Drew would be playing for in a year and a half—was him and Drew.

As they moved out into the pool area, music playing, waiters serving food and drinks, Drew immediately spotted a tall guy with a shaved head, a crowd of people around him, laughing loudly at something somebody had just said. It was Stu Jarvis, who'd played college ball with Mr. Gilbert at USC and who did work for Nike now.

Drew wondered what Stu Jarvis would think if he knew that Mr. Gilbert liked to refer to Nike as "the mob" when it was just him and Drew talking. Telling Drew that once the time came, there'd be no choice, he'd have to wear Nike shoes.

"Basketball version of being a made man," he'd say.

Mr. Gilbert walked Drew right over to Stu Jarvis now.

"Now, this is a social event, Nike man," he said to his old friend. "So no business talk tonight—I mean it. There's plenty of time down the road for you two to get to know each other a *lot* better."

Stu Jarvis did the same kind of lean-in King had done with Drew before the game. Though in his case it was more like a lean-

down, because Stu went six six, at least. Mr. Gilbert had said he'd played three years in the league for Golden State, before the anterior cruciate ligament in his right knee, his ACL, had ripped like a raggedy shoelace.

"Tough one tonight," Stu Jarvis said. "That shot at the end should have fallen. Where I sat, I thought you had it as soon as the ball left your hand."

Drew knew he couldn't possibly mean that. Couldn't possibly be sincere. *Maybe it figures that he works for a sneaker company,* Drew thought. *Because the man's acting like somebody trying to sell me a pair of shoes.*

"Should have been able to get a better look," Drew said. "*I'm* better than that."

Stu Jarvis put his arm around Drew the way Mr. Gilbert had, laughed. "Yeah," he said, "you are."

Just a little edge to him, behind the smile, giving him a little jab the way Mr. Gilbert had.

"But twenty-two, sixteen, eight still isn't a bad night," Stu Jarvis went on, reciting Drew's stats. "Most guys would kill to have numbers like that, and here you are acting as if you stunk the joint out. And you still had the confidence to take the last shot."

"Well, thanks, Mr. Jarvis," he said, trying to sound modest. Hearing Lee's voice inside his head, one of Lee's favorite lines about him, the one about how nobody faked sincerity better than True Robinson.

"The other kid tonight, all he does is shoot," Stu Jarvis said. "You, son, are a *playa.*"

"Thank you," Drew said again.

"I'm sure you get asked this all the time," Stu said. "But I gotta ask something, just 'cause I got so many coaches on scholarship who are gonna be begging me for some skinny on you tomorrow, knowing I was with you tonight."

"Ask away."

"Any of their schools might be starting to get your attention yet?"

"I'll let you in on a secret," Drew said, lowering his voice.

"Hit me."

"The only school I'm worried about tonight is Park Prep. And how they ended up with more points than we did."

Drew couldn't help but think, *I'm as phony as this guy is.*

Stu Jarvis laughed and said, "Well, there *is* a reason why they keep score in sports," and then walked off, heading in the direction of another one of Mr. Gilbert's friends, the center fielder for the Dodgers, who hadn't lost their game tonight.

Next Mr. Gilbert wanted Drew to spend some time with an *LA Times* guy Drew recognized from the locker room, one who told him he'd finished his story at what he called warp speed.

"Of course," the guy said, "it wasn't the story I came here looking to write tonight."

He was smiling as he said it—everybody here seemed to be smiling at Drew. But his eyes weren't. It was almost as if Drew had let him down, too, in addition to himself and his teammates and his school.

Maybe even his mom.

"Sorry," Drew said. "I was sort of looking for a different ending myself."

"That's the problem with sports," the reporter said. Drew had been told his name and had forgotten it already. "We can't make it come out the way we want it to, even in a high school game."

"Maybe next time," Drew said.

"Let's hope so," the reporter said.

Not saying it in a mean way, just with an edge. The same edge Drew had heard in the Nike man's voice. Letting him know that, even though it was a high school game, they treated you differently when you lost.

He started to move off, but the reporter put a hand on his arm.

"Listen," the *LA Times* guy said. "I want to tell you something before you go: I want to be your go-to guy in the media."

"Go-to guy," Drew said.

"I want it to be me instead of somebody from ESPN, or *Sports Illustrated,* or Fox. I want to get with you now and stay with you. You got something to say, I want you to say it to me."

"Even when I lose?" Drew said.

"As long as that doesn't happen too often," the guy said, and laughed, as if somehow that was funny.

"I'll work on it," Drew said.

"I'm serious. When you're ready to write your first book, I want to be the one with the tape recorder."

Now, that almost made Drew laugh, the reporter coming right at him this way, talking about writing books when Drew had almost no interest in reading them.

Drew stayed with him for a few more minutes, gave him his phone number and his e-mail because he didn't see any harm in that, and finally broke loose, feeling the way he did on the court when he broke loose from a double-team.

He found Mr. Gilbert and told him he was fixing to leave.

"Not yet," Mr. Gilbert said, trying to make it sound casual instead of like an order. "Just a few more people to charm," he added. "So the evening isn't a total loss."

Another diss. Mr. Gilbert wasn't even trying to pull his punches now.

"Can't you charm them for me?" Drew said. "You got more than enough charm for both of us. And you're always telling me you know me better than I know myself."

But he let Mr. G pull him over and get him talking with a woman Drew knew was the weekend sports anchor on KTLA, the one who reminded him of Megan Fox. And who smiled at him until she noticed the quarterback from USC, one everybody was talking about for the Heisman Trophy, on the other side of the pool.

Drew watched her go, shaking his head. Amazed at these people. Knowing they were treating him differently than they would have if he'd made the last shot. Acting like they were his friends, but all of them, in their own ways, letting him know the deal, that they liked winners better.

Even Mr. Gilbert had been different with him tonight.

But Drew knew something: this was his world now, like it or not. People giving him fake smiles and him giving them fake smiles back. This was the Los Angeles you always heard about.

Land of make-believe.

When it was just the two of them, Drew asked Mr. Gilbert if he could leave now, asking for permission like he would from his mom.

"I'll text Eddie," Mr. Gilbert said. "He'll meet you out front."

Drew said, "You sure this is no bother? I could have Lee come get me."

Knowing Lee would.

"Hey," Seth Gilbert said, "I'm not taking away your car-and-driver privileges just because you threw up a brick like that at crunch time."

When Drew got outside and checked the time on his cell, it was only eleven thirty. He knew there was plenty of time to get to Lee's house. He was about to text him, tell him to save him a couple of slices or else . . .

But he didn't.

He got into the front seat of the car next to Eddie, not wanting to treat Eddie like a chauffeur, even though he pretty much was in this case.

"Would you mind taking me all the way home?" he asked.

Knowing he wasn't going straight home the way he wasn't going to Lee's.

He was going to Morrison Park.

TWELVE

Just being at Morrison made Drew feel better.

He looked down and realized he still had his game sneakers on, had forgotten to put on the pair of old blue Nike Cortez shoes, nylon with the white swoosh, that he had in his locker. But he didn't have his ball with him, so it didn't matter that just being in Morrison gave him his usual late-night urge to walk over to the lighted court and start shooting around.

Drew stopped and sat down on one of the swings in the kids' playground, even though he was too big for it, heard the creak of the chain, the small noise sounding loud in the big quiet of the late night.

Maybe, Drew thought, *it's not the court that I like the best here.*

It's the quiet.

Not having anybody talking to him or acting like they were laughing with him when they were the only ones laughing—and fake laughs at that, to go with their fake smiles. Not having people ask him questions. Not having to tell them what they wanted to hear.

Maybe he liked Morrison in the night because nobody wanted anything from him here. He didn't have to play the part of teamman Drew here, humble Drew. Nobody bossed him around the way Mr. Gilbert had tonight, like Drew was one of his waiters, almost like he wanted to punish Drew a little for losing the game. And Drew had just let it happen, had just taken it until Mr. Gilbert allowed him to leave.

Even though the day was coming when he wasn't going to let anybody even *think* they were bossing him around, telling him where to go and what to do, whether they were fake smiling or not.

For now, Drew Robinson knew he had to pick his spots where he could be his own self.

Though on nights like this, he wasn't sure who that was anymore.

He didn't stay on the swing set for long. It was moving up on midnight now, he saw that when he turned his cell back on. A little earlier than when he usually showed up here with his ball. As soon as the phone was back on, he could feel it vibrating. It had to be texts from Lee, wanting to know where he was.

Drew turned the phone back off.

If people could reach you on your cell anytime they wanted, then you weren't really alone, were you? And now there were all the stats on Twitter. But why wouldn't they be tweeting, from LeBron on down, the world having convinced them it was hanging on their every word?

Drew walked over to the small patch of trees where he and Lee had hidden out the night they'd come to watch the guy. Nobody was on the bad court, not yet, and maybe not ever tonight. No matter. Drew sat down, prepared to wait.

A few minutes later, he saw headlights, turned and saw it was a police car making a slow turn in the parking lot near the playground. Had to be Archey and Delano, looking past the playground and seeing that the lighted court, Drew's court, was empty tonight.

Drew closed his eyes when the cruiser was gone, tired all of a sudden, like everything that had happened in the game and at the end of the game and after the game had finally worn him out. He felt the energy coming out of him, like air coming out of a basketball when you got a needle stuck in it . . .

Drew closed his eyes.

He didn't awaken until he heard the bounce of a ball.

THIRTEEN

Drew had made up his mind on the way over: if the ghost guy was there tonight and ran away again, he was going to run him down and find out who he was, why he'd come to the game.

Why he'd left his court to come watch Drew play on his.

Why he'd looked as if Drew had let him down more than anybody else in the gym.

Drew got up, moved up behind a tree closer to the bad court, to get a closer look. The guy had taken off his sweatshirt tonight, was wearing a black T-shirt with his jeans, like he wanted to blend into the night. But he had the same Lakers cap, same old Air Jordans he'd been wearing the other times.

Same game.

With some new moves tonight, almost like he was adding elements to his game. *Before long,* Drew thought, *I'll be able to come up with a scouting report, like I'm getting ready to play him in a real game.*

He couldn't take his eyes off the guy.

It was as if he was playing an imaginary game of one-on-one, like the ghost guy was up against another ghost, not merely dunking or flying through the air, but playing with a purpose. He'd back in sometimes and then shoot fadeaway jumpers. He'd take the ball back to the top of the key, dribble left, then make this blinding crossover dribble back to his right, not dunking the ball, just laying it in.

Drew got lost in watching him all over again, but finally decided that if he didn't make his move, he might be here all night.

So he came out of the trees.

"Hey," he said, keeping his tone casual, not wanting to scare him off like he did before, not really wanting to have to chase him after having played every minute against Park Prep.

The guy was about to shoot a three when he heard Drew's voice and froze. Just stayed in that pose, like Drew had snapped a picture of him on his phone.

He didn't run.

Instead he looked at Drew and said, "You should have passed."

FOURTEEN

He didn't say it in a mean way, just sounded as disappointed as he'd looked when the game was over. Ball cocked on his right hip. Staring right at Drew, hard, with no expression on his face, lit only by the lights from the court in the distance.

Drew said, "I don't even know you. And now you're my coach?"

The guy said, "Not your coach. Just somebody who knows the game."

"And I don't?" Drew said. He knew as soon as he said it how defensive his words came out.

"Nope, that's not the problem," the guy said. "In fact, the problem is that you *do* know the game."

"You're gonna talk to me about one shot, when the guy I was playing against hoisted up about a hundred tonight?"

"Shooting the ball was the best way he had to help his team win the game," the guy said. "You're better than that. Better than *him*."

Drew felt himself getting hot, knowing he was taking the bait, picking a fight almost even though they were just talking. Conversating, as Lee liked to say.

"If my game bothers you so much, why'd you even come to the game tonight?"

"Who said your game bothers me? You better grow a thicker skin, boy, you're going the places you want to go."

"Right," Drew said. "What are you, a fortune-teller from the park, telling me where I'm going?"

The guy ignored that, just said, "I wanted to see you in a real game, not just messin' around like you do here. I wanted to see you handle yourself when something was on the line. When the ball you was playing—" He stopped himself, wagged a finger, like he was correcting himself. "When the ball you *were* playing mattered."

For the first time, Drew thought he saw a hint of a smile from him, there and gone faster than a fly.

Drew said, "You've been watching me play *here*?"

"What," the guy said, "I can't spy on you the way you spy on me?"

Just then, he flung his arms out, like he was going to fire a hard chest pass at Drew. Only the ball didn't go anywhere, just hung in midair before he reached back and caught it with what Drew noticed were huge hands.

Drew hadn't been able to help himself, had flinched when he thought the ball was coming.

"Funny," he said.

"You're the one who's funny. Still too stubborn to admit that you played the fool on that last possession, even though we both know it's your job to feed the hot hand, to *always* give it up if somebody else has a better shot."

This wasn't going the way Drew had imagined it would, and he told himself to get out of there, just walk away, stop letting someone he didn't even know get under his skin.

But he stayed right where he was.

"You obviously know my name," Drew said. "What's yours?"

The guy didn't answer right away, as if deciding whether he wanted to tell. The blank expression back on his face.

Drew was thinking, *That's my game face.*

Finally the guy said, "You can call me Donald."

"That a first name or a last name?"

"It's a name."

"Okay, *Donald,*" Drew said. "So why did you come and watch me play tonight?"

"Like I said. See with my own eyes whether you were for real or for hype."

"And you'd know the difference?"

There was something about this guy's attitude. All during the game, Drew had to deal with King Gadsen's trash talk. Now he was dealing with another kind.

"If you don't care what I think, why are you here? Ask yourself that."

"I wanted to know who you are," Drew said. "I couldn't care less what you think about me."

"That so?"

"Yeah," Drew said. "It is."

"Okay, we've established why you said you came here. But why are you *still* here? Could it be because you *do* care what I think?"

Drew didn't say anything, not wanting to admit he was right.

The way he was right about the last play of the Oakley versus Park Prep game.

"Okay," Drew said. "You tell me now: am I real or am I hype?"

"I'd grade you about half-and-half," Donald said, putting out his big left hand, palm down, making a wavy motion with it like Drew's grade could go either way.

Drew said, "Even on a night when I didn't play my best game, I was two boards shy of a triple double."

"I'll try to contain my excitement."

"I'm just sayin'."

"The more you talk like a numbers hanger," Donald said, "the more your grade goes down. If you'd passed the ball like you should have on the last play, we wouldn't even be havin' this conversation, now, would we?"

Drew couldn't help himself now. He took a step forward. "Tell you what," he said. "I still got my game sneakers on. If I'm such low-class hype, why don't we play some one-on-one? We can do it here in the dark or over in the light, your call."

"You're not hearing me," Donald said. "It's not a one-on-one game, you against that boy King. It's five-on-five."

"You think I don't know that?"

"I think you forgot that tonight, turned it into a one-on-one game at the worst possible time. That wasn't nothin' but your ego, takin' over the game as much as you did."

"You make that sound like some kind of crime," Drew said.

"Not a crime," Donald said. "How old are you?"

"Fifteen," Drew said, "going on sixteen."

"You better watch that stuff, starting right now," Donald said, "or before you know it, you'll be the one telling fortunes in the park."

Drew heard Lee's voice inside his head now.

"Wow, another playground legend who never made it out of the park," Drew said. "Trying to give me advice."

The guy was staring at him harder than ever.

Stared until he finally said, "Yeah, boy. I'm a real legend."

FIFTEEN

Then he just turned and walked away, basketball under his arm.

Drew let him go. Maybe it was because he knew this wasn't the last conversating they were ever going to do. Or maybe he was too tired from chasing King Gadsen around in the second half to even *walk* after the man.

Knowing he had more questions than answers, even though he'd met the man now. Especially the answers Drew wanted about how the man who called himself Donald had ended up here.

Donald telling Drew to make sure he didn't end up here, too.

Like I'd ever end up some old park player, Drew told himself.

He walked home from Morrison, trying not to make too much noise as he came through the front door, knowing his mom was sound asleep by now. Ten o'clock was the latest she made it during the week unless Oakley was playing a rare seven o'clock game. The only way Darlene Robinson was awake past ten was if she'd

TiVo'ed something on her bedroom television set and it ran past her bedtime.

She had left him a note on the table where they both kept their keys.

Honey:

Even you can't win them all.

Still love you.

Mom

At least she didn't want to analyze the game like she was on ESPN, didn't want to lecture him about how he should have passed. But then she never thought her boy did much wrong in basketball. She saved her criticism for other things, like his head getting too big or his grades being too small.

Drew went into the kitchen and fixed himself a big bowl of cereal, Lucky Charms, and when he finished it, he filled up the bowl again, no milk this time, and ate the cereal up like it was candy.

Wondering if Mr. Gilbert was worrying tonight about his diet, about getting him a nutritionist.

Way past midnight now, but he was still too wired to go to sleep.

He shut the lights in the kitchen, went to his room at the very back of the ranch-style house, closed the door, opened up his laptop—not the Dell he had when they were still in New York, but the MacBook Pro Mr. Gilbert had bought him as a present when they moved in, calling it a housewarming present.

"I just like it because it has the word *pro* in it," Mr. Gilbert had said when Drew found it there on his desk, all the stuff from the Dell having been transferred already.

Drew went online now, saw more messages from Lee wanting to know what had happened to him. The most recent message, from a few minutes ago, was the YouTube link to the video showing Drew attempting the last-second shot against Park Prep.

Sending Drew to the place where he could watch a shot that could have been Lee's. *Should* have been his, if you believed Donald.

Drew felt himself getting hot all over again thinking about the guy, even now, alone in his room. Mostly getting hot about the guy's know-it-all attitude.

You know why I took the shot? Drew wanted to tell the guy. *You know why I took it whether Lee was open or not?*

Because I believed I could make it, that's why.

That part was right, whether his decision making in the moment had been wrong or not. Drew had *never* been afraid in basketball, of taking the big shot or anything else, from the time he was the smallest kid on the playground back in the Bronx.

It was one thing to knock down open shots the way Lee had for just about the whole thing, but something else altogether, almost like a whole different game, when it was all on the line. When everybody in the gym was looking at you.

Was Lee capable of making the big shot? Was he *really*? Drew didn't know that about him, not yet, anyway. Neither did Lee.

Maybe they both could have found out tonight. They didn't. So what?

I'm not just not afraid to take that shot, Drew thought to himself, alone in his room.

I'm not afraid to miss it, either.

Drew pushed away from the desk now, put his head back, felt himself finally winding down, finally dialing down the emotions of the night. He briefly considered doing some research for his English paper, the one he'd fooled Mr. Shockey into thinking he was all jacked up about.

But there was no need.

Lee was already on it. He was doing the heavy lifting, as usual.

Drew Robinson was never going to cheat, never going to have it come out later that somebody had taken a test for him or written a paper, like had happened with other guys. School wasn't important enough for Drew to cheat at. Still, from the time they became boys, Lee had made it clear that he'd do whatever Drew needed.

"You're still gonna have another year at this school after I've gone off to college," Lee had said one time before basketball started. "But this is it for me, my last chance to win a championship. Remember what Drew Brees said to the guys in the huddle, before he took the Saints down the field in the fourth quarter of the Super Bowl against the Colts? 'Let's be special.' Now we've got the chance to do something special, and I'll do whatever it takes. You drag me across the finish line on that, I'll help pull you through junior year."

It wasn't as if Drew was going to him all the time, asking for help. He didn't want Lee to feel as if he was taking junior-year classes all over again along with his senior-year classes. But when Drew did have to pick it up—like now, with Mr. Shockey—Lee was all over it.

Which meant this paper on playground stars—playground legends—would be like a lot of others they'd teamed up on. Lee would do most of the research, highlight the important stuff he thought Drew should use, even outline it for him.

Then, after Drew wrote the paper himself, Lee would go over it one more time, fixing up the punctuation, and hand it back to him before it went to the teacher.

So Drew knew he didn't need to sweat the start of this paper. It was really just for fun that he went to Google and tried to find out about some old-time basketball star named Donald. First name or last.

Came up empty.

Then he played around a little bit, with "playground legend," but what he mostly came up with was Larry Bird, because they used to call him Larry Legend.

He tried "Donald" and "Legend" and mostly came up with different kids on Facebook, kids named Donald calling themselves legends.

Or legen*dary.*

Lee would probably end up doing most of the work on this, but Drew had to admit he wanted to know, *Who was this guy?*

SIXTEEN

Drew and Lee and the Brandt twins, Tyler and Jake, were walking down the hall the next morning, between first and second period, arguing about whether you'd take Kevin Durant or Derrick Rose if you were starting a team and could only pick one of them, when they saw Callie Mason coming in the other direction.

"Mayday, mayday!" Lee said, at least not shouting it out. "Callie alert."

"What's that supposed to mean?" Drew said.

"You better run now, dude. Or you may have to actually *talk* to the girl."

Tyler said, "Drew got a little thing on Callie?"

"Get *out*," Jake said.

Drew said, "Maybe Lee's the one who does, not me. I got no issues with the girl one way or the other."

Lee grinned. "Define issues."

None of them, not even Lee, knew how right they were, Drew thought. He'd done his best not to let on what he really felt about Callie and how she made him feel—like he was back to being the smallest kid on the court.

But *no* way he was going to give them the satisfaction of being right. Or making him feel weird about running into Callie and her friends in the hall—one of whom he knew was named Lizzie, but couldn't for the life of him remember her last name. The other one he only knew as number 12 from watching the girls' practice.

He'd been sneaking around and watching them more than Lee even knew.

They were about ten feet away from the girls now, and neither group had room to pass. Drew could feel Lee and the Brandts watching him, wanting to see what he'd do, or say, as if they wanted to see how uncool the always cool Drew Robinson could be in that moment, all because of one off-the-grid cute girl.

So what he said to Callie, in a voice he didn't even recognize, was this: "Whooo, me, you are lookin' fine today, girl."

And he knew instantly he'd fired up a brick. Hundred percent.

He heard Lee, right there on his shoulder, groan quietly.

He saw Callie's eyes get big.

"Girl?" Callie said.

It would have been better if she'd acted mad. Or just ignored him, like she hadn't heard, and kept on walking. Instead, Callie did something worse.

Way worse.

She burst out laughing. Right before she did a pretty good impersonation of the dumb street voice Drew had used on her.

"You lookin' *fine,* girl," she said to her friends, Lizzie and number 12.

Who laughed, too.

Now Callie went to a high-pitched, girly-girl voice, saying, "OMG, Drew Robinson noticed I'm a . . . girl!"

Drew turned to Lee, looked at him hard, as if saying, *Save me.* Not this time. Lee just grinned. Drew was on his own.

But Drew had nothing, other than the heat on his neck, the *embarrassment* he was feeling.

All he could do was step aside, let Callie and her friends pass.

Then he heard the girls laughing again before they disappeared around a corner, heard the same laughter Lee and Tyler and Jake heard.

The Brandts, even though they didn't know Drew as well as Lee did, weren't that kind of bros with him, knew enough not to say anything more.

Even Lee waited about a minute, before finally saying, "Butter. My man is so smooth you want to spread him sometimes like butter."

The Brandts started to giggle, before Drew glared them out of that.

"Don't," Drew said, then he turned to Lee and pointed and said in a voice that had even more snap in it, *"Don't."*

Lee couldn't help himself, though. He had one more bullet left in the chamber. Took his voice way down low, like a DJ at a party, and said, "You lookin' *fine,* girl."

Then they were all moving toward the locker room, everybody laughing except Drew Robinson. Who wanted to move, all right.

All the way back to New York.

They were at Lee's house a couple of hours later, in his bedroom, the subject of Callie having been declared off-limits for the rest of the day—and, if Drew had his way, it would be forever.

Lee's room was about three times the size of Drew's. And as big as the apartment he remembered growing up in Crotona in the Bronx. Drew's bedroom back then was as small as one of Lee's walk-in closets. That was when Darlene Robinson was still working as an operator for the phone company.

By now, Drew had explained to Lee why he hadn't come over last night, telling him he wished he had, not gone to some boring party and then over to the park to get disrespected by the old hooper who called himself Donald.

They were on the floor now, Lee holding his computer in his lap while Drew showed him what he'd found on his own laptop last night.

"The only guy who fits his description happens to be dead," Drew said.

Lee brightened. "Dude!" he said. "You're back to where you started. With a ghost!"

"A guy called Urban (Legend) Sellers," Drew said. "From Sacramento."

Lee grabbed Drew's computer, put it on his lap. "But it says here that Urban Sellers died in a fire in Los Angeles ten years ago."

"And his name wasn't Donald," Drew said.

Lee had his nose practically pressed to the picture of Urban Sellers he'd enhanced on the screen.

"You can't tell too good from this," he said. "This guy has more hair and even a full beard. Never could have played for Coach D."

"But it doesn't matter whether he looks like him or not," Drew said. "Because the guy's *dead*."

"And our guy is alive."

Drew said, "And maybe just a legend in his own mind."

According to the obituary in the *Los Angeles Times,* they'd started calling him Urban Legend, or just Legend, back at Sacramento High in the 1980s. That was before he got into trouble with cheating in school and drinking and drugs and found himself in Europe. And then he disappeared for a long time before ending up dead in a fire that ate up a shelter for homeless people in South Central Los Angeles.

There was a link to some old video of him on YouTube that showed Urban Sellers apparently taking the first three-point shot in high school history. His sophomore year.

In the obit, it had said that Sacramento High had moved up its opening game a night so he *could* get the first official three-point attempt.

Urban Sellers had missed.

But that wasn't what made Drew and Lee watch the video over and over. It was what happened *after* he missed. When he blew past everybody else on the court, took off from behind the free-throw line, caught the ball with his right hand, as high as the top of the backboard, and jammed it home.

Drew and Lee went from there to Google Images, looking for a better picture of the young Urban Sellers than the one in the *Times*. But in almost all of them, he was wearing oversized shades of some kind to go with his full beard. It was that way even with his yearbook picture. Not just shades in that one, but a Dodgers cap.

And Drew knew exactly why his school would let him pose that way.

Because he had the numbers.

The game.

According to the story, Urban (Legend) Sellers had averaged thirty-five points a game in his three years on varsity for Sacramento High, eleven assists, and nine boards.

Yeah, Drew thought, *you put up numbers like that, they let you take any kind of picture you want for the yearbook.*

"I mean, this *could* be the guy I saw the other night," Lee said. "Just an older, skinnier version."

"Only it can't be," Drew said.

"Because that would make him an older, skinnier version of a dead guy."

Drew nodded. "Tough to get around that."

"So maybe this guy Donald in the park, maybe he just *wanted* to be a legend," Lee said.

Drew said, "Let me see the video of the dunk again."

They watched it again, Lee freezing Urban Sellers at the highest part of his jump, when he'd put his left arm behind his back just to make the dunk showier, more memorable.

"Well, when this guy *was* alive, he definitely did *not* stink," Lee said.

"The guy in the park has ups like that," Drew said.

"Ups, dude. But not like Legend's."

"The guy in the park looks smaller than him. Like he shrunk back inside himself."

"Smaller or just skinnier?" Lee said.

"Both."

"Okay," Lee said, "we gotta stop now."

"Why?"

"Because this guy can't be our guy," Lee said, "unless you do believe in people coming back from the dead."

"It's just that Donald carries himself like a player, you know? Talking down to me the way he did, like he knows things about ball that I don't."

"You gotta let it go, what he said to you," Lee said. "About passing the ball."

Lee still playing wingman on what he knew was Drew's team.

Then Lee had an idea. "Y'know, if we really want to know more about this dude, we should ask Coach D. He must have heard about him when he coached in Sacramento at McClatchy High."

"Would've been before Coach's time," Drew said. "And he didn't grow up in Sacramento, remember? He grew up in Oregon someplace."

"Still," Lee said, "if he coached in the same city and this Legend Sellers guy was that big a deal, he must've heard about him."

"Yeah, that makes sense. Let's ask him at practice tomorrow."

Drew still didn't know if he was more interested in the dead Legend or the one at Morrison Park.

The one at Morrison—Donald—had told Drew not to end up like him. In the park, he meant. But what about Urban (Legend) Sellers, who didn't even make it back to the park, who'd pretty much died on the street?

Two Legends. One dead, one alive.

Both of them were telling Drew not to end up like them.

Coach DiGregorio said, sure, he'd heard of Urban Legend, everybody in Sacramento—at least everybody of a certain age—had heard of him.

When Coach asked why they cared, Drew said it was for the paper he was working on. When Coach heard that, his eyes lit up like Drew had just made a pass or a play.

"That's what *I'm* talkin' about," he said, his excitement level going from zero to sixty. "I knew I had myself a real student ath-a-lete waiting to bust out."

Coach D said he never actually saw Urban Legend play, that he hadn't thought about him in years until he found out he'd died the way he had.

"He's the flip side of all the guys who made it," Coach said. "The guys who made it to college, or the Final Four, or to their hundred-million-dollar contracts in the pros. Guys like—"

"I'm gonna be," Drew said, finishing his thought.

"Yeah," Coach said. "Like you're gonna be. Guys like Legend, they're not only the flip side in basketball. It's more like they're the *dark* side."

Coach said it was amazing how often Sellers's name came up in conversations once he got to Sacramento. If a McClatchy kid put up a triple double in a game, they'd remind you in a game story that Urban Sellers had *averaged* a triple double for a whole season. If one of his kids went for forty in a game, they'd tell you how many times Sellers did it.

Like that.

"And by then," Coach said, "nobody knew what had happened to him. It was like he'd fallen off the face of the earth."

"Maybe 'cause he had," Drew said.

"No matter how good a kid was in Sacramento," Coach said, "there'd always be somebody to say, 'Yeah, but you should've seen Legend back in the day.' One year, my best player said he felt like he wasn't just competing against the other best players in the league, he was going one-on-one with a ghost."

Drew and Lee just looked at each other when he said that.

"Finally," Coach said, "I went over to talk to his old coach, Fred Holman, about him. He'd retired the year before I got there, but he was a kind of legend himself as a high school coach, the way John Mabry is at Park. I had to know if a guy I'd never seen was as good as everybody said. If maybe he had some film I could watch."

"Did he?" Drew asked.

"He did."

"And?" Lee said.

"Let me put it in language you two will understand," Coach said, grinning. "He was filthy. I sort of knew how the kid had gotten messed up, because people talked about that in Sacramento, too, but Coach Holman didn't want to talk much about it. He said there was an old proverb that covered what had happened to Mr. Sellers, as he called him, the one about how the dogs bark, but the caravan moves on. One thing he said that I'll always remember: he started losing the boy when Sellers started *believing* he was a legend."

Lee said, "You know anybody like that, Coach?"

"You mean a big star who's bought into his own hype? Nope, not me."

"Funny," Drew said. "You guys could have your own show on Comedy Central."

Coach said, "Seriously? If you want to do this paper right, you ought to talk to Coach Holman about Urban Sellers."

"Right," Lee said. "Since I've become Drew's personal driver, I'll run him up to Sacramento this weekend."

"Who said anything about Sacramento?" Coach DiGregorio said. "Santa Monica. He's got a small house there now."

Coach said Fred Holman was in his early eighties now, but still sharp. He even showed up for some coaching clinics in the area from time to time. And still full of opinions about everything, mostly how he felt the modern game of basketball had become more like some video game.

Drew said, "But if he didn't want to talk about this Urban Legend guy with you, why would he want to talk about him now?"

"Maybe he doesn't," Coach said. "Or maybe it'll be different now that Urban's dead. Whatever. I'll give him a call and see if he'll talk to you. He must know who you are."

Lee grinned. "Doesn't everybody?"

SEVENTEEN

Two nights later, Oakley played Christian Hills on the road, and compared to the Park Prep game, the Red Bull energy of that one, this felt like a preseason scrimmage.

Oakley jumped out ahead 24–4 at the start, and Christian Hills never cut the lead under twenty points for the rest of the game, even *after* Coach DiGregorio had cleared the bench and it was officially garbage time.

Cleared the bench except for Lee, who begged coach to let him stay in and play point after Drew was done for the night.

He promised not to showboat or run up the score. Promised Coach he'd play the right way over the last six minutes.

"Just let the offense run through me for a little while," he said at a time-out. "Show you I can be a pass-first guy."

And he did, dishing out five assists the rest of the way, a couple of them beauties, after he broke down the defense like he was doing his best impression of Drew, penetrating inside before kicking the ball back outside.

In the locker room, he said to Drew, "So that's what it feels like to be you."

Drew put his arm around Lee's shoulder and said, "Keep telling yourself that."

It was a Friday night, and they were all on their way to Lee's house after the bus dropped them off back at Oakley. This time Drew went along. Mr. Gilbert hadn't even been at the Christian Hills game, had said he had some business out of town. So Drew ate pizza with his teammates and got involved in one of those video games where you teamed up to kill aliens. All in all, one of those nights when he felt like one of the guys.

Even though he hadn't been one of the guys for a long time. Sometimes, at parties like this, he'd look over and catch Lee staring at him and wonder if Lee knew the exact same thing.

Much later, when Lee was driving him home, Drew asked to be dropped off at Morrison.

Lee sighed, making it like the saddest sound anywhere. "Man, you put those blinders of yours on, you don't take them off, no matter what."

"I just want to know who this guy is," Drew said.

"What if it turns out he's just some nobody?"

"Then at least I'll know that," Drew said.

He didn't tell Lee that he had been in the park the last two nights, both times waiting until two in the morning for some sign of Donald before giving up and walking back home. He was starting to feel a little bit like one of those celebrity stalkers. But then he told himself Donald was the one who'd come to Drew's game, admitted he'd seen Drew shooting around at Morrison late at night.

So, what—they were stalking each other?

It was around midnight when they pulled into the parking lot at Morrison, and the police cruiser, with Archey behind the wheel, was just pulling out. Drew told Lee he didn't have to stay this time.

"Forget it," Lee said. "A wingman is a wingman, even on some dopey stakeout."

No sign of Donald or anybody else.

This time Drew didn't hang around until two; he gave up a few minutes after one, telling Lee it was his own dang fault, maybe he'd chased the guy off for good.

When they pulled up in front of Drew's house, Lee said, "Can I ask you something?"

Now Drew was the one who groaned. "Please don't ask me again why I'm so interested in this guy."

"Wasn't going to."

"Good."

"But if I ask you something else, straight-up, will you give me an honest answer?"

"I don't lie to you, you don't lie to me," Drew said.

"And you promise you won't take it the wrong way."

"Dude, it's late," Drew said. "You know how long it takes me to fall asleep."

Lee took a deep breath, then he said, "I'm just wondering if the reason you won't give up on this guy is because he hated on you a little bit after the Park game. And nobody ever hates on you, unless they're playing against you, the way King was."

Drew turned in the front seat so he could face him, his hand still on the door handle, and said, "What are you now, Coach, worried that I'm starting to believe my own hype? That I think of my*self* as some kind of legend?"

"Do you?" Lee said in a soft voice.

Drew didn't get mad.

"No."

"You sure about that?" Lee Atkins said.

"You're supposed to be my best friend," Drew said.

"I am," Lee said.

Drew said he'd talk to him in the morning, got out of the car, walked into the house, knowing as he did that he'd never answered Lee's question.

Coach DiGregorio called Drew late Sunday morning and told him he'd just talked to Fred Holman, who said he'd be happy to talk to Drew if he could get himself to Santa Monica.

Drew called Lee right away, even though he knew that on weekends, Lee Atkins could sometimes sleep until the middle of the afternoon if he didn't have anything better to do.

"You gotta get up. We're going to Santa Monica to meet Urban Legend's old coach."

Lee mumbled something in his sleep-croak that Drew didn't understand.

"What?" Drew said.

"I said the scavenger hunt continues," Lee said. "Be over in an hour."

"Don't go back to sleep," Drew said.

"What, and miss all the fun?"

The ride to Santa Monica was no fun, not because of what Lee had said to Drew when he dropped him off Friday night and not because Lee was wasting perfectly good sleep time driving Drew over there.

It was because Lee had somehow found out what Drew had done on Saturday afternoon: snuck over to Oakley to watch the girls' team play. Done that even though Callie had laid him out in the hallway the other day.

It meant the twenty-mile drive to the address near the Santa Monica pier felt like about two hundred miles to Drew, especially since the traffic for a Sunday afternoon was more like rush hour during the week.

So Drew had to hear about Callie Mason for an hour and twenty minutes, most of it spent crawling along on the 405 and then I-10, the Santa Monica Freeway, as the GPS woman's voice directed them to the address that Coach D said was just down from the pier and from the hotel called Shutters on the Beach, on Pico.

"How many times do I have to tell you?" Drew said. "I got no interest in Callie Mason. And, just for the sake of us conversating, if I ever did, why would I after the way I acted like a donkey in the hall that day?"

"It would be better for everybody," Lee said, "if you'd just admit it. Maybe even to her."

"Why? So she can laugh at me again?"

"Dude," Lee said, "it's not like she had a choice. It would have been like trying not to laugh at *The Hangover.*"

"Why are we still talking about this?" Drew said. "Didn't we agree this would be off-limits?"

"For a day," Lee said. "I think I might have agreed to that one day. But it would be selfish of you to deny me the pleasure of busting on you. Besides, all you got to do is change your attitude."

"Did you say something to her?" Drew said, whipping his head toward Lee. "Did *she* say she doesn't like my attitude?"

Lee grinned wide now and said, "Got you. Took you to the iron and threw one down on you."

Drew didn't care.

"Did somebody tell you that for real?" he said.

Lee pointed.

"We're here," he said.

Fred Holman met them at the door of a tiny house that didn't look anything like the other, bigger houses on the block, almost like it had been shoehorned in.

Or like the old man was just living in a shoe, Drew thought.

Coach DiGregorio had said Holman played in the original NBA, back in the 1950s, but even with that, he was smaller than Drew expected, maybe five eight, tops, with thin white hair and bright blue eyes that seemed young to Drew somehow. Even in his mid-eighties, the man seemed to carry himself young, not shuffling around the way you saw old guys do at Morrison in the daytime, the ones who sat around on benches and drank their coffee and just watched the world go by.

He was wearing a V-neck sweater over some kind of golf shirt, jeans on his skinny legs and an old pair of Basket sneakers from Puma. White with a blue stripe.

Holman shook hands with Lee first, then turned to Drew and said, "So you're the hot kid, huh?"

Motioned them into the house with a wave of his hand.

Small as the house was, there was a cool view of the ocean from the back patio. Way down to the right, Drew could see the famous Ferris wheel, part of the amusement park on the pier.

Holman was telling them as they made their way to the patio that his daughter was a casting agent in the movies—"divorced," he said, "aren't they all in Hollywood?"—and that she'd wanted him to move with her to Brentwood after he fell and broke a hip a couple of years ago.

"If you're in the motion-picture business," the old man said, "everything's a big drama. She pictured me falling the next time and not being able to get up."

Drew didn't see any signs of him limping, thought what he saw instead was a pretty nice bounce in the old guy's step. A bounce to his whole *self,* really.

There were small pitchers of lemonade and iced tea waiting for them on a table on the deck. Without asking, Coach Holman poured a little of both into each glass, stirring it up with a spoon. It was a drink that Mr. Gilbert liked, iced tea and lemonade, what he called an "Arnold Palmer," named after a man who, he told Drew, had been a famous golfer.

"It's really an honor to meet you, sir," Lee said.

Coach Holman said, "You said that at the door, son."

He was grinning. But Coach D said Fred Holman didn't win more than seven hundred games by being warm and fuzzy, that he was still a hard case.

"Sometimes he just repeats himself until he can think of the next thing he wants to say," Drew said.

"I coached more than a few like him," Holman said, taking the chair with the best view of the water. "Sometimes I'd finally ask them when they were going to *stop* talking so I could *start*."

They all sat there for a moment now, Lee acting like he was afraid to talk, looking out at people walking on a path set back from the beach, or jogging, or skateboarding.

"Couldn't afford this house if I wanted to move here nowadays," Fred Holman said. "Like I was here and they built all the nice houses around me. People keep asking, do I want to sell it? But where would I go?"

Then he said, "What were you thinking with that shot against Park, you don't mind me asking?"

Even him, Drew thought.

"I thought it gave us our best chance to win," he said, not wanting to get into it. "Just didn't work out."

"You *think*?" Fred Holman said.

"All due respect," Drew said, "I didn't come here to talk about myself."

Fred Holman said, "Why are you so interested in talking about Mr. Urban Sellers?"

Drew and Lee looked at each other, and Drew nodded, as if telling him, "You take it." So Lee, talking fast, the way he did when he got nervous, told Coach Holman about the paper Drew was writing, and how they'd found out about Sellers almost by accident.

"So it's his paper," Holman said, giving a nod at Drew.

"Yes, sir."

"And you're here as, what, his coauthor? Ghostwriter?"

Ghost. The word kept popping up.

"I guess you could say," Lee said. "Me being a senior and all, and us being teammates and all . . ."

The words just drifted toward the beach.

The old man focused on Drew now and said, "He's just another guy taking care of you, isn't he?"

"We're friends," Drew said.

"I can see that," Holman said. "You ever help him out with any of his papers?"

"No, sir," Drew said.

"So it's a give-and-take relationship," the old man said. "He gives, you take."

"Not on the court," Lee said, smiling. He believed he could make anybody like him. "Out there, he gives, and I take."

"Not against Park," the old man said.

It got quiet again, except for the sound of music playing from the beach, the sound of the gulls in the air, some kind of maintenance jeep on the sand out near the water.

"Why don't you boys tell me what you know about Mr. Sellers?" Holman said. "Or what you think you know."

Lee rattled off what they'd learned from the Internet about

Sellers's career. How he was supposed to be on his way to Nevada–Las Vegas to play for a coach named Jerry Tarkanian, known as a guy who'd take any kind of outlaw player, a good coach who won a national championship at Vegas.

Lee didn't tell Urban Sellers's story in any kind of order, just jumped around, trying to recite what he and Drew had found. How the NCAA accused Sellers of having somebody take the SATs for him, even though they could never prove it.

How Coach Holman finally kicked him off his team his senior year of high school, halfway through, by which time he wasn't going to class at all, had given himself no chance to qualify for any four-year college anywhere because of his lousy grades.

How six months later he had some high school diploma nobody believed was real, and ended up in junior college. But he couldn't last there, because he got caught paying somebody to take his tests for him.

Drew picked up the story then, told how they'd read that Sellers couldn't get a tryout in the NBA, even though they were taking high school kids in those days, because he let himself get fat and out of shape after busting out of junior college. So he went to Europe, played in France and then in Greece, but got into all kinds of trouble—including jail trouble—for drinking and drugs.

Then hurt himself falling down a flight of stairs in a bar fight in Greece.

After that, he just disappeared, Drew said, until he died in that fire in Los Angeles.

"And what is it you'd like me to tell you?" Fred Holman asked. Looking right at Drew now, not Lee.

"How he threw it all away like he did, I guess."

"How, or why?"

"Either way," Drew said.

"Only he knew the answer to that," the old man said. "I kept hoping he'd figure it out before it was too late."

Drew said, "Coach DiGregorio said that you told him you started losing Legend—"

The old man said in a sharp voice, "I never called him that, not one single time."

"Coach said you thought you started losing Urban Sellers when he started to believe he *was* a legend."

"I said that, yes."

"But if he was as good as everybody says, he was—"

"He was better."

"If he was *that* good, couldn't somebody stop him?"

"Make him see what he was throwing away?" the old man said. "Make him realize what a gift he had?"

"Yes," Drew said.

"You mean like you realize?"

"I'm not saying I'm him," Drew said.

"Let me ask you something," Fred Holman said, angling his chair more toward Drew, focusing those eyes on him harder than ever. "You spend as much time in the gym as you used to?"

Drew said, "Yeah. I guess so. Sure."

"Don't sound sure to me."

"I put in the time," Drew said. "Nobody ever handed me anything."

Feeling as defensive as he had in the park with Donald.

"Nobody ever handed you anything until now," Holman said.

"I'm not sure what you mean by that . . . Coach."

Hadn't they come here to ask *him* the questions?

"There's all sorts of ways for people to *lose* their way, no matter how good they are. And you are good, son. I've seen that with my own eyes."

"You've come to watch me play?"

"Three or four times," he said. "I can still get around."

"Coach didn't tell me."

"I didn't tell *him,*" Coach Holman said. "I wanted to see for myself what all the fuss was about."

Drew waited and then finally said, "So how am I doing?"

"You don't need to wait for college," the old man said. "You're already there. It's not about the game anymore. It's all about you."

Drew felt the way he did when he ran into a pick nobody had called out. Getting slammed like this from some old coach who used to be somebody.

I didn't come here to talk about me, he thought. But he didn't say that, just cleared his throat instead and said, "'Scuse me?"

There had been nothing mean in the way Coach Holman had said it, no change Drew could see in his manner. But he wasn't looking to be some kind of good host now. "You heard me, son,"

Holman said. "When you get to be my age, you got more important things to worry about than hurting somebody's feelings."

He smiled as he kept saying mean things. "If I just went by what I see, you're just another knucklehead who thinks his teammates are what Jordan used to call them: his supporting cast."

Drew said, "But I'm averaging a double double, points and assists—"

Now the old coach snapped at him. "Don't give me numbers, kid. Don't *ever* give me numbers. What do they call you—True? If you want to be true to your talent, you'll listen to what I'm telling you."

He was, what, twice the age of Donald in the park? Being twice as hard on Drew.

Lee jumped in now, trying to change the subject. "About Legend," he said.

The old man looked back out at the water, like he was trying to see something in the distance.

"Mr. Sellers was another one who stopped working at being the best player he could be about this same time in his life," the old man said. "Decided he didn't have anything more to learn on the court, the way he didn't need to learn anything in the classroom. He used to always tell me, 'I worked hard to get here. Why can't I have some fun?' And I'd say to the boy, 'To get *here*? You're not anywhere yet.'"

"But he wouldn't listen?" Lee said.

"Not until it was too late."

"Did you stay in touch with him?"

"You mean until he died?"

"Yes."

"I did stay in touch with him, as a way of keeping a promise I made to him."

"What promise?" Lee said.

"I used to tell him that he'd hear my voice in his ear, no matter which one of us died first."

Just like that, he stood up.

"Nice to meet you boys," he said.

He was telling them that the interview—not that it had been much of one—was over. Like class being dismissed.

Drew stood up, too. He was close enough to reach out, offer the man his hand. But didn't.

He just looked at him and said, "Not that you care. But I'm not him."

"Didn't say you were, son. I'm just trying to tell you I see a lot of him in you. Or vice versa."

"You don't know me," Drew said, standing his ground.

"Better than you think."

"Off a handful of games?"

"No," Fred Holman said. "Off all the games I've ever seen."

One last time, Lee tried to lighten the atmosphere on the deck. "You know, we really didn't get a lot out of you about Urban Legend."

"Nobody ever really has," the old man said, and led them back to the front door.

Neither one of them spoke until they were on the freeway, when Lee reached over and turned down the volume on the satellite radio.

"Don't let him wreck your whole day," Lee said.

"I'm not."

"What you said to him right before we left is right," Lee said. "He *doesn't* know you."

Drew had been staring out the window. Now he turned and faced Lee.

"Why do you suppose so many people think they do all of a sudden?" he asked.

NINETEEN

His mom was in the sunroom at the front of the house on Forest Cove Lane when he came in. She asked him how it had gone in Santa Monica.

"Learned some stuff," he said, "even if it was from a mean old man."

"No love?" she said, grinning at him over her reading glasses.

"Hey, Mom," he said, knowing he sounded testy, "I don't need the whole world to love me."

"Easy there, tiger. I was just playing."

"Sorry."

"My boy home for dinner?"

"Probably not," he said. "No school tomorrow, remember?"

"You have plans?"

He took a deep breath, let it out slowly, knowing she wasn't going to like the answer to that one any more than she usually did. But he knew better than to lie. Doing that with Darlene Robinson was a way of opening himself up to house arrest, no matter how big a basketball star he was.

"Robbie's throwing a party."

"You don't even like Robbie."

"Make my life go easier, 'specially with his dad, if he would like me a little more. Lee's gonna pick me up in a while."

"Lee's going to a party at Robbie's? I thought Lee *really* didn't like Robbie."

Over his shoulder, not wanting to talk about this anymore, he said, "Who's researching a paper today—me or you?"

The last thing he heard from the sunroom was the sarcastic voice of his mom, saying, "Party at Robbie's. Good times."

Drew hoped.

He hadn't told his mom that the real reason he was going to Robbie Gilbert's party wasn't to get Robbie to like him more, just Callie Mason.

Robbie Gilbert was tall enough to be a basketball player, taller than Drew, and had played some with Lee growing up in Thousand Oaks. But he'd stopped when he got to Oakley.

"Sports have rules," Lee said on the way over to the Gilbert house. "And Robbie wasn't much better at rules than he was at basketball. He's always sort of known his best talent was being Mr. Gilbert's son, from the time I first met him, in first grade."

"You know the deal," Drew said. "I just don't want the guy hating on me."

"You ever think there's some things you can't control?" Lee said.

"Nah," Drew said.

When they arrived, Drew was surprised to see there were more people tonight than there had been for Mr. Gilbert's party after the Park Prep game. But that was Mr. Gilbert's show, not Robbie's. Drew knew from previous experience that if this was anything like Robbie's other parties at the house, Mr. Gilbert was probably upstairs in his soundproof study, hiding.

Robbie spotted Drew and Lee from across the swimming pool when they had made their way out back. He was wearing what he usually did, a black T-shirt and old-looking jeans with holes in the knees. Drew knew the jeans cost a couple of hundred dollars at least to look that way.

"Hey," Robbie said to Lee, without even looking at him, as he gave Drew a lean-in hug.

It was then, over Robbie's shoulder, that Drew saw Callie, in a crowd of girls near the diving board, looking back at him.

"What's good?" Robbie yelled at Drew over the music.

His mood seemed different, better than it had been at the breakfast table the other day. Maybe he was trying to make things better with Drew. Or maybe it was just part of the show. It was hard with Robbie sometimes, trying to figure out what was a pose, what was real, when he was messing with you, when he was just having fun.

"Check you out later," he said to Drew. "Right now, gotta go do my host *thang*."

Drew watched him make his way to the end of the pool where Callie was and put his arm around her shoulder. Watched as Robbie leaned over and said something into her ear that made her laugh.

Lee saw, too.

"Funny guy, that Robbie," he said.

"Just doing his host *thang*," Drew said. "Like he said."

"Really?"

Drew's eyes were still on Robbie and Callie, on Robbie's arm around her shoulder.

"They're just talking at a party is all."

"Really." Lee drew the word out, not even trying to make it sound like he was asking a question this time.

As if Robbie could feel them staring at him now, he looked across the water, smiled and waved with his free hand.

Lee said, "He's using Callie to mess with you."

"I got no claim to Callie Mason," Drew said. "Dude, you're reading way too much into it."

Lee said, "Sometimes I think you forget how well I can read *you*."

They walked around a little bit after that. The party was catered—of course, it was the Gilberts'—and Drew and Lee found the stations where they were serving cheeseburger sliders, filled a plate with those, found an empty table, and ate. Some other seniors from Robbie's rich-boy crowd spotted them, pulled up chairs for a while, talked basketball with them like they actually cared.

Beyond where the DJ was set up and a temporary dance floor had been laid down, Drew saw the lighted basketball court, nobody on it tonight, not even fooling around. For a second, even on a night when he'd said he wanted to get away from thinking about basketball, Drew imagined himself out there by himself, the party over, everybody else gone.

Maybe just Callie watching him shoot around.

He got up from the table, walked around the edges of the party, trying to see where she was, if she *was* still with Robbie. Wanting somehow to get a few minutes with her, find a way to act as comfortable with her as Robbie had.

He had made it look as easy as Drew made things on the court.

When Drew couldn't find her in the crowd or on the dance floor, he went to get himself a soda at the bar next to the cheeseburger station.

He waited to get to the front of the line.

When he had his drink, he turned around and there she was. Startled, Drew nearly spilled his soda on her blue shirt.

"Hey," he said.

"Hey, Drew." She looked around. "Where's Lee? I never see one of you without the other."

He didn't know whether she meant it as a dig or not, but he took it that way.

"Where's Robbie?" he said.

Idiot, he thought as soon as he said it.

"No clue," Callie said. "Why would you ask me that?"

"You look nice tonight," Drew said.

She was wearing a white dress that showed off her figure, her long legs.

"Not lookin' *fine*?" But she was smiling as she spoke. No harm, no foul.

Drew put out his hand, saying, "Peace?"

She shook it.

"Peace," she said.

"Thank you *so* much." He felt like you do when you get a do-over on the playground. "You want me to get you something to drink?"

"I'm fine."

They both just stood there, Drew not knowing what to say, hoping Lee would come back and rescue him, start talking so he didn't have to.

Except it wasn't Lee who showed up.

It was Robbie.

Robbie with his loud voice, like he was trying to be heard over Kanye, over the whole party. No volume switch on his voice you could turn down, ever.

"Wait a second. You trying to hit on my date?"

Drew knew he was imagining it, but felt all the eyes at the party on him, just like that.

"Just saying hi," Drew said.

Which was about all he really *had* said to Callie.

"I don't know," Robbie said. "I heard you might be sweet on Miss Callie."

Callie said, "Robbie, mind your own business."

He does know, Drew thought. He didn't know how. But Robbie knew.

"I should've seen this coming," Robbie said, not letting it go. "The two best basketball players in the school, like, in the same backcourt"—turning to the crowd—"if you know what I mean."

Drew said, "C'mon, man, give it a rest, okay?"

But Robbie was enjoying himself. Like he was on stage, just without his band. Drew noticed that there were more kids in the immediate area than there had been a couple of minutes ago.

"Wow," Robbie said. "My man True has a freak on for Callie."

He was trying harder than ever—trying too hard, Drew thought—to be the show at his own party. Or just trying to show Drew up.

"Shut it," Drew said.

Drew was tired of this. Robbie Gilbert didn't get to embarrass him, not even at his own house, at his own party.

"I'm just having a little fun."

"Maybe you are," Drew said. "I'm not."

"If you can't take a joke—"

"Shut it now," Drew said.

"And I'm going to do that . . . *because*?"

"Because I'm telling you to."

"Oh, I *forgot,*" Robbie said. "Everybody's supposed to do what True Robinson wants. Did you know that, Callie?"

"Leave Callie out of it," Drew said.

This was another way of looking bad in front of her, Drew knew it. But couldn't stop himself. A bad day that had started with the mean old coach was ending worse.

"I can speak for myself, thank you," Callie said. "Though I can't imagine why I'd want to speak to either one of you at this particular moment."

She was the cool one, even now.

"I didn't mean it that way," Drew said. "I just . . ."

It was like his words just dropped out of the air.

"Can't talk to the girl?" Robbie said. "I thought you could do anything."

Was he drunk, acting this way?

"This is the last time I'm going to tell you to shut it," Drew said.

"Or what?" Robbie said. "You gonna take me to the basket?" For some reason, Robbie laughed now, like he'd cracked himself up.

Drew took it as if he were laughing at him.

He stepped forward, but that was as far as he got, because Lee was there now, a death grip on Drew's right arm.

It had turned into a scene, and Lee was trying to get him out of it.

"Hey," Lee said, "I thought parties were supposed to be fun."

Robbie said, "Looks like the only one not having fun here is Number One."

Before Drew could respond, Lee was walking him away, back toward the main house, keeping that firm grip on his arm.

Drew didn't turn around all the way to the house, but he didn't have to. He could feel Callie's eyes on him the whole time.

TWENTY

Drew was tired of listening to people who thought they were experts on him or his game, as if they thought looking at him on a basketball court gave them the ability to see right inside him.

The season had been going along fine; everything had been going along fine. But now, just like that, he was sick of just about everybody: old coaches, dead legends, ghosts in the park. *Girls.* And especially guys like Robbie Gilbert, who thought his daddy liked Drew better. Boo hoo.

Drew was just going to tune out all the noise and play his game. What, there was a problem with it all of a sudden? Really? If there was so much wrong with it, if he was such a bad guy and a bad teammate, then why did everybody in the world want him to come play his one-and-done year of college basketball for them?

How many other *juniors* in high school who weren't even sixteen years old yet, who didn't even have their driver's license yet, could say that?

So he made up his mind: in two nights, he was going to take everything out on Conejo Valley Christian, Oakley's next opponent.

Let his game do the talking, like always. Let his *game* answer all of them. Coach Holman acted like numbers didn't count in sports?

Then tell sports to stop keeping score.

Drew was still mad at the world the next day at practice.

He was guarding Ricky Colson, the sixth man for Oakley, a guy who could play both guard positions if he had to, and small forward. He was playing point for the second team at the end of a scrimmage, and Tyler was playing with him, to make the sides more even.

And even though Ricky hadn't called out a play, Drew knew what was coming just by his eyes—a high pick-and-roll. Trouble was, Drew read it too late.

Drew bounced off Tyler's pick and landed on his left shoulder. Hard.

When Tyler offered a hand to help him up, Drew snapped at him. "You're supposed to set screens in practice, not make me feel as if I just got hit by a car."

Tyler kept his hand out, like he couldn't believe Drew was really mad.

Drew ignored it, got up on his own. It was the same as slapping Tyler's hand away.

"What," Tyler said, "nobody's supposed to touch you? Maybe we should put a different uniform on you, like they do with quarterbacks in football."

Tyler was also a tight end on the Oakley football team.

"Maybe you should just focus on basketball," Drew said, "and think what this team would look like if I got hurt."

It ended right there. Coach D came running in from half-court, blowing his whistle like a ref, saying practice was over, telling them that was about enough fellowship and bonding for one afternoon.

Drew iced the shoulder as soon as he got to the locker room and again when he got home. It was still sore, but not nearly sore enough for him to even think about sitting out the Conejo game. No way.

What had happened with Tyler just made him more chafed at the world.

Mr. Gilbert figured it out, though. Drew was out on the court earlier than everybody else before the game, shooting around by himself, one of the managers feeding him the ball. Just trying to see if the stiffness in his off shoulder was going to affect his shot.

"Hey, you okay?" Mr. Gilbert said when Drew came off the court.

On game nights, a seven o'clock game tonight, he was at the gym earlier than Coach DiGregorio was sometimes. Like the gym was just an extension of the man's office.

"Good to go," Drew said, just wanting to get back inside the locker room, get his headphones on, listen to some tunes, change out of his T-shirt and sweatpants and into his uniform. "Looking to have a big night," he said.

"You look like you're favoring your left side a little bit."

Sometimes the man's eyes were better than a zoom lens on a camera.

"Got a little stinger at practice yesterday. Wasn't no thing."

"Just remember, rule number one is don't get hurt."

"I forget, what's number two?"

"See rule number one." He put his hand on Drew's right shoulder. "So let's not be rolling around the floor tonight, got it?"

"Got it."

"I'm serious."

Drew grinned, wanting to get out of there. "Don't I know."

"I *am* serious," Mr. Gilbert said. "Nothing's going to happen to you, not on my watch. From now until you pick your college, we want them to keep talking about you, not somebody else. Might even get the next game against Park Prep—your chance for redemption—on ESPN2."

Last game of the regular season.

"Cool," Drew said, then told Mr. Gilbert in a nice way that he needed to go get ready for the tip and pulled away, wondering what it was going to be like, having the man in his ear the rest of his life.

The Conejo Valley Wildcats had made it to the semifinals of the league tournament the last two years, losing to Park Prep both times. But they had graduated most of their best players last season and now were starting three sophomores and two juniors. They had only managed to split the six league games they'd played so far.

Not only were the Wildcats inexperienced, they weren't particularly big. Oakley had a size advantage at every position on the court, including Drew's at point, something that didn't happen all the time.

On paper, the game should have been easy.

It wasn't on the court.

With four minutes left in the half, Oakley was down fifteen points. The Wildcats—they just had "Cats" on the front of their uniform—wouldn't miss, Tyler was on the bench with two fouls, Lee had missed all six of the three-pointers he'd attempted, and Brandon was in the locker room having a twisted ankle looked at by the trainer.

As loud as the gym had been for the Park Prep game, tonight all the noise was coming from the one pocket of the place where the Conejo fans were sitting, yelling their heads off, stomping their feet, sometimes making it sound as if this were a home game for them, as badly as they were outnumbered.

The Oakley fans seemed too shocked at what they were seeing to do anything but sit on their hands and hope things got better.

Drew was the only one keeping the Wolves in it, despite the fact that, with no one else hitting the shots, he often found himself double- or even triple-teamed on defense. There always seemed to be a crowd in his face every time one of his teammates would swing the ball back to him.

But somehow he kept finding ways to create space for himself and get his shot. The only help he was getting on offense was from Ricky Colson, who'd replaced Brandon at power forward and managed to get some easy baskets inside when Drew wasn't firing away from the outside.

Drew looked up at the clock and did what he always did in a game, whether his team was winning or losing: imagined the next four minutes as a game all by themselves. Told himself that all Oakley needed to do to *make* this a game was win these four minutes, see if they could win it by enough to cut the Conejo lead under ten going to the locker room.

He pulled Ricky aside and told him his plan.

"We just have to stop the bleeding for now," Drew said. "Because if we're down twenty at half, we're not winning tonight."

Ricky grinned. "I'll hang with you," he said, "just like always. Know why?"

"Why?"

Ricky said, "'Cause it's been working for me, that's why."

From there to the end of the half, Oakley went on a 12–2 run. Drew scored the first ten points, but on the last play before the horn, three guys on him, already up in the air, the whole gym sure he was going to score one more time, Drew passed.

Ricky came off a back screen just in time, and what might have looked to be an air ball from Drew turned out to be a perfect lob pass that Ricky—who had serious ups—caught off to the side of the rim and threw down.

Highlight reel dunk.

Now there was some Oakley noise in the gym.

They were still down five points; the scoreboard said so. But Drew could see in the faces of the Conejo Cats, just the way they walked off the court, that they felt as if they were behind now.

Drew would have been happy to start the second half right then. He'd taken one spill early in the game, drawing an offensive foul but paying full price for it, landing on his sore shoulder. But for now, he was feeling no pain because of the rush of the last four minutes.

He wasn't the one in the hurting now. The guys on the other team were. And he wanted to make it worse for them once the second half started. He wasn't losing this game now, no way.

No excuses.

On his way back onto the court for the second half, Drew noticed Callie sitting with some friends about halfway up the bleachers, across from the Oakley bench. He made sure he didn't make eye contact with her. *What did she say the other night? I can speak for myself?* Drew wondered what she had to say about the way he was playing tonight.

Not that he was going to ask.

He didn't need her or anybody else to tell him what they thought about his game tonight. He was doing what he'd always done: trying to win the game.

Only the Cats wouldn't go away. Hadn't given up because of the way the first half had ended. Even after Oakley took an eight-point lead with about seven minutes to go, and Drew thought they had to be done *this* time, they came back with eight points in a row and tied the game again.

Coming out of a time-out, Lee said, "Shouldn't they have realized by now that we're better than they are?"

Drew said, "Maybe we could text them."

With twenty seconds to go in the game, Lee's man made a crazy three to put Conejo up by three. But Drew, who had forty points by now—out of the seventy Oakley had scored—pulled up on the break even though he could have driven the ball all the way to the iron, totally feeling it by now, and made a three of his own.

Game tied again, 70 all.

Fifteen seconds left.

Conejo was out of time-outs, but it didn't matter. Everybody in the gym knew what they were going to do, run the clock down as far as they could for the last shot, so that even if they missed, Oakley—which meant Drew—wouldn't have time for a last shot of their own.

But Lee had his own idea about how the game should end, and it didn't include giving Conejo a shot.

He knocked the ball away from his man without fouling him, a clean steal. The ball ended up loose near half-court, Drew the closest player on their team to it.

Drew saw the ball, saw Lee streaking toward their basket at the same time.

Because he could see everything.

Including the clock. Ten seconds left.

All Drew had to do was dive to get the ball. Dive and slap it in Lee's direction for the game-winning layup.

Only Drew didn't dive.

Instead, he pulled up, thinking about his shoulder, remembering how much it had hurt when he landed on it in the first half, hearing Mr. Gilbert's voice in his head, telling him to let somebody else roll around on the floor tonight. Telling him not to get hurt.

Rule number one, for Oakley's number 1.

He would tell himself later that he really thought he had enough time to pick the ball up and pass it to Lee.

Didn't matter.

Because Lee's man appeared out of nowhere, not chasing Lee the way he should have been, chasing the ball, flying past Drew like he was launching himself into a racing dive in swimming.

He was the one who saved the ball from going out of bounds, slapping it to Drew's now-open man.

Who caught the ball in stride, turned, took one dribble and buried a three.

Conejo 73, Oakley 70.

The horn sounded.

Game over.

Drew felt sick.

Of all the things you could fault him on in basketball, for all the times people had a right to say he was hogging the ball—at least before he made one of his no-look, highlight-reel passes—nobody had ever once faulted him on effort.

No one had ever said he didn't give 100 percent.

I should've gone for that ball, he thought.

I *should have been the one laying out for the ball the way the kid from Conejo Valley did.*

I should never have put us in a position where the other team had the ball in the air at the end with a chance to beat us.

Drew stood there watching the players from the other team celebrating their Hollywood ending, his eyes still seeing everything at once.

He saw Callie turn away when she spotted him looking at her.

She was too good a player herself not to know what she'd just seen.

Drew saw Coach D's back as he headed quickly toward the locker room.

He couldn't find his mom. If she was still at her seat, she was being hidden by the Conejo Valley Cats.

Now he started walking slowly toward the locker room, a forty-point game having turned to mud. As he did, his eyes once again took him to the top of the Gilbert Athletic Center, way up in the far corner.

Same corner as before.

Somehow he knew that Donald was up there before he even saw him.

And he was looking even more disgusted than after the Park Prep game, shaking his head slowly from side to side. When he saw Drew staring up at him, he stopped shaking his head, put his hands out in front of him like an umpire making the "safe" sign in baseball.

He was right, of course.

Drew *had* played it safe.

Never again, he told himself.

Never again.

Drew was in and out of the locker room before Coach even came out of his office to give them his post-game thoughts, always delivered with a stat sheet in his hand, one he already seemed to have memorized by the time he started talking to them, win or lose.

Drew just threw on a warm-up jacket, pulled an old Mets cap over his eyes, stuffed his phone and his wallet into his pockets, left the jeans he'd worn to the game and his Rihanna T-shirt hanging in his locker.

He didn't even take time to explain to Lee what he was doing or where he was going, just said, "I got to get out of here. *Now*."

The way the game had ended, it was worse than if he'd choked by missing a wide-open shot or a free throw.

So Drew was on the move. Out into the parking lot, around to the front of the gym, where fans were still exiting. He pulled the Mets cap down even lower, hoping nobody would bother him as long as he just kept moving, stayed away from the crowd, most of whom were Oakley fans and wanted to get away from the gym as much as Drew did.

Like they were leaving the scene of a crime. Same as Drew.

And there, on the other side of the street, limping slightly, head down, was Donald.

Drew decided to follow him, follow him even if he was taking the two-mile walk back to town. See where he went, maybe even find out where he lived. He was going to find out who the guy *was,* once and for all, why he kept showing up, why he kept waiting to catch Drew's eye only to look disappointed.

He didn't seem to be in much of a hurry and never looked back. Drew stayed a block behind, on the other side of the street, ready to hide behind a lamppost or tree if Donald did turn around.

Right before they reached the start of downtown, the first stores, Donald took a right, toward the old train station, which had been renovated into an indoor shopping mall and food court. Lee and Drew sometimes went in there for lunch when both of them had the same free period.

As Donald went past that, Drew still hung back.

First you go looking for him in the park in the middle of the night, Drew told himself. *Now you follow the guy all the way from school.*

But Lee had been right.

Drew had put his blinders back on as soon as he saw the guy after the game.

If there was a poor side of town in Agoura Hills, they were in it now. Donald walked past check-cashing stores and a couple of bad-looking bars, then past the bus terminal. Not the Southern California you saw in TV shows.

Up ahead there was an old residence hotel that Lee had pointed out one time, the Conejo Valley Hotel, the front of it looking like something built a hundred years ago. Or more. Lee had told Drew it was the oldest building in town.

Donald walked up the steps and through the double doors.

Drew hung back, waited a few minutes, until he was sure the coast was clear, and followed him in. There was a bald white guy behind the front desk, watching television on a small set.

Drew didn't know how much of a story he needed to make up to find somebody at the Conejo Valley Hotel, so he kept it simple.

"Excuse me. I just saw a guy I thought I recognized walk into the lobby. I was wondering what room he might be in."

"Name?"

"Donald," Drew said.

"Donald who?"

"It's kind of funny," Drew said, "and you gotta believe me, but I've only ever known him as Donald." He smiled. "Long story."

The guy didn't even open the ledger in front of him, just said to Drew, "This isn't the Four Seasons, kid. But we don't give out room information unless you got a full name. Which you ought to have, him being your friend and all."

"We just know each other from playing ball in the park," Drew said.

Nothing.

Drew decided to try something, because it couldn't hurt.

"Hey, I forgot my manners," he said, putting out his hand. "I'm Drew Robinson. From the Oakley team."

"Drew Robinson!" the guy said. "From Oakley!" The guy pumped his hand.

Drew tried to look embarrassed, thinking that what he was doing was taking the guy behind the desk by the hand to where Drew wanted him to go.

Then the guy behind the desk said, "Kid, I don't want to burst your bubble, but I didn't care about my high school team when *I* was in high school." He went back to watching his show.

Drew went outside, walked down to the train station, sat down on the bench. He'd followed Donald all the way to this hotel. He knew the man was in there somewhere.

Now, how did he find him?

Did he have to find a way to look in the manager's guest book, one that was sitting right there on his desk? He could run any kind of play on the court he wanted, fake guys out of their shoes. Yet he couldn't handle some night manager at some run-down hotel?

It was getting late, and there was hardly any traffic on the streets in front of him. Drew didn't care how late it was. He was on a mission now, the blinders on, wasn't going to waste the time he'd spent following the man.

No way. He'd already lost one game tonight.

He wasn't losing another. Wasn't losing Donald.

He sat there and looked up the street at the Conejo Valley Hotel, saw the lights in most of the windows, saw one light get turned off. The man was in one of those rooms, he told himself.

Which one?

Wasn't like he could go back now to the guy behind the desk, tell him the truth, tell him he was trying to solve a mystery.

Outthink the guy, Drew told himself. *The way you outthink people every time you play a game. At least until you don't dive for the ball . . .*

Well, he would just have to find some way to dive headfirst now.

It was then that he saw the skinny young guy come out of the hotel, dressed in what looked like a cheap bellman's outfit, probably the only bellman they had in the place.

Drew was up and moving right away.

"Excuse me?" he said.

The skinny guy was startled at first. Drew's voice was as loud as a siren on the otherwise empty street.

The bellman, if that's what he was, turned around. Then it was like he was about to say one thing, but changed his mind when he got a good look at Drew's face.

"Drew Robinson?" he said.

Yes.

"That's me."

"Dude, I've seen you play."

He's not much older than I am, Drew realized.

"Thanks," Drew said. "Listen, I need a favor." Grinned. "What's your name?"

"Josh," he said. "I got out of Westlake Village High a couple of years ago. I go to the community college."

"Cool," Drew said, trying to act like he cared. "Nice to meet you, Josh."

Think fast.

He took a deep breath and let it rip.

"Anyway," Drew said, "it's a long story, but there's a guy staying here, older dude, I played some ball with him over at Morrison? He never told me his last name, we were just bros in the park, you know? But I saw him walk into the hotel tonight, and the guy behind the desk wasn't much help . . ."

Drew tried to look as helpless as he felt.

"Vic," Josh said. "He wouldn't throw water on you if you were on fire."

"Tell me about it."

"Can you describe the guy?"

Drew did the best he could.

"I know him." Josh said, "That's the old dude with all the books. I brought him up some coffee once. He's in 3G."

"Fresh," Drew said. "One more thing? Is there another way I can get up there without going through the front door? I don't want Vic to think I'm a stalker or something."

"I can't believe I'm with Drew Robinson," Josh said, and then took him around to the service entrance, showed him where the back stairs were.

Drew was already moving toward the staircase as Josh was saying good night. When he got to the third floor, he found 3G, heard what sounded like jazz music coming from inside.

Knocked on the door.

TWENTY-TWO

This time there was something in the man's eyes Drew had never seen before. If it wasn't fear Drew was looking at, it was close enough. Like what he really wanted to do was run. Shove past Drew and just escape into the night, run with whatever his old legs still had left in them.

Instead, he took a deep breath and said in a tired voice, "You followed me."

"Followed you good."

"And you're feelin' good 'cause you found me."

Drew shrugged.

"Good for you. Now leave."

"You know I can't do that. That I'm gonna stay with you now."

"'Cause you think this is, what, some kind of game?"

"In a way, yeah. Maybe."

"Well, it's not. To you maybe. Not to me. You don't want to get into my business."

"Not your business. Just who you really are."

The man shook his head.

Drew said, "You gonna let me come in, by the way?"

He thought he saw the man smile.

"It's not what I do."

"Do what?"

"Let people in. Been doing a much better job at keeping them out. Least till now."

"So is your name really Donald?"

"Partly."

"You're partly named Donald? Give it up, okay? If I partly found out about you, I can find out the rest now."

And just like that, he did seem to give up, like he was quitting a game of one-on-one. Or a fight. He leaned himself against the door frame, almost like he needed it to hold himself up. Then he said, "Urban Donald Sellers. Least before the world changed my middle name to Legend."

TWENTY-THREE

So it was true.

"You're him."

"Used to be him. Past tense. Back when that was my biggest problem. Me being me. Never got the hang of that, not till it was too late, anyway."

Drew knew how dumb it was going to sound, but said what he wanted to say anyway.

"You're supposed to be dead. It was one of the headlines after that fire: 'Death of a Playground Legend.'"

"Trust me," Urban Sellers said, "that Legend had been dead a long time before that shelter went up in flames."

They were still facing each other in the doorway, Legend just inside the room, Drew in the hall.

"That Legend," he continued, "died a long time ago. Of natural causes. Starting with the natural cause of stupidity. And he's gonna stay dead, with or without your help."

"Ask you again," Drew said. "You gonna let me in, or we gonna stand out here all night?"

"Might as well," he said. "Maybe then you'll leave me be."

"You mean like you've let *me* be?" Drew said.

Legend motioned him into the room.

The inside was nothing like Drew expected.

Starting with how clean it was, like it shouldn't even have been part of this old run-down hotel. It didn't fit, the way the run-down hotel didn't seem to fit the town.

The bed was made up nice, no wrinkles showing. No clothes or towels on the floor. Nothing at all, then, like Drew's room at home, no matter how many times Darlene Robinson marched him back in there and told him to clean up, that she wasn't his maid and God hadn't put her on this earth to pick up after him.

No TV in this room.

No laptop that Drew could see anywhere.

Just a small CD player on the table next to the bed, discs stacked neatly in their cases beside it. Drew was close enough to read the top one: *Kind of Blue,* by Miles Davis.

Drew knew his mom liked Miles Davis, recognized the sound of the man's trumpet because he'd heard it so much growing up.

But it wasn't the familiar music that struck him, the neatness and order of the place.

It was the books.

Books everywhere.

They were piled on top of an old green footlocker that Urban

Sellers had shoved against a wall next to the bathroom. In other places, they were just stacked against the walls, going nearly all the way to the ceiling. On either side of the one window in the room, they were in shelves that Drew wondered if the man might have built himself. On the desk were more books, and some of those old-fashioned Mead Square Deal black-and-white tablets, the kind Drew remembered from grade school, with a place for your class schedule on the inside cover.

There was barely enough room in one corner for an old recliner chair, fake leather, Drew could tell, black tape holding it together in some places, a reading lamp next to it.

The only other chair in the room was a swivel chair pushed up to the desk. Urban Sellers motioned now for Drew to sit himself there. He got on the bed, grimacing as he forgot to put the weight on his right knee.

"You like to read," Drew said.

"Do now."

"You didn't when you were my age?"

"Didn't think I had to," he said. "Thought there was others supposed to take care of that the way they took care of everything else except playing ball."

Drew had so many questions he didn't know where to begin, but Urban Sellers asked one first.

"Why'd you have to know so bad?"

Drew shrugged. "When I get fixed on something . . ." He shrugged again. All he had.

"Got to have what you got to have," Urban Sellers said.

"'Cause I'm so spoiled?" Drew said. "We on our way back to that?"

"You *are* spoiled," Sellers said. "But spoiled doesn't have anything to do with this. It's about who you are. One of the things that's gonna at least give you the chance to be great. That thing I had once before I lost it. The thing on the court that makes you sure nothing or nobody is gonna get in your way. Even when you mess up like you did tonight. When you *give* up."

"I know what I did. Or didn't do."

"Everybody makes mistakes," Legend said. "You just gotta stay away from the big ones."

They sat there eyeballing each other.

"Does anybody else know you're alive?"

"Hardly anybody," he said. "And that's the way it has to stay, provided I can trust you."

"You can."

"Because if I can't trust you . . ." Legend stopped right there, tired all of a sudden. Like he'd lost his place. "If I can't, it won't matter you found me, 'cause I'll be gone."

"I didn't come here to run you off."

"But you got the power to do that now, boy. Like you got the power to name your future."

Drew looked around the room, at the books, like he was looking at Urban Sellers's world.

"I read about you," he said. "You had the same kind of power once. You weren't supposed to end up like this."

"Now, that's where you're wrong. I figure this is exactly how I was supposed to end up."

Drew said, "Why'd you let everybody think you died? *How* did you?"

Legend leaned back, staring at the ceiling.

"There was somebody had crashed in the room I'd been living in. Somebody who showed up that day, needing a bed. Big guy, about my size. A brother. Burned up as bad as everybody else, the place went up that easy. In the papers the next day, it said they thought it was me, and I let them. Nobody was gonna turn it into one of those *CSI* shows." He still had his eyes closed, telling it. "I just let Urban Legend die once and for all, 'cause I knew nobody was gonna miss him. 'Specially me."

Drew got up. It was a way of filling the silence that was in the room now, the silence between him and the end of the man's story. He made himself seem busy looking at the titles of the books all around him.

Even some school-type textbooks, the kind Drew only opened up as some kind of last resort these days. And there was a copy of *The City Game,* by Mr. Pete Axthelm, on top of one of the stacks. Drew picked it up.

"You read this?" he said.

"I did. You?"

"Yeah."

Urban Sellers said, "You read outside of school? On your own?" Sounding surprised.

"If it's something I think might be fresh. My friend Lee gave it to me."

Not wanting to tell Legend that it was the only book he'd ever read outside of school.

"Recognize anybody in it?"

Drew felt himself sag. "I'm not like them, if that's what you mean."

"You mean the crash-and-burn guys like *me*?" Urban Sellers said.

"I'm not gonna end up in a room like this, if that's where you're going with this."

He was sorry as soon as the words were out of his mouth, falling out of the air between them like some forced shot. It was then that he noticed the old basketball Urban Sellers had been using behind the recliner. Seeing it there, knowing what the man could do with it, only made Drew feel worse.

"That came out wrong," he said.

"No, son, it did not come out wrong. It came out exactly the way you meant. And don't worry about hurting my feelings, because I don't have those anymore."

With that, he got off the bed, forgetting again to put his weight on his right knee, pulled another face.

"Time for you to go," he said.

"But I just got here."

"And now you're out of here," he said. "You got school in the morning, if you're still bothering to go to school. And I got work."

"You've got a job?" Drew knew he sounded as surprised as Urban Sellers had when Drew told him he read books.

"I do."

Sellers walked past him, opened the door.

"I'm gonna say this again, straight up," he said. "If you tell anybody about me, where I live, who I *am,* you'll never see me again."

"What about Lee? My friend? Can I tell him?"

"Nobody."

"I'd trust Lee with my life."

"Doesn't mean I have to trust him with mine," Legend said. "Anybody shows up here asking questions, looking for me, I'm gone. And this time, nobody will ever find me again."

"You're serious."

"If I'm lyin'," he said, "I'm dyin'. All over again."

"Okay," Drew said.

"Your word really count for something?"

Drew couldn't remember anybody ever asking him that question before.

"Yes, sir, it does," he said. Hoping it did.

Urban Legend Sellers put out his big right hand, one that Drew knew by now could make a basketball look as small as a baseball.

Drew shook it.

Sellers didn't let go right away.

"Your word, Drew Robinson," he said.

"I give you my word," Drew said, like he was swearing on a Bible.

Then he added, "What do I call you? I can't think of you as anything except Legend."

"I told you," the man said, his voice soft, like the jazz music behind him. "That Legend died a long time ago. The only legend on me is the one about how I threw it all away." He looked hard at Drew and said, "Don't you do the same."

When Drew finally left the little room, the door closed so quickly it nearly hit him in the back on his way out.

Drew walked to the train station, got himself a cab, quietly let himself in the front door at home so as not to wake his mom.

It seemed as if that night's game had been played a week ago, because of what had happened after it. Following Urban Legend to his room, to where his life had taken him after he'd played all his ball for Coach Fred Holman.

But there was something about the man that made it impossible for Drew to feel sorry for him. A sort of pride. Living with his books in that little room, the whole world thinking he was dead, having forgotten him a long time ago.

David Thompson, the one they once called the Skywalker, who'd had his own fall, he was still around, Drew knew that, having checked him out on Google. He was off somewhere living his Christian life. Trying to help young players not make the same mistakes he'd made. Thirty years after he had played his last game at North Carolina State, he even went back there and got a degree in sociology.

What did Urban Sellers have? An old ball and those books and some memories?

And that pride. The one thing he'd managed to hold on to, along with his ability to play himself some *mad* ball.

Maybe that's what I'll find out someday, Drew thought.

Maybe the swagger is the last thing to go.

TWENTY-FOUR

This was one of the days when the girls got to practice first.

So Drew had to wait a couple of extra hours to get back in the gym the day after the Conejo game, get back out there, start putting the ending to the game behind him. And when he finally did, Drew Robinson was on fire, playing the scrimmage at the end of practice like it was the state finals, even getting into it with Lee under the boards one time when Coach put Lee with the second team to give them more offense.

They both had their hands on a rebound, both were fighting for it, and even after Coach blew the whistle, they *kept* fighting. Drew, who was stronger than he looked, finally ripped the ball away, sending Lee flying into the basket support, a surprised look on his face.

But he didn't say anything. The look on Drew's face must have told him all he needed to know.

Even when practice was over and Drew should have blown off

enough steam, he couldn't let go of last night's game, the humiliating way it had ended for him, the way he had to watch helplessly as the kid's shot was tracking for the basket.

He hadn't just let his team down, he'd let himself down. Listening to Mr. Gilbert like he had, Mr. Gilbert telling him to be careful, not get himself hurt. Only you couldn't play basketball careful. Or afraid.

He should have listened to himself, and he hadn't.

When everybody else left the court, a couple of minutes after eight o'clock, Drew stayed out there, shooting at one end of the court, then dribbling to the other as if he were on a breakaway, throwing the ball down, then shooting at that basket for a while.

Lee came back out from the locker room looking for him, asking if he wanted a ride home.

"I'm good," Drew said.

"I can wait," Lee said.

Friend to the end, even after practice was over.

"Nah," Drew said, trying to sound casual. "I got some things I need to work on by myself. And I don't want to wait to go over to Morrison at midnight."

"You sure you're good?"

"Don't worry about me," Drew said. "I'll call you later."

When he had the gym to himself again, he pushed himself even harder than he had in practice. Ran the court more, made pull-up J's. Still on fire, wanting to dunk the ball tonight.

He'd dribble as fast and hard as he could, stop at the free-throw line, breathing hard, pretend the ref was handing him the ball like it was a game, knock down two free throws.

Then go to the other end and repeat the drill. Then again.

Until a voice stopped him.

"I can't tell—are you winning or losing?"

Callie.

TWENTY-FIVE

As usual, he didn't know what to say to her.

He just stood where he was at the line, dribbling the ball, as if somehow that could pass for conversation.

Basketball, he thought. *The only language I'm really fluent in.*

He saw that Callie was in basketball shorts, a pale blue UCLA T-shirt, some really fresh kicks, white Nikes with a blue swoosh on them that matched her T-shirt.

Finally Drew managed a "hey."

Tool.

Power tool.

"Hey, yourself."

Drew nodded at her. "You look like you're fixing to play. But you guys finished a while ago."

"My shot needs work."

Drew said, "No, it doesn't."

"How do you know?"

Drew, feeling himself relax just a little, said, "You know what they say about me. I see things."

He hadn't watched a lot of women's basketball, not even college, even when that one team, the University of Connecticut, was winning what felt like a thousand games in a row. But he couldn't imagine there could be a high school girl anywhere—or college, for that matter—who had as much game as Callie Mason did.

"Ten for twenty-four our last game," she said. "I'm better than that. But I kept putting it up there, like Kobe on a bad night."

"If you want the gym to yourself," Drew said, "I can leave."

Another brilliant move, he thought. *Give her the chance to bounce you.*

"No, you don't have to leave," she said. "I was just surprised to see you, I thought everybody was gone. Though you looked as if your own practice was still going on."

"How long have you been here?" he said.

"Long enough to see you stepping on it as if you had Coach in your ear."

"I didn't like the way last night ended."

"Not diving for that ball, you mean?"

Getting right to it.

Before Drew could respond, Callie smiled again, put out her hands. "Sorry," she said. "Sometimes my mouth says something before my brain gets a chance to stop it."

Drew didn't care. Didn't even mind what she'd said. They were talking. Just the two of them. Nobody else around.

"You don't have to apologize for saying the truth," Drew said, realizing as soon as he did that he sounded a little like Legend. "I should have been on the floor for that ball."

"It's like my dad says," Callie said. "Woulda, coulda, shoulda. Next time will be different. Now, pass me the ball."

Drew did.

"You sure you don't want to shoot around by yourself?" Drew said. "I was about to pack it in."

Callie was walking toward him, dribbling as she did, right hand, left hand, back and forth, saying, "Hey, if you want to leave—"

"No," Drew said, way too fast.

Callie said, "I mean if I have to work out with somebody, well, I *guess* you'll do."

Drew felt himself relax a little more. All of a sudden, something that had seemed harder to him than speaking Spanish in Spanish class—speaking to this girl—wasn't.

Drew told Callie he was plenty warmed up already, so he stood under the basket and rebounded for her while she started taking shots from outside, missing her first one and then making so many in a row Drew lost count.

Her shot was as pure as Lee's, her form perfect, as far as Drew could tell. Drew felt himself smiling again, this time to himself, thinking, *Yeah, Callie Mason's form is pretty much perfect in all ways.*

"What are you smiling at?" Callie said as Drew threw her a two-hand chest pass at the top of the key.

"Nothing," Drew said. "Maybe just thinking basketball is back to being fun today."

"Every day," she said, and made another shot, nothing but string. She seemed happy, too, showing off her game to Drew this way.

"You could play on the boys' team," he said.

"They have a decent point guard," she said. "And, what, girls' basketball isn't good enough for me?"

"You're just too good, period."

Callie stopped now, out on the left wing, ball cocked on her hip. "You think a girl will ever play in the NBA?"

Drew hadn't ever thought about it much, but he saw her looking at him.

"Within ten years," he said. "Sooner, if it turns out to be you."

"Suck-up," she said.

"I mean it."

Callie said, "I'm not one of those people you have to say what you think they want to hear." She hadn't moved, was still staring at him, intent. Like she knew things about him, even though this was the longest they'd ever been together.

"I mean what I say," Drew said.

"Okay," Callie said and drove the ball to the basket now, drove right past Drew, kept going underneath the basket, made a sweet little reverse, lots of spin.

"I'm ready," she said.

"For what?"

"To play you in H-O-R-S-E."

TWENTY-SIX

"You want to play *me* in H-O-R-S-E?" Drew said.

"Don't sound so surprised. You see anybody else around here for me to play?" she said.

"Okay, then," Drew said. "I guess it's on."

"*So* on," Callie said.

Drew tossed her a bounce pass, like she was supposed to go first. The ball came right back at him, almost like it hadn't touched her hands.

"No favors for the girl," she said. "We shoot for it."

They both stepped to the free-throw line. She missed, Drew made.

"You sure you don't want to go first?" he said. "Early lead might be the only one you get."

"Maybe," Callie said, "since you don't have to dive for any balls in H-O-R-S-E."

Drew, who had been ready to take his first shot, a jumper from the left side, stopped. "Don't you usually have to wait for the game to start before you start trash-talking?"

"Trash-talking is what you and Robbie did at the party," she said. "This is just me setting you up."

The girl looking for an edge. Drew knew the best players were always looking for an edge, whatever they could get, even in a pickup game like this.

Drew missed the jumper.

Callie collected the rebound, dribbled outside to the three-point line, turned, and made her first shot.

Now Drew had to match. His shot felt good when he released it, tracking on the basket all the way. But it was just a little too hard. Bounced off the back rim.

"H," Callie said, no change of expression, getting to the rebound before Drew could. She dribbled into the lane, called "lefty, bank," and put up a teardrop from about ten feet away that caught nothing but net and would have made you think she was left-handed if you didn't know better.

Drew tried to look casual as he dribbled in now, but went off his wrong foot, his right foot, and released the ball too soon, knowing he looked clumsy and hating it.

Missed again.

"H-O," Callie said and then, as if she couldn't help herself, added, "Ho, ho, ho."

She laughed, so did Drew. But he didn't really mean it. Even here, with a girl he liked and wanted to like him back—he still couldn't believe it was just the two of them—he could feel another Drew showing up in the gym.

The one who hated losing, pretty much at anything except schoolwork. Might even hate losing more than he liked Callie Mason. His mom liked to talk all the time about people having good angels and bad angels. All in their own selves. And when it was time to win the game, when it was what Reggie Miller called "winning time," he'd always thought of the Drew Robinson who hated losing as a good angel.

But was it that time now?

He remembered this movie he'd seen on ESPN about Reggie. His sister Cheryl was in it, too, because when they were growing up, Cheryl had been more of a basketball star than Reggie was. Cheryl went to the Olympics way before Reggie did.

Cheryl had grown up giving it to her little brother good at the family hoop, every chance she got.

Callie was acting like Cheryl Miller today, not missing until she'd made her first eight shots in a row; Drew felt lucky to hang with her on each one. Like she'd turned into the Cheryl Miller who'd scored a hundred points in a high school game one time.

When she finally missed, Drew took control and sank a deep three.

Callie missed again.

"Knew it probably wouldn't be a shutout," Callie said.

Drew didn't say anything, just went to the other side and made another three.

Callie missed again.

Game tied.

Drew tried to go lefty now, prove to her that she wasn't the only one who could make shots with her off hand. But he missed.

Now Callie walked to the free-throw line, turned her back to the basket, bounced the ball once, took a quick look over her shoulder, put the ball up.

Nothing but string.

Like it was no thing.

Drew tried the same shot and missed everything.

"H-O-R," Callie said. "Not a real horsey yet. Maybe a cute pony."

She was as good as he thought she was from watching her in games, maybe better.

Annoyingly good.

In a way girls could be, whether they were basketball stars or not.

When Callie missed again, Drew went a little deeper into his bag of shots, into his own game. Went on a drive from the right corner, up in the air, looked like he would shoot it on the right side, pulled it down, glided to the left, made the reverse with his left hand.

As good as Callie was, she didn't have hang time like that—few *guys* did, truth be told—and she ended up shooting the ball too soon. It was like the rim blocked it.

They were even again, three letters apiece.

Then they both made five shots in a row until Drew missed a jumper.

Callie went *back* to the line, made *another* over-the-head blind shot.

"You fixing to beat me with your trick shots, instead of straight up?"

"How'm I tricking you, if it goes in?" Callie said, putting a finger to her cheek, like she was confused.

Drew missed again. Now he was at H-O-R-S. It meant she was a letter away from beating him.

And in that moment he knew how much he didn't want her to. Didn't want to lose to a girl.

Even *this* amazing girl.

There was no conversation now. Drew couldn't help himself. The bad angel was in the gym. He knew it was dumb-guy stuff happening here, he really did.

He just couldn't stop it.

He could see Callie wanted to win as much as he didn't want to lose. But she missed a twenty-footer. Drew went and got the ball, took it out to a distance he knew by now was beyond her range. Pointed to the spot where he was standing. Called "no dribble."

Drew had always had strong wrists. The kind baseball sluggers had, the ones who could yank a ball out of the park without even swinging hard. Drew was like that. Could flick the ball a long way, no sweat—it was another reason he was such a sure passer. He stood there now, flat-footed, like he was at the line, even though he was nearly thirty feet from the basket, and calmly buried the sucker.

She went and got the ball, staring at him again, both of them knowing she couldn't reach from here.

But she didn't complain. Too proud. As proud as Drew. The ball didn't come close to the basket.

They were both at H-O-R-S.

And just like that, the air in the gym had changed, they both knew it. Both of them wanted a silly game of H-O-R-S-E. Maybe it wasn't dumb-guy stuff after all.

Just jock stuff.

Neither one of them talked. There was just the bounce of the ball and the sound of their sneakers on the floor.

Drew's shot. One more letter for the game.

And now he really couldn't stop himself, his bad self, even with this girl he'd waited the whole school year to spend this much time with. Wanting her to like him.

He still did. Want her to like him. He just liked winning a whole lot more.

There it was.

Like it or not.

He went to half-court, threw the ball out ahead of him, high in the air, so he could get the bounce he needed. A show-off shot even if he'd been playing against Lee or Brandon.

The great passer throwing himself a perfect pass.

Caught the ball in perfect stride on his way up. Then showed the girl what he hadn't shown her yet. That once he took off like this, he could just keep going up, all the way through the roof if he wanted. And right now he wanted. In the worst way. Like he was being propelled into the air and into the moment by some jet engine inside him. Like he had that kind of roar inside him now, one he had to let out when he caught the ball above the rim and threw it down.

"Come *on*!" he screamed.

When he came down, he gave his chest a hard pound, surprised at how good the dunk had felt. Thinking that even Callie had to be impressed by a throw-down worthy of the Slam Dunk competition on All-Star Saturday Night.

But when he turned around to see, throw her the ball, all he saw was her back.

She was already walking out of the gym.

TWENTY-SEVEN

Two days later.

Drew and Lee were in Lee's rec room, which would have fit right in at Mr. Gilbert's house. There was a big-screen in there that seemed as wide to Drew as a basketball court.

In the game they were watching, Steph Curry—who just got better and better—blew down the lane, blew past the defense, seemed to shock everybody on the Lakers, Kobe even, by throwing one down instead of passing the ball or pulling up to shoot it.

Drew groaned.

"You got a problem with that move?" Lee said.

"No, it was fresh to death," Drew said. "It just reminded me of *my* brilliant move against Callie."

"Sweet," Lee said. "Let's talk about that some more."

Drew had called Lee as soon as he got home, told him about the whole disaster with her, the way the game had started . . . the way it had ended. Told him the whole story, right through his dunk, not sugarcoating any of it.

Told him how he couldn't help himself, how he turned into a jerk when he thought he might lose. Couldn't stop himself.

"That shot against Callie was worse than the one I took against Park," Drew said.

"Dude," Lee said. "You *dunked* on the girl? I'm just asking—but how did you stop yourself from ripping your shirt off afterward, like you were the Incredible Hulk?"

"Thanks for making me feel better."

"What are friends for?"

"How could I have been so stupid?"

Lee said, "And you haven't run into her one time since?"

Drew shook his head. It wasn't like he was trying to avoid her. Maybe—more likely—she'd been avoiding him. Not that Drew would have known what to say if he *had* run into her.

So he was all the way back to where he'd started.

"Good job by me," Drew said. "Took me about five minutes of H-O-R-S-E to turn my sorry butt into a *horse's* butt."

"Actually," Lee said, "as I think this over, it might turn out to be a good thing."

Drew lifted his head. He was on one couch facing the screen, Lee on another.

"How do you figure?" Drew said. "Because I didn't tear up my ACL coming down after my big slammer jammer?"

"No," Lee said. "Because you're acting like a normal guy for a change."

"What am I the rest of the time, some kind of freak boy?"

Lee sat up, facing Drew. His serious face on. Like he was at the foul line and needed to knock down two.

"No," Lee said. "But you're True Robinson." Putting air quotes around the name. "You're the next thing, son, the one they all come to see, they all want to talk to, the one we all want to play ball with. Or against. You're legendary already."

It made Drew think of Urban Legend Sellers. He'd wanted in the worst way to tell Lee about the meeting in the hotel room, but had managed to keep his word so far.

"Oh, yeah," Drew said, "I'm huge. Ask Callie."

"My point!" said Lee. "It takes a girl to make you into a regulation high school junior. Turns out girls make you crazy the same as they do everybody else!"

"You don't seem to have a problem."

Lee didn't, not with girls. All the cute girls at Oakley wanted him to give them the nod.

"I'm the exception," Lee said. "The way you are when it comes to hooping."

"I'm still not feeling it," Drew said. "This being a good thing."

"Trust me."

"No."

"I can fix this with Callie if you let me."

"No!"

"Seriously, dude, let me talk to her. It's clear you can only communicate through basketball, as tragic as that sounds."

"Maybe she just doesn't like me."

"At least not the way you want her to like you."

"Yeah."

"But now we've sort of established that you have no idea how to make that happen."

"Yeah," Drew said again.

Lee said, "Maybe we can start with you not trying to impress her with how good you are at basketball. 'Cause I'm thinking she already knows that."

"Hey," Drew said, "she wanted to win that game as much as I did."

Lee turned off the sound on the big screen. "You want to know what Bob Knight's wife used to say when he wouldn't let something go," Lee said.

"Do I have a choice?"

"Instead of telling him to stop beating a dead horse, she'd just say, 'The horse died.' Get it? And us talking about a H-O-R-S-E game." He started laughing. "Dude, I crack myself up sometimes."

"Glad you're enjoying this."

Drew leaned back, tried to keep his mind on the basketball game, watching Steph Curry keep getting a step on Derek Fisher, watching Kobe get his usual step on everybody. Both of them making it look so easy.

Drew thinking, *I can't even get past a girl.*

Their next game, against Westlake Village High, a nonleague game, did make him feel like his usual self.

He didn't see Callie anywhere in the gym. Or Urban Legend

Sellers. Mr. Gilbert wasn't there either, having told Drew he had "commerce" to take care of in Las Vegas this weekend.

Only Drew's mom was there, which made it a little bit like it used to be when he was growing up, looking up in the stands when New Heights was playing in Albany or Syracuse or someplace, and his mom was the only face he recognized. Every time there was a stop in the action, she'd work on one of her crosswords.

Maybe that's why he wasn't playing to the crowd today, wasn't losing himself in some playground sideshow against somebody like King Gadsen. Today Drew played basketball the way he was supposed to play it. The way everybody was.

Basketball that began with one good pass.

He still took his shots when they were there. But today they had to be wide-open looks or a clear path to the basket. Drew made sure that nobody else on the Wolves had a better look than he did.

Westlake Village's Warriors tried every defense on him: man-to-man, double-teams, box-and-one, a couple of tricked-up zones. Nothing worked, not today. It was Drew who was in the zone. Or on a mission, to find the open man.

The open man had always been Drew's best friend in the world, at least in a basketball game.

By halftime, he had twelve assists and Oakley was up twenty on the Warriors, who were always a powerhouse in their public school league and were favored to win the league again this season. In the locker room, Lee said, "I've heard of guys being on fire shooting the ball. But never dishing it."

"Taking what they're giving me, is all. Like always."

"Then *please* keep taking," Lee said. He had nineteen points at the half, his game average for the season, right on the number. "Take from them, give to me."

In the end, Drew had twenty-five assists for the game, the most he'd ever had, high school or junior high or even with New Heights. Oakley won going away, and Coach D said afterward that if he hadn't taken Drew out with four minutes left—for what he called "humanitarian" reasons—Drew might have been the first guy he ever heard about getting to thirty assists in a game.

"Guy did it one time in the NBA," Drew said. He didn't know stats the way Lee did. But he knew this one. "Scott Skiles, the Bucks coach, did it when he was playing."

When Lee dropped Drew off at his house, it was still only four. Drew announced that before they could even talk about a plan for later, he was going to take a nap.

"You?" Lee said. "Sleeping? When it's still light out?"

"Got tired today," Drew said, "trying to raise your dag-gone scoring average."

Lee had ended the game with thirty-two points.

"Well played, Mr. Robinson," Lee said, and fist bumped him and left.

Drew went upstairs and tried to close his eyes in the quiet, empty house—his mom was off shopping with some friends. No go. Then he thought about actually working on his paper for Mr. Shockey. The due date on that was coming up fast.

Couldn't motivate. Still not sure how he was going to handle telling Legend's story without giving him up.

He tried to watch a college game on TV, couldn't motivate on that.

Finally, he realized something: He wasn't tired at all. Playing the way he had today made him want to play *more.* So even though it was still light out, even though he usually wanted to be sure about his alone time when he went to the park at night, he grabbed his outdoor ball and headed for Morrison.

When he got there, he went straight for the bad court, because there was a pickup game just finishing up on the good one, the kids high-fiving each other, laughing, collecting their stuff.

Drew steered clear of them, walking along the tree line, Mets cap pulled down low, and didn't start shooting around until they were gone.

When he did, still on his high from the game, he wasn't True Robinson, wasn't some kind of basketball superhero. He was the little Drew, the one who could only get himself into games back in New York, on bad courts like this, because of the way he could pass the ball to the bigger kids.

That's who he'd been today.

Once the other kids were gone, the only company he had in the park, other than some parents and small kids on the playground, were a couple of orange Agoura Hills trucks, maybe a hundred yards away, doing some Saturday work in the area where the new pool was going in. There were two trucks and a huge yellow backhoe, digging rocks out of the hole in the ground.

His mom had told him how the town had raised money for the

pool project and wanted it in by the summer when kids were out of school.

"That pool won't be for the country club boys and girls," she said. "It'll be the best kind of place for kids."

Drew knew where she was going, he'd heard this speech from her enough times growing up, when she'd drop him off at a youth center like Morrisania, near Yankee Stadium.

"A safe place for them to go when their folks aren't around," she'd say. "The kind of place you're going to build when you start making money in the NBA."

"Gonna build you a house first," he'd say.

"Just remember where you came from," his mom would always finish.

Drew thought about that now. *Where I come from,* he thought, *and where I'm headed are worlds apart.*

He shot for a half hour straight, finally sat down with his bottle of blue Gatorade, toweled off. He thought about putting the buds from his iPod into his ears, listening to music while he played, like he did sometimes.

But he didn't need music to get him going today.

This had been a good basketball day, best of the season. Drew wished Callie had been there. Maybe she was still mad at him.

He got up and went harder than before, nobody bothering him, the workers paying him no mind. It was mostly just straight-up shooting, Drew working on his stroke, believing that the weakest part of his game was his pull-up, mid-range J. Nobody would have believed that if he'd said so, but Drew knew the strengths and weaknesses of his own game the way he knew his phone number.

To be the player he wanted to be, the player he *had* to be, he needed to be able to knock down that shot like it was a layup. And he couldn't, not yet.

Callie had a better pull-up than he did, at least in games. Drew had seen it for himself.

So that's what he worked on today until he finally gave himself another break, chugged down the last of his Gatorade, got ready to walk home, call Lee, think about the two of them making their dinner plans.

He looked back over at the pool workers. It seemed they were about to call it a day themselves.

It was then that Drew saw him.

Urban Sellers, in dirty work clothes, old gloves covering those big basketball hands, looking tired and old, looking *whupped,* climbing into the back of one of those Agoura Hills trucks, as if it took all the strength he had left.

Drew stood there staring.

This time Drew didn't follow the man.

He didn't want to.

TWENTY-EIGHT

Mr. Gilbert was standing in the middle of the court while Drew warmed up for the game against Garner, acting like he owned the place.

Which he did.

"Haven't been seeing too much of you at the big house," he said to Drew.

Drew was shooting three-pointers, one of the team managers rebounding for him. "Would've come over on the weekend," he said, "but you were in Vegas, doing your commerce thing."

"I meant you haven't been around much, period," Mr. Gilbert said. "Dude, I'm not feeling you lately."

That was another one of his ways, talking like a kid. *But why not?* Drew thought. *He thinks he's part of the team.*

"Trying to catch up on some schoolwork," Drew said.

He had actually started writing on Mr. Shockey's paper, using a fake name for Legend.

Mr. Gilbert laughed now. "Right," he said.

"I mean it," Drew said. "I got this paper due, about old-time playground guys. I've been learning a lot about them, the history of them and whatnot."

"What*ever*," Seth Gilbert said, dragging out the last part of the word. "Just remember: high school's just your part-time job. High school *ball*, that's the day job."

Drew kept shooting as he talked, grinning as he said to Mr. Gilbert, "You better not say that in front of my mom. She says that if I've only got this year and then two more in school, she wants me to make the most of them."

"Just go out there and *school* Garner tonight, that's all I care about," Mr. Gilbert said. "And let's shoot the ball a little more. Nobody ever passed their way to the league."

"Jason Kidd," Drew said, the name just coming out of him, even though he knew Mr. Gilbert didn't like to be debated on basketball things.

"Eighteen points a game at his best, seventeen points," Mr. Gilbert said, having the numbers right there. "And all those triple doubles. He was a lot more than a pass-first guy."

"But that's what I've always been," Drew said.

Mr. Gilbert said, "Never forget something, kid: I know your game as well as you do. Maybe better sometimes." He wasn't smiling now or playing. "Shoot the ball tonight." Mr. Gilbert shook his head, like he was disgusted with Drew. "Maybe you're spending too much time in the park, living inside your own head too much."

"What?" Drew said.

Mr. Gilbert said, "Don't worry, I got eyes on you even when I'm not around. You don't think I know you've been shooting around with some old dude over at Morrison?"

How could he know that? Did the cops tell him? But how would he even know the cops?

Drew tried not to act surprised, just shrugged, like it was no thing, started dribbling toward the free-throw line, ending the conversation that way.

"Shoot it tonight," Seth Gilbert said one more time.

He did. He made the first four outside shots he took, and it was like that gave him an excuse to keep shooting, on his way to thirty-five for the night, just six assists, in a game against Garner that Oakley finally won by six. Drew even knocked down a three in the last minute after Garner had cut Oakley's lead to a basket.

On the way off the court, Drew said to Lee, "Was I too much of a ball stopper tonight?"

His way of asking if he'd been too much of a gunner.

"Nope," said Lee, who'd ended up with just eight points. "We needed you to be shooting it tonight. The rest of us couldn't throw the ball into the ocean from the beach."

Drew didn't tell Lee that wasn't the reason, that this had been another time he couldn't get Mr. Gilbert's voice out of his head. Another time when he'd let Mr. Gilbert be the boss of him, not just the boss of his mom.

After the game, Seth Gilbert was waiting for him outside the locker room, excited, even giving Drew the kind of chest bump Lee would after a good play.

Behind Mr. Gilbert, Drew could see Lee and Brandon shaking their heads, like they couldn't believe what a tool the man was sometimes.

"Do we win tonight if you're not hoisting it up there?" Mr. Gilbert said. "That's the True Robinson I'm talking about. Whole truth and nothing but."

"No, sir."

Drew just wanted to get into the locker room, but agreeing with Mr. Gilbert made his life easier, on and off the court.

"Who's your basketball coach and your life coach?" Seth Gilbert said.

"Man whose last name is on the gym."

"I'll wait for you," Mr. Gilbert said, "take you over to the house."

"Can't tonight," Drew said. "Got a little more work to do to get out from under that paper."

It was true, just not in the way Mr. Gilbert might think. He was going to work on the paper because he was going to see Urban Sellers. Drew had looked for him in the gym, but didn't spot him, second game in a row.

But he wanted to see him. Wanted to spend time with him more than he did with Mr. Gilbert.

He knew it was weird, 100 percent.

It was still the whole truth. Nothing but.

Not much media around tonight, not even close to what they'd gotten for the game against King Gadsen, but the ones who were there still had questions for Drew.

It occurred to him sometimes that it was going to be like this for the rest of his playing life, the postgame questions no different from the ones he got now. Just more people wanting answers.

Lee started calling the reporters the "True Crew." And he timed how long Drew spent with them after games.

"Fifteen minutes tonight," he said to Drew as they walked out of the locker room. "Not so horrible."

"No matter what happened in the game," Drew said, "they all want to know if I'm gonna stay home for college or go off to Kentucky or Duke or Carolina."

"And they keep coming at you."

"Like waves to the beach."

"No matter how many times you tell them your focus is winning a league championship and a state championship for your school."

"Word," Drew said.

Lee said, "You want to go get something to eat in town?"

"No," Drew said, "but would you mind dropping me?"

They had reached the door to the parking lot, and Lee was about to push it open.

"Drop you where?" he said. "Or should I say, drop you *why*?"

"It's no thing," Drew said. "But can I ask *you* not to ask *me* why?"

"No," Lee said.

"No?"

"Of course I can drop you wherever," Lee said. "I'm your wheel man, you know that. But I almost always know where you are, day or night, like I got one of those electronic anklets on you."

"Just not tonight. Okay?"

"You still ghost hunting?"

Drew hated lying to Lee, hated lying to him as much as to his mom, but he didn't see any other choice. "No. There's just something I gotta do." He grinned. "But if this is sketching you out, I can always walk."

"After you drop thirty-five on Garner? What kind of teammate would do that, even to a secret-keeping weasel?"

Drew didn't like keeping secrets and did feel like a bit of a weasel, sitting on something as big as the guy they thought dead being alive, information he knew would light Lee up like he was a rocket.

But a promise was a promise.

There was no conversation in the car until Lee dropped him in front of the Starbucks on Kanon Road.

"Curbside service," Lee said. "No tipping allowed."

"Thanks."

"No, thank *you.*" Not happy with Drew, not trying to hide it. "You sure you can get home after you do whatever it is you're doing?"

"Got cab fare."

"Wouldn't need it if I was with you."

"See you tomorrow," Drew said.

He shut the door. Lee drove away. Drew knew he wouldn't circle back, follow him. It would be, Drew knew, a violation of Lee's strict bro code. Lee wouldn't sneak around, even when he thought Drew *was* sneaking around.

As usual, Lee Atkins was a much better friend to Drew than Drew was to him. Probably always would be.

But a promise was a promise.

He went into the Starbucks, got himself a giant Frappuccino with whipped cream, the whole thing as sweet to his sweet tooth as an ice cream sundae. And he always ordered a "giant." Couldn't bring himself to order in Italian like everybody else.

He drank it through a straw on the way to Urban Sellers's hotel. Wondering if he'd been at the game tonight without Drew seeing him. Hoping that he hadn't, because Drew knew he'd shot it too much. The game he was sorry Legend had missed, if he'd missed it, was the one against Westlake Village, when he'd passed nearly all the way to thirty assists.

But he wasn't looking for him tonight to talk about basketball, he wanted to ask him more about his job, about his life, about how after all the promise he'd had—all his potential—he'd ended up living in a run-down hotel.

How he ended up working on some park crew.

Drew walked through the lobby, up the stairs, down the hall, knocked on 3G.

No answer.

Knocked harder.

Nothing.

There had been no point in calling first. Drew hadn't seen a phone in the room. For some reason, he didn't see the man owning a cell. Or maybe he did have a cell, some little throwaway phone. Nothing like the iPhone Mr. Gilbert had given Drew for Christmas.

Drew knocked on the door again, but stopped when somebody from behind a closed door nearby told him to knock it off out there. Drew walked back down the stairs to the lobby, feeling let down, wanting to talk to Legend in a way he didn't want to talk to Mr. Gilbert tonight.

Even Lee.

Maybe Legend was just out having a late dinner somewhere. Or with a friend. Did he even *have* friends? Did he have a *life*? Or just this room, his books? His job off a truck, helping build a pool.

Better question: *Why do I care so much?*

But Drew knew the answer to that one. He knew, all right. His real nightmare, True Robinson's true nightmare, wasn't just falling down a flight of stairs the way David Thompson had. The way Urban Legend had after a bar fight in Greece.

The bottom of Drew's nightmare was a room like this. A life like this.

A ghost of someone who should have made it big.

He sat on a bench in front of the hotel for a while, feeling silly. Looked down at his hand and saw that he was still carrying his drink, that there was a little left. He sucked it dry.

Drew thought about getting a cab at the train station, but didn't. Tonight he walked all the way home in the cool night air, wondering what Urban Legend thought about at this time of night, before he went to sleep.

Wondering what his dreams were like. Or his nightmares.

The rest of the way home, Drew kept telling himself the same thing, over and over again, like he was trying to scare a bogeyman away.

I'm not him.

Not him.

Not.

Him.

TWENTY-NINE

All the other juniors, whether they were sixteen yet or not, talked all the time about getting their driver's licenses. If they weren't talking about getting their licenses, they were talking about getting permits, starting the process.

Drew wasn't like them. He had his permit, but hadn't done much with it, had been out riding in a car one time with Mr. Gilbert, and both of them said they'd do it again real soon. But they never had.

Oh, he wanted to drive, all right, have the freedom of all that, and not have to rely on Lee—or Mr. Gilbert or his mom—to take him places.

But the truth was, all those people wanting to take him places—*knowing* he had people who wanted to take him places—chilled him out on the whole idea of driving. Made him less gigged up about it than the other kids in school. Maybe having his own personal car service, Lee or Mr. Gilbert's man Eddie, whenever he needed it was just one more part of being True Robinson.

As always, he thought of that guy, True, as almost another identity, the way he knew Magic Johnson used to talk about the Magic part of him and the Earvin part. People wanted to do things for True Robinson, get him stuff. The kind of stuff that would be coming his way his whole dag-gone life.

For now, he just enjoyed the ride in all ways, putting off driver's ed, not even thinking about scheduling a driver's test. He was still months away from turning sixteen, anyway.

He'd worry about it all after basketball season, even the car Mr. Gilbert had promised him when he finally did have his license.

Drew and Lee were at Mr. Gilbert's house now on Saturday night. They had the place to themselves except for the help, because Mr. Gilbert and Robbie had flown in a private plane to Phoenix for a Jay-Z concert and didn't plan to come back until morning.

Lee had been talking about the whole license thing, couldn't believe Drew wouldn't get after it. Drew told him what Mr. Gilbert always said, that he was going to buy Drew a new car a year until he could buy his own once he got to the pros.

"But don't they have rules about cars and things once you get to college?" Lee said.

Drew gave Lee the same kind of look he put on when they found out there was no check at the diner.

"Rules? Mr. G says those are for the other guys," Drew said.

"Sorry," Lee said. "I forget sometimes."

Drew said, "Mr. G said not to worry, there's always ways around the rules, that whatever car he gets is going to be in his name."

"That's why if it was me," Lee said, "I'd be getting my license *tomorrow* if I could."

"It isn't you," Drew said. "I can wait until after the season. Besides, Mr. G. says I can get behind the wheel of one of his cars anytime I want."

"Riding with him, you mean."

Drew grinned, shook his head no. "When it comes up, he just gives me that look like we're on the inside of the same joke and says, 'You really do need to take the Moz for a spin one of these days.'"

His Maserati.

"What'd you drive when he took you out that time?"

"Mercedes."

"My dad's got one of those," Lee said. "But, dude, a Maserati? It's like being at the controls of a rocket ship."

Drew said, "Mr. Gilbert says I might as well start getting the feel of a ride like that now, seeing as how I'm gonna have a whole fleet of my own someday."

They were getting ready to watch a movie in Mr. Gilbert's private theater, which was in one of the cottages behind the swimming pool—six rows of cushy red seats, a movie-theater-size screen. Mr. Gilbert's *casa* being Drew's *casa,* like always. He knew that if he called up to the main house, one of the chefs on call 24/7 would whip them up something to eat.

Have it down there a lot faster than if they ordered Domino's.

But they had already chowed out on pizza in town. As they were coming out of Pizza Nosh, on Canwood, Lee had asked if there was anyplace Drew wanted to be dropped tonight, asking if he had any secret spy-type missions planned.

Drew had said, "Nah, I'm good."

The Brandt twins, Tyler and Jake, were having some kind of party, and Drew and Lee had said they might drop by, but knew they weren't going to, even though Tyler had let Drew know that Callie might be there.

"Why should that matter to me?" Drew had asked.

Tyler had grinned and said, "I'm just passin' on the intel."

Drew and Lee had agreed this ought to be a chill night. Kick it and watch the movie—Mr. Gilbert always had copies of new movies even when they were still in theaters. Nowhere they wanted to be, no games for four days.

But Drew was restless, even in Seth Gilbert's private theater, knowing he should be feeling like he was living the dream, his best buddy next to him.

He always got restless between one game and the next.

As cool as he tried to be, about everything, when eyes were on him, Drew knew how much these games meant to him. No matter how many times he told himself he was just passing through Oakley, the way he was going to pass through his one-and-done year of college, no matter how many times Mr. Gilbert told him to be careful, not get himself injured over some high school game, Drew *knew*: he was only happy, for-real happy, when there was a game going on.

Now there was no game until Wednesday.

His paper on the playground legends was due, and he hadn't even got past half of a first draft. And this time, because of his promise to Urban Sellers, he couldn't ask Lee for help.

It was one of the things Drew wanted to ask Urban Sellers, if there was a way to tell the story and not break his promise. Only he couldn't find the man. He'd been back to the hotel twice more—both times on the sneak from Lee—and both times Urban Sellers hadn't been there.

Where did a guy go who seemed to have no life to speak of? Drew couldn't figure it out. That was one thing. Then there was Callie, who'd barely nod hello to him when they passed in the hall. She was colder than New York in the wintertime.

Drew found himself getting too jumpy to make himself sit still.

He got up out of his cushy theater chair and said to Lee, "Let's go for a drive."

When they were pulling down the winding driveway, long enough to have its own name or number, Lee looked at Drew from the passenger seat and said, "You're sure this is okay?"

"Taking the car or me driving it?"

"Both."

"We're fine as long as I keep it under the speed limit and we don't get pulled over," Drew said. "And as for taking the Moz, I already told you he said I should take it out for a spin one of these days. So this is the day."

Because of the times Eddie had driven him in the car, Drew was familiar with what Mr. Gilbert called the "eye candy" on the dashboard, starting with the old-fashioned clock, a traditional clock with a short hour hand and long minute hand, not the digital clock most other cars had. It was just one more way the car was telling you it was different.

The speedometer wasn't digital, either, and working the radio was so complicated Drew wasn't sure he'd ever be able to get that down, especially when he was trying to drive at the same time—which was okay because he didn't want any music tonight, anyway, didn't want any distractions.

He just knew that if he ever drove this car for real, he'd have to take some kind of driver's ed class just to find stations he liked.

When he'd told Mr. Gilbert that one of the reasons why he was in no rush to get his license was because he was in no rush to sit in a classroom for a bunch of hours, Mr. Gilbert had said, "Don't worry, when the time comes, I've got a guy to handle that."

But for now, Drew was the guy, the guy sitting behind the wheel of the man's Moz, remembering how to work the shift paddles on the Formula One steering wheel, starting to feel as if he were driving a race car for real.

On the open road in the night, not some school parking lot.

He stepped on it a little now, pushing Lee back in his seat, thinking, *This is what I feel like in the open court, like nobody can keep up with me.*

"You remember we cannot, in a million years, no way, get pulled over, right?" Lee said.

He sounded more nervous than Drew had ever heard him.

"Relax," Drew said. "This is *fresh.* You can drive it on the way back, if you want. See what this baby's got."

"I know what it's got. And what it's got, we shouldn't have. Because what it could do is *get* us arrested."

"It's not like I'm taking it out on the 101."

"Well, there's good news."

Drew said, "We'll just turn it loose on some back roads, then go back."

"No," Lee said, "no turning loose. Driving the speed limit is what we're shooting for."

"Got it."

Then he stepped on it a little more, laughing as Lee fell back into the seat again.

Drew said, "Just sit back and enjoy the ride."

"Not happening."

Drew slowed down as they came out of Thousand Oaks, on their way toward Westlake Village, not wanting to head toward Agoura Hills. He felt himself getting more comfortable doing this, not feeling as nervous as he had when they'd pulled away from the house, starting to feel that control he did on the court, when he could make things happen the way he wanted them to.

This was like driver's ed for the life he was going to have.

"Maybe we should think about heading back," Lee said.

"Little while longer."

They were on Route 23 now, heading toward the Pacific Coast Highway.

Drew said to Lee, "Aren't you the guy always telling me I should act like a normal kid? What's more normal than this, wanting to get out and drive a hot car?"

"Drive one," Lee said, "or carjack one?"

"Just trying to be like a kid taking Daddy's car for a little joyride."

More like a sugar daddy, in Mr. Gilbert's case, Drew was aware enough to know that. His real dad, Miles Robinson, had walked out on Drew and his mom when Drew was a baby. He said he was going to get a bottle of red wine and never came back. But then his mom had always said that Miles had never come all the way back from the first Gulf War, from what he'd seen there. When Drew was ten, they got the call from the Veterans Hospital in Miami, telling them that Miles Robinson had finally passed from complications from liver disease.

The things you thought about in the night, out here on the empty road, things that flew into your head as the night flew by you.

He could go a long time without thinking about the dad he'd never known. Now here he was.

Just like that, Drew stepped on it again, hard this time.

THIRTY

Dude, you *got* to slow down," Lee said.

"In a minute."

Lee said, "You just had your minute, going from zero to ludicrous."

Drew wondered if Lee even knew that the Maserati had a Ferrari engine under the hood. Mr. Gilbert had told Drew that the first time he'd been in the car, sitting where Lee was sitting right now, pulling his seat belt tighter.

Drew could hear Mr. Gilbert's voice inside his head—again—telling him, "Just punch it and it goes. Ultimate combination of power and luxury."

Drew surprised himself, handling the curves the way he was, even without much light on this road in the night, though there wasn't much to see on the 23 in the daytime.

He was up to sixty now.

"This isn't funny," Lee said. "Or fun."

"Speak for yourself."

Seventy.

That's when they both heard the siren.

Drew looked into the rearview mirror, saw the flashing lights of the police car. And he knew they weren't going to be the friendly cops at Morrison Park, cruising past the basketball court to check up on him.

This was going to be about speeding, about not having a license, about somebody else's car.

About not being sixteen.

When Drew was able to speak, he sounded more like he was twelve. "I can't get into trouble for this! I can't!" He looked at Lee, bug-eyed. "This could screw up *everything.*"

"Relax," Lee said. "It's gonna be all right."

"All right?" Drew screamed at him. "I'm not talking about *this* stupid ride. I'm talking about my ride to the *pros*! Are you *hearing* me?"

"I'm hearing you loud and clear," Lee said. He looked over his shoulder. "When we get around the next curve, pull over right away."

"What good is that gonna do?"

"Just do it. This is still a Maserati. They're not gonna catch us right away. We've still got time."

"For what?"

They came around the corner now, still going fast, losing the lights of the cop car for just a moment, the sound of the siren fading out like calls on your cell phone could fade out. Lee yelling at him to slow down, but Drew out of control in this moment, the opposite of who he was on the basketball court—

The other car wasn't supposed to be there on the side of the road.

Wasn't supposed to be in the way, warning lights flashing, a guy in backseat of it, talking away on *his* cell phone.

As well as he thought he'd done tonight behind the wheel, Drew wasn't an experienced driver yet. But even in what felt like the worst moment of his life, he still had the same reactions as on the court. He avoided the car right there in front of them, turned the race-car wheel hard to the right, barely avoiding the car, but having no chance—none—to miss the first tree.

Drew sideswiped it as he hit the brakes hard, hearing the terrible sound of the tree scraping across the right side of Mr. Gilbert's Maserati. His right knee slammed hard into the dashboard—it felt as if somebody had clubbed it with a baseball bat.

Now the siren was close again, the sound earsplittingly loud, the cop car coming around the curve.

Lee was already unbuckling his seat belt, doing the same to Drew's, not even asking if Drew was all right, just grabbing him by the shoulders, shoving him toward the passenger seat, sliding underneath and getting behind the wheel.

"What . . . ?" Drew said.

"If one of us is going to get in trouble for this," his friend said, "it's gonna be me."

Even though one of the policemen back at the station recognized Drew, they did everything by the book. But that had already started back at the scene of the accident, Drew and Lee both taking Breathalyzer tests to see if either one of them had been drinking alcohol, even though both of them had told the policeman questioning them that they never drank, no sir. The two policemen at the scene had also asked Lee what he was doing driving a car that didn't belong to him, but Drew jumped in and said they had permission, they could check with Mr. Gilbert if they wanted, gave him all of Mr. Gilbert's numbers, which they called in to the station.

Now they were at the station, the policeman questioning them, looking at Drew first, then Lee, then saying, "What were you two thinking?"

Lee said, "We weren't thinking, sir. What I did was stupid."

What he did. Not the two of them. Just him. Wanting to take it all.

"You're going to lose your license for a good long time, son," the policeman said to Lee.

The name on his badge read "Saunders."

"I know that, sir," Lee said. On their way back to the station, Lee and Drew in the backseat of the police car, Lee had whispered to Drew that it was going to be "yes sir" and "no sir" no matter what the cops said to them.

"You know how lucky you both are?" Officer Saunders said.

"Yes sir," Drew said, not wanting Lee to take it all, feeling guilty already. "We're just not feeling too lucky right now, sir."

Then Saunders dialed Seth Gilbert's office and told him what had happened and then finally said, "So they did have permission?" And told him what the damage was and where his Maserati was and hung up.

Now Drew felt at least a little bit lucky on the worst night of his life, just because Mr. Gilbert had backed their lies with a lie of his own.

Lee left first with his parents, neither one of them saying too much, Drew seeing just from the looks on their faces what it was going to be like for Lee when he got home.

Drew's mom got there about ten minutes later. She asked Drew if he was all right, and he said he was, and then she walked past him to where Officer Saunders was sitting, and talked to him in a low voice, nodding a lot, turning and glaring at Drew a couple of times.

Then she took Drew by the arm, as if he was five again, and walked him out of the police station and to her car.

Opening up this way when she finally started talking to him again: "What were you possibly thinking?"

When Drew had called, waking her up, telling her as fast as he could what had happened and where he was, she had first asked if they were both all right.

Once she found out they were, it was as if she had gotten mad and stayed mad and maybe was going to stay mad the rest of her life.

After a while—the ride home taking so long it was as if they were driving all the way back to New York City—she found so many new ways to ask what he and Lee were thinking taking the man's car that Drew had lost count.

When they stopped for a light or at a stop sign, she'd turn slightly in her seat and give Drew another mean look before she started driving again.

Finally she said she had nothing more to say. But Drew knew his mom well enough to realize that sometimes her silence was worse than her yelling.

And the scary part for Drew was that she was only this ripped at him because she thought he'd somehow allowed Lee to take the Maserati.

It wasn't until Drew and his mom were inside the house, door shut and locked, that she went off again, talking about what could have happened, how badly they could have gotten hurt.

Or worse.

He knew she was as scared about that as she was mad, but he wasn't about to offer that opinion to her.

He just stood there in the front hall and took it as long as he could until he finally said, "I'm not apologizing anymore." Adding, "Sorry."

"Now you're going to give me a little of your True Robinson lip and attitude?" she said.

Drew almost told her that she didn't mind him being True Robinson when he was playing ball and helping them get the life they had here now. But he knew better.

She went to her room, and he walked down to his. Like boxers walking back to their corners. Drew wasn't feeling hurt by the things she'd said to him. He knew this would pass, maybe even by morning. She never stayed mad, not at him.

Nobody really did, except maybe Callie Mason.

No, he wasn't suffering from some case of hurt feelings. It was worse than that—he had to stand there and take her being this mad at him for the wrong reasons, not knowing the truth. She had no idea how mad she should have been.

Drew was ashamed.

Ashamed that he was just standing by, letting Lee take the weight like this, for the speeding, for the damage to Mr. Gilbert's fancy car. All of it. All because his friend had just been along for the stupid ride.

Drew not just ashamed, but sad.

Sad all the way into his bones, because he knew he didn't have it in him to be even half the kind of friend to anybody that Lee Atkins had been to him tonight.

Alls I can do, Drew told himself, *is keep a secret.*

He closed the shades in his room, trying to make his room even darker than night. Two in the morning by now and Drew not even thinking about trying to sleep.

Not *wanting* to sleep.

Asking himself, *What* was *I thinking?*

Maybe this was one of those times—*another* time—when he'd thought the rules didn't apply to him because of the way he could play basketball.

Drew reached over, grabbed his cell off the nightstand, hit Lee up on his speed dial.

Lee picked up right away, answered in a low voice Drew could barely hear.

"Yo."

"How is it there?"

"Bad. There?"

"Same."

"Here's how bad it is here: my dad says he hasn't even decided what my punishment's gonna be."

Drew said, "What do you think Coach is gonna do?"

"Suspend me."

"For real?"

"You weren't here last year. Ricky got into some trouble on

Facebook, trash-talking a Park kid. Coach said he crossed the line and gave him two games."

"Two games wouldn't be so bad."

"'Less he thinks this is worse," Lee said. "Which it probably is."

"He wouldn't suspend you into the tournament."

They both knew it started in four games.

"Might."

"Wow."

Drew was talking in the same low voice, knowing that if his mom heard him talking on the phone, it would probably set her off all over again.

After a long silence from both of them, Drew said, "I could explain what really happened to Mr. Gilbert, maybe he could talk to Coach before he even does anything to you."

"Righhhhhhht," Lee said. "'Cause Mr. Gilbert is gonna be so happy with me."

"But he always says one of his goals in life is to keep *me* happy."

"Like that's his real job," Lee said.

Drew thought, *Lee could be talking about himself.* But what he said was, "Man, I can't let you do this."

"We already went over this."

"I want to go over it again," Drew said.

"We'll be fine, even if he suspends my butt for the rest of the season. But we're just another team without you. Like all the other teams we ever had at this school that weren't good enough."

"See, that's the thing," Drew said. "If we go to Coach and tell him what really happened, he *won't* suspend me."

For the exact same reason Drew thought he could take the car out, even without a license. Because the rules didn't apply to him.

"We're not gonna find that out," Lee said. "We already lied to the police. It's not like we can go to Coach now and say that it's all right to lie to the police but tell him the truth because it might help out our team."

He knew Lee was right. *Lee's right, and I've got nothing,* Drew thought. Tired all of a sudden. Like the whole night had caught up with him the way the cops had.

Lee said, "You still there?"

"Barely."

"This stays between us, like we agreed. You don't need something like this in the papers, on ESPN, on your permanent record."

Drew said, "Iverson went to jail and still got to go to Georgetown."

"You're not him."

"Maybe I just lie better," Drew said. "My mom's always told me that a lie is halfway 'round the world before the truth gets its boots on."

"Oh, good," Lee said. "More parental wisdom—just what I need about now. Get some sleep. I'll see you at school." Lee paused and said, "That would be right after my mom drops me."

Drew put the phone back on the nightstand. His knee was hurting from where it had hit the dash. He thought about getting some ice. But decided that if his mom heard, found out he *had* got himself hurt, she'd start acting like her hair was on fire all over again.

Only one thing to do.

Drew got off his bed, got his ball out of his closet, quietly opened his back window, climbed out, started walking to Morrison Park.

Limping slightly.

Just like Legend.

THIRTY-TWO

It was funny, Drew thought on his way over to Morrison, all the times Mr. Gilbert had told him not to get himself hurt, not to dive for loose balls. And how he'd listened to him.

Now he banged up his knee on the man's own car.

What was I thinking?

Drew knew. He wasn't thinking. He was just doing what he wanted and getting Lee to go along. Now he'd gotten hurt and hurt Lee in another way. Letting Lee clean up the mess.

Drew wondered if there'd always be somebody around to clean up his messes.

Legend had talked to him about mistakes. Now Drew had made one. Only it hadn't cost him, it had cost his best friend. And the only way he could figure out how to deal with it was to go play himself some ball.

Even on a sore knee.

When he got to the park, he sat down on one of the swings to rub the knee, knowing he really should be back home icing, not playing ball to make the dag-gone world go away, make him feel better.

He was still sitting there, rubbing on the knee, when he heard the bounce of the ball.

He got up and walked in the direction of the bad court and, like the first night, Legend Sellers was just *there.* And for the first time since he'd seen those flashing police lights—heard the siren—Drew did feel better.

Drew didn't sneak up on him this time. Didn't watch from the shadows. Just started bouncing his own ball to let Legend know he was in the area.

As always, the man was cool, acknowledging him with a nod, like they were supposed to meet up here in the middle of the night.

Legend said, "You wouldn't have been able to cover me like this when I still had my legs underneath me."

"Been looking for you at your hotel, but haven't been able to find you."

"I heard."

Drew came out on the court, no warm-up, one bounce, made a three. When he jogged after the ball, Legend said, "What happened to your leg?"

Drew thought, *Do I trust him?*

But Legend had trusted him so far with his secret that he was still alive when the world thought he was dead. So Drew told him what had happened, wondering how he'd react, if he'd start fussing on him the way his mom had.

He didn't. Just stared at Drew and said, "Had to blow off some steam, didn't you? Feeling like if you didn't, you might explode."

Drew stared back. "How did you know?"

The older man made a growly sound, which Drew took to be his version of laughter. "How do I know?" he said. "Because I do, that's why. Because I was you once, remember?"

Then he turned and went back to shooting jumpers. Drew did the same. Talking to each other in a different way, without words. Drew put down his ball, and the two of them shared Legend's. One would shoot until he missed, then rebound for the other. No judgments from this man about what Drew had done tonight. Maybe because this night wasn't even close to the kinds of mistakes Legend had made in his life.

All there was between them right now was basketball.

Once, they both stopped at the same time to massage their sore knees.

"You put any ice on that 'fore you came?" Legend said.

"No."

"Idiot."

"Yeah," Drew said. "All night long."

They went back to shooting until Legend finally said, "Enough." They sat down in the grass. Legend had a big jug of water and offered it to Drew. He drank some and handed it back and leaned on his elbows.

"I saw you," Drew said. "Working on your crew."

"Know that. Saw you, too."

"So that's your job."

"It is," Legend said. "Not ashamed of it, either, if that's where you're going, like seeing me in my dirty work clothes somehow made you feel sorrier for me than you already do."

"I didn't say any of that."

"Didn't have to," Legend said. "It's honest work and gives me a paycheck, regular. Helps me to save up a little bit at a time." He grinned. "As you saw at the hotel, it isn't like I got myself a lot of high overhead."

"Saving up for what?" Drew said.

Legend paused and then in a quiet voice he said, "For school."

"For real?"

"For real," Legend said. "Now that I can finally read, I got myself some unfinished business." Then he held up a finger and said, "I *have* myself some unfinished business."

Drew said, "What's that mean, you can finally read?"

"It means what it means. When I first got to high school, I couldn't read, at least not anything like I was supposed to."

Drew sat up, stretched out his sore leg, turned so he was facing Legend. "But if you couldn't read—"

"How'd I get by? People took care of me, because of the way I could play ball. This come as a big shock to *you*?"

Drew thought instantly of Lee. No, it was no big shock to him.

Then he remembered what he'd read about Legend Sellers, being accused of having somebody else take the SATs for him, even though he denied it up and down and they could never prove it.

He didn't tell him that, didn't want Legend to think he'd followed him through the Internet the way he'd followed him to his hotel the first time.

Legend said, "I didn't start getting a real education until . . ." Now he smiled all the way in what little light there was. "Till I reached the afterlife." He stood up again, tossing the ball from one big hand to the other. "Why am I telling you all this?"

"Because I tell you stuff."

"Maybe so," Legend said. "Eventually I want to find my way to some kind of college."

"But if you did that," Drew said, "wouldn't you have to tell people you were still alive?"

"Haven't thought that far ahead yet," Legend said. "For now, I just sneak in the back and audit some night classes at the Thousand Oaks Community College."

"So that's where you were those times?"

Legend nodded.

Drew, excited now, said, "Listen, Mr. Gilbert could probably make a couple of calls, get you enrolled at Thousand Oaks no problem."

He got the growly laugh in response.

"Now you're getting ahead of *your*self," Legend said.

"How?"

Legend looked down at the basketball in his hands, slowly turned it over. "Because I never graduated from high school," he said.

Drew wanted to know how that was possible and tried to ask, but Legend said enough about him, he wanted to know how Drew had picked this particular night to act dumber than the rocks Legend had been pulling out of the ground at Morrison.

"I told you."

"You told me about getting behind the wheel, not what put you there."

"You said you knew I felt like I was gonna pop."

"But not *why*."

By three in the morning, Drew had told him all of it, even the part about Callie and the H-O-R-S-E game. Told it as honestly as if he were telling it to himself inside his own head. Told it in a way he'd never told it to anybody else, not even Lee.

Because he wasn't sure even Lee would understand it.

But he knew Legend would.

He even told Legend that he'd kept the secret about him being alive from everybody so far, including Lee.

"You want some kind of trophy for that to put with all the others you've probably won?"

Drew should have known by now to stay on his guard, because Legend could give him a quick elbow to the ribs like that.

"I just wanted you to know I could do what I said I was gonna do," Drew said.

"Woo hoo!" Legend said.

"Laugh at me if you want," Drew said. "I didn't know my word meant something to me until it *did.* It would be easier for me to tell, because I got this paper due now, and I need the grade. But I don't know how to do it without calling you out."

There was another long silence. Drew could see it wasn't something that bothered Legend. Maybe that was because he was alone so much, had lived inside his own head for so long. In this life that he'd made for himself, the one he called his afterlife.

Legend said, "And you can't get your boy Lee to write your paper for you, because you'd have to tell on me."

"Word," Drew said.

"So I'll help you," Legend said.

"You'll help me write my paper . . . about you?"

Legend nodded. "Maybe there's a way we can write it together," he said. "See if there's a way to do it right. Get the story right. Even if we have to tell your teacher. Let me think on that. But if I'm ever gonna find out if I can handle a real school, it might as well be now."

"At my school?" Drew said. "Working with my English teacher?"

"You got any better ideas?"

"No," Drew said, he sure did not, remembering something his mom had told him once, about how once a good idea got inside your head even the United States Marines couldn't get it out.

Then Drew said, "But that would mean trusting somebody besides me."

Legend actually laughed out loud now. "Hale, boy, you put it that way, I could probably trust anybody after trusting you."

Drew said, "You ever think about what the worst thing would be, if you did come back to life?"

In the sky there was the sound of a night bird.

"All the time," he said. "Sometimes I think, 'Go ahead, Urban. Nobody's even gonna care.' But then I think about the world we live in now, how they'd probably eat up a story like mine. I don't want that spotlight back, even for a day."

"But if I fix it that you could somehow take courses at Oakley, you'd think about it?"

"They'd probably want to see if I had any dang eligibility left."

"I mean, for real," Drew said. "I don't usually have much use for teachers, but Mr. Shockey's one of the good guys. Even I'm smart enough to see that. And probably the only one in the school who'd know who you used to be would be Coach."

"My old coach knows about me," Legend said. "Coach Holman. He's the only one besides you. He helped me get myself back on my feet, helped me get this job. Gave me some money at the start when I didn't have any."

Drew felt his mouth fall open. "Wait a second, he knew all along?"

Legend nodded. "Knew I could trust him," Legend said. "Came the time when he was the only one in the world I could trust."

Drew said, "So what name do you use at work?"

"Donald Sellers."

"So that's who you could be at school."

There was a long pause. Drew thought he saw the same look he'd seen that night when Legend opened the door to 3G at the hotel. That fear.

"Don't do anything yet," Legend said finally. "I got to think on this."

"But you won't run."

Another pause.

"No," Legend said "I won't run. You got *my* word. As your friend."

Drew felt himself smiling then, feeling this dumb smile on his face. But not feeling dumb in that moment. All he'd ever done in his life was look up to basketball players, LeBron and all the rest of them. All the guys with the ball in their hands, the ones who really knew what to do with it.

Maybe he *should* have been looking up to somebody like Lee Atkins. Who really knew how to be a friend.

Or a guy like Donald Sellers, who knew how to come back from the dead.

THIRTY-FOUR

Lee's parents had called Coach DiGregorio the first thing that morning, after they'd spoken to the principal.

The principal, Mr. Flachsbart, said that while Lee's behavior had been reckless, to say the least, it was also out of character, and that he thought that the Atkinses could handle any punishment they thought should be handed out. Mr. Flachsbart—known as Flax to the Oakley kids and generally considered to be pretty cool—joked that his office took on a lot of different forms, but that he didn't think traffic court was supposed to be one of them.

Lee didn't get off as easily with Coach at the team meeting he called before practice.

It was the old "higher standard" thing for his players.

Wasn't anything they hadn't heard before. How they knew he applied a higher standard to them, even in terms of their grades, than the school did for the rest of its students. Billy DiGregorio said that his high school coach had treated *his* players that way, and his college coach had done the same.

"You're the next in that line," he said, "when you step out of line. Or cross one."

Coach didn't raise his voice, but they could all see how hard he was working not to lose it in front of them. The way he'd be during a game when he didn't want a ref to see how much he wanted to strangle the guy.

He'd told them one time about a line an old coach named Jimmy Valvano had used on a ref.

"Can you give me a T for what I'm thinking?" Valvano said to the ref, according to Coach's story.

"No," the ref said.

Valvano had said, "Well, good, because I think you stink."

Coach D kept his voice down and said, "This is about the team. And only about the team. Because in the end that's all any of us have: each other. Nothing else means squat."

Standing there in the middle of their lush-life locker room, best in their league by far. Arms crossed in front of him, not focusing on anybody's face. Mostly just staring straight ahead.

But Drew knew: the cop had been nicer last night after they got Lee to roll down the window of the Maserati.

Coach said, "It was just one other person with Lee when he decided to take a car *that did not belong to him and that he did not have permission to drive* and turn it into the Riverside road race. But the fact of the matter is that he might as well have had the whole team piled in there. Because he took *all* of you for a ride last night."

Then he got to it, how close they were to the end of the season, how Oakley had never won the regular season title in their league, much less the league championship. The one he'd been by-God brought here to win. Talked about how there were just three games left in the regular season and how if they won out, they *would* win the regular season and get home court for the playoffs.

"Three games," he said, "the last one against Park. Park—the team that always wins the gol-dang regular season and every other gol-dang thing."

Coach's wife had asked him to get through the year without swearing like a rap record.

He stared at Lee now. "Three games you are going to miss, young man."

"But Coach," Drew said, before he could stop himself.

Coach wheeled on him and said, *"Don't. Talk."* In a tone of voice Drew couldn't remember Coach ever using on him.

"Lee and his . . . passenger got lucky," Coach said. "A couple of yards more the wrong way, and we're having a different conversation today, about something much worse than one of my players missing a few games," Coach said.

He zeroed in on Lee again and said, "You and everybody else on this team can thank their lucky stars neither of you was injured."

Drew thought, *If he only knew.*

His mind already trying to figure a way to cover up what had really happened—one more thing that had really happened last night—when his knee hit the dash.

A knee that wouldn't stop hurting, even though he'd gotten up early—after having hardly slept—to ice it for an hour.

"I know some of you, maybe all of you, think this punishment is too harsh," Coach said. "And it doesn't take a mind reader to know most of you are wondering if the punishment would have been *as* harsh if it'd been Drew behind the wheel."

Drew felt the air come out of him, and wondered if everybody else in the room could *hear* it come out of him.

Could Coach possibly know the truth?

"The answer is yes," Coach said. "Because nobody is bigger than the team."

He was done then, telling Lee he could watch practice, even help him out. Drew wondered if that would make it even worse for Lee than being sent home.

But that wasn't the big thing right now. The big thing, Drew knew, was finding a way to get himself sent home—he couldn't practice on his knee the way it was feeling right now. It took all the effort he had not to limp.

He made it through warm-ups all right. Then Coach announced that they were going to practice against the 3–2 match-up zone St. Thomas was going to throw at them in their next game.

Three plays into the scrimmage, Drew made sure to cut way too close to a pick Tyler Brandt had set for him, like cutting too close to a corner in the hall.

Down he went.

Tyler, one of the best guys on the team along with his twin, was kneeling next to him before Drew even had a chance to grab for his left knee, the one he'd hurt in the car.

"Dude," Tyler said, "I am so sorry. You okay?"

"My bad," Drew said.

He didn't want to take another teammate down with him, one this week was enough.

"Wasn't watching where I was going," Drew said. He was rubbing his knee with both hands, thinking that he'd never faked an injury in his life to get out of practice, but this was different. The injury was real—it was the reason that was fake.

Drew was pretty sure that there wasn't anything seriously wrong with his knee, that it was just a bad bruise. He wasn't even thinking about missing the St. Thomas game.

He just knew it wasn't going to get better with him practicing on it.

Now Coach was there, kneeling next to Tyler.

"Just a ding?" Coach said.

"Yeah."

"Take the rest of the day off," Coach said. "I'm pretty sure that cracking that 3–2 zone isn't going to be like cracking the Da Vinci code."

"Who's he play for?" Drew said.

"Go ice," Coach said.

"Done."

Ice, Drew thought as Lee walked with him to the locker room. No matter how much you heard about all these medical breakthroughs in sports, and how guys came back from injuries faster than ever, old-school guys like Coach—and even Legend—thought the miracle cure for everything was ice.

When they got to the locker, Ana, the team trainer, was waiting for them, wanting to check the knee out for herself.

"Boy," she said, "this swelled up fast."

"You know me," Drew said, wanting her to change the subject. "I do everything fast."

She went for ice.

When she was in her trainer's room, Lee said, "You sure that didn't happen last night?"

Drew shook his head. "That's crazy talk," he said. "I'd rather hit a tree than Tyler Brandt anytime."

Lee seemed to buy it. A good thing. It would, Drew knew, just make Lee feel worse if he thought he'd caused an injury, too.

It wasn't much, Drew thought.

At least I did something for Lee today.

The next day, his first free period, Drew went to see Mr. Shockey.

Counting the weekend, his paper was due in four days. Drew had gotten an e-mail from Mr. Shockey that morning before school, gently reminding him of the deadline, saying how important a good grade was and hinting at the possible "consequences" of a bad one.

Drew had spent so much time worrying about Legend lately, even before he'd gotten behind the wheel of the Maserati, that he hadn't spent nearly enough time worrying about the consequences of getting a bad grade from Mr. Shockey. Forget about Coach's higher standards.

Drew had to meet the regular standards at Oakley if he wanted to stay eligible for basketball. He knew he could do it, stay away from a D in English. Just hadn't done it yet.

"So," Mr. Shockey said once Drew had closed the door to his office behind him, "you got that paper pounded into shape yet?"

"Mr. S," Drew said, "I swear on my life I've done more research on this than anything I've ever *worked* on in my life."

"Glad to hear it," Mr. Shockey said. "But you didn't really answer my question. How close are you to being done?"

"It's comin'," Drew said. He fidgeted a little in his seat, mostly to get his left leg stretched out in front of him. "But that's not what I wanted to talk to you about."

Without thinking, he rubbed his knee. Mr. Shockey saw that and said, "Did Tyler bang knees with you, or hit you with a baseball bat?"

"Oh, you know," Drew said. "I'll be *aight*."

As soon as he used the worldwide hip-hop version of *all right,* he saw Mr. Shockey wince. Like Drew had hit *him* with a bat.

Mr. Shockey didn't say anything, just sighed and let it go. This wasn't one of his classes. "So what do you want to talk about?"

"It's like this," Drew said.

Then stopped. He'd been thinking hard on how he wanted to present this. Now here it was. Showtime.

"The thing is," Drew said, "there's this guy I met. Kind of the playground legend who made me want to write about playground legends."

It was a made-up version of the Legend Sellers story. Like one of those movie versions of a true story. When they'd say, "Based on actual events."

Drew didn't tell him all of it, where Legend was from, how he was supposed to be dead. Just got right to the part about him wanting a high school diploma.

"How old is this guy?" Mr. Shockey said.

"Forties," Drew said, "in there."

"And he wants to go to school . . . *here*?"

"One English credit, one math—I think that's all he needs."

"A man who's been away from school for, what, maybe thirty years, and now he gets religion about education?"

"You could say."

"And I don't want to sound like I'm stuck on this . . . but he wants to clear his courses at Oakley?"

"It was my idea," Drew said. "I figured that you and me and Mr. Gilbert . . ."

Drew knew he really didn't need Mr. Shockey if he had Mr. Gilbert stepping on this, but he was trying to be polite. Be the good Drew.

The pleaser.

Now he wanted to see where Mr. Shockey would take this. He didn't have to wait long to find out.

Mr. S slapped both hands down on his desk, smiling. Happy. Like Drew had surprised him by putting a done-deal paper on that desk.

"I love it!" Mr. Shockey said, something he'd say in practice when Drew would throw some kind of pass like he was a magician pulling a quarter from behind his ear.

"For real?"

"I will work with any high school student who wants to improve, even if they are as old as I am," he said, then stood up. "Bring him around. And Mr. Nichols will have to meet . . . you haven't even told me his name."

"Donald."

Mr. S didn't even bother asking for a last name. "Bring Donald around." He smiled again and said, "Tell him we're going to kick it old school. Just at this school."

"Good one," Drew said.

"He must be a good friend."

Yeah, Drew thought.

Yeah, he is.

He couldn't wait to tell Legend, even thought about skipping a few classes to do it. Knowing he could get away with that, as usual. But he waited. There was a late practice today because the girls had the gym early, so after his last class, he took the school bus that dropped kids in town at the train station. He would've run the rest of the way to Legend's hotel if his knee hadn't stiffened up on him again.

But this time when he got to the lobby, Vic, the night manager, stopped him. He was wearing the same T-shirt, watching the same TV, a game show this time.

"Looking for your friend?" Vic said.

"Yeah, but I'm kind of in a hurry, if you don't mind," he said, heading for the stairs, talking at the guy over his shoulder. "I know which room he's in by now, thanks."

"Kid." Stopping him with his tone.

Drew turned around.

"What I'm trying to tell you is," he said, "that room is empty."

"What does that mean?" Drew said. "Empty?"

Vic said, "The guy checked out." He shrugged and turned back to his set, where Drew could see people jumping up and down and hugging on each other. "He's gone."

THIRTY-FIVE

Drew could only think of one thing to ask, picturing the room the man said was empty now.

"What about the books?" Drew said.

"What books?"

"The books he had in his room."

"Must be in the boxes downstairs. Said he'd come back for them. Then he paid up and left. Like I told you: the guy was gone like the wind."

Drew was still picturing the books and that old basketball he played with at Morrison. All Legend really had.

"You ask him where he was going?" Drew said. "Why he was just up and leaving?"

"Kid," the man said, "let me explain something to you. I'm the manager of this dump, not a concierge."

Drew walked past him, walked outside, taking deep breaths, trying to process what had just happened. *I won't run,* Legend had said.

Only now he had.

Drew had trusted him. *Same as he trusted me,* Drew thought. *He asked me to keep his secret, keep my word, and I did. Why couldn't he keep his in return, instead of running?*

All the way home, walking on his sore knee and not even caring, Drew wondered if he still needed to keep Legend's secret, wondered if you were obligated to keep your word when somebody else didn't keep his.

Wondered if there was some kind of rule about that.

He thought about a lot of things, trying to figure out his next move. The player whose moves on the court always came natural.

When he got to his room, his mom not home, he called Mr. Gilbert and asked if Eddie could come get him. Mr. Gilbert said sure, then laughed and said, "Of course he won't be picking you up in the Maserati. Don't know if you heard, but it's in the shop."

"Funny," Drew said, and then asked if Eddie could leave right away—it was kind of important.

When he got to the house, Mr. Gilbert didn't ask what he needed, just wanted to talk about the knee.

"You never leave practice," he said, "the way you never take yourself out of a game."

"Caught Tyler just right," Drew said. "And you know how strong that boy is. If it's still yakking at me tomorrow, I'll take one more day off, just to be on the safe side."

"If it's still hurting tomorrow, we're going to have the best orthopedic guy in LA take a look at it."

"No," Drew said. The words coming out on fire. He didn't want the top orthopedic guy in LA to take a close look at him and wonder how Drew could have gotten a bruise like that clipping a teammate.

"It's just dinged, is all," Drew said. "Not like I took a bullet."

"Blah, blah, blah," Mr. Gilbert said. "If you're not out there for practice, you and me are taking a ride."

"Figgeritout," Drew said. "I'm not gonna do anything that would jeopardize the season."

"I don't care one way or another about this season," Mr. Gilbert said. "I'm looking at the next one. And the one after that."

Drew knew what he had to say to end this. "Don't worry," Drew said. "We both got our eye on the prize."

"Well," Mr. Gilbert said, giving Drew his cocky grin, "at least when you're not playing NASCAR with one of *my* cars."

Mr. Gilbert had been cool about the accident from the start, even though Drew knew he wouldn't have been nearly as cool if he'd known Drew had been the one behind the wheel and had gotten himself hurt because of that.

Drew wondered how the man would have reacted if it had been Robbie taking one of the fancy cars out for a joyride.

"Stuff happens," Mr. Gilbert had said, and had even tried to plead Lee's case with Coach, saying that he'd done a lot worse in high school. With Mr. G, you could never know whether he thought trying to get Lee's suspension reduced was the right thing to do or whether he thought doing that made him look good.

Or maybe he just didn't want to get mad at Lee because he

thought Drew might not like that, another sort of star treatment for Drew.

Which never seemed to end, no matter how much you were the one in the wrong. Legend had said that the only time the star treatment ended was when you no longer were one.

"So what's on your mind tonight?" Mr. Gilbert said. "You needed to come over?"

"I need a favor," Drew said, "and my mom is still too mad for me to ask her."

"That's all?" Mr. Gilbert said. "You sounded like it was something serious. You want a favor, you got it."

"But I didn't tell you what it is."

Mr. Gilbert gave him a look, like he couldn't believe what he was hearing. "True," he said, "this is me. Your all-around man."

"Sorry, sometimes I forget how generous you are."

Laying it down now.

"So what can I do you for?"

"I need Eddie to drive me down to Santa Monica," Drew said. "To see a guy." Then he added, "For a paper I'm working on."

When Coach Fred Holman opened the door and Drew told him why he was there, Holman said, "He's dead, is where he is."

Drew could only imagine, standing there, not being asked to come in, what it must have been like to play for this guy. When Coach John Wooden, the famous old UCLA coach, had died a couple of years before, Drew had read some of the stories about how people used to go see him at his little place in Encino like they were going to see some holy man at a shrine. He didn't see that happening with the old coach standing in front of him, looking at Drew like he'd come to sell him something.

"You're the only one who knows he's alive besides me," Drew said.

Fred Holman looked to be wearing the same clothes he'd worn the first day, the same sweater even.

"You should have called first," he said.

"I just wanted to get up here and see you as soon as I could."

"You want me to help you find him," Coach Fred Holman said. "Give me one good reason why."

This time the truth came out easy.

"Because I'm his friend," Drew said.

THIRTY-SIX

Coach Fred Holman told Drew he could show himself out—the Lakers were about to play the Suns, and he wanted to watch.

"But before you go, you ought to know something," he said to Drew. "He's run before. And when he finally turned up, it turned out he'd been in a place I should have known to look for him."

"I'm not sure what you're telling me."

"It's not rocket science," Fred Holman said. "You've scouted the man. Haven't you *learned* anything?"

Drew felt like the old man was trying to help out, 100 percent, but he still made it sound as if he were telling Drew to get off his lawn.

But that was it. The old man didn't even offer to shake hands before Drew walked out the front door and got into Mr. Gilbert's car, safely in the passenger's seat this time.

On the way back to Agoura Hills, he thought about what the old man had meant, almost making it sound as if Legend might be hiding in plain sight. But it wasn't as if he had all this free time on his hands to go searching for him. He had three regular season games left and a knee to manage without letting on how much it was hurting him, because there was no way he was coming out of the lineup, not with Lee already out.

He knew what these games meant to Lee.

Plus, he had the paper to finish.

He wound up working on that when he got home, worked on it late into the night, revising it, acting like the student his mom wanted him to be. Working on it all by himself, no help from Lee.

No help from Legend.

He'd decided that he was going to tell the reader—Mr. Shockey, in this case—from the jump that Donald wasn't his subject's real name, that he was a real person, a player the world had pretty much forgotten. Given up for dead, so to speak.

Writing about a playground legend, he treated it like a playground game, establishing the rules.

He didn't say what city Legend was from, didn't say where he'd played his high school ball. Just said he was a perfect example of how everything could go all sideways and haywire on you, not just your basketball but your whole dag-gone life.

Two A.M., he was still writing.

Trying the best he could, in his own thoughts and words, to get to what he thought about "Donald," what had happened to him.

And the more he wrote—surprised at how into it he was now—the less it was about some grade he was trying to get, or what Mr. Shockey was going to think about what he was writing.

Drew simply wanted to get this *right*.

Before he shut down his laptop at a quarter to three, he read everything he'd written since he'd gotten home from Coach Holman's house, and it was like the words had been written by somebody else.

Sometimes he wasn't sure whether he was writing about Legend or about himself.

Drew turned out the light, got into bed, closed his eyes, tried to clear his mind. But his mind was still busy.

Full of this one thought: he was ending the season pretty much the same star player—the *playa*—he'd been when the season started. But somehow, something he never saw coming, he hoped he was turning into a different person.

Maybe that was why, when he was done writing the paper, he wrote one more thing before he went to bed. An e-mail to Callie Mason he should have written a lot sooner.

One that just had two words in it: "I'm sorry."

Oakley beat St. Thomas, no worries, ending up winning by twenty. Drew sat out the last eight minutes while guys off the end of the bench finally got some real burn. He was happy with the win, and even happier that nobody seemed to notice, not even Lee, that he was playing the game at a different speed than usual.

Mostly no one questioned Drew's health because by the time

St. Thomas came out of its match-up zone near the end of the first half, Drew had already torched them for twenty-four points, going five for five from beyond the three-point arc.

It hurt, but he knew he would have hurt all over if he hadn't gone on the floor this time.

By the time Drew sat down for good, he was glad Coach didn't need a full game out of him tonight.

Glad the team didn't.

It was when he was sitting at the end of the bench next to Lee—Lee in his blazer and tie and khaki pants—wanting to ice but no way to do that without people noticing, that he saw Callie. She was sitting up in the stands.

It was the first time he'd seen her there since the H-O-R-S-E game.

He told himself not to get his hopes up, knowing her being there might not have anything to do with him. After all, she still hadn't responded to his apology. Drew had wondered if he'd sent the e-mail to the right address.

Maybe she didn't care whether he was sorry or not.

But at least she was there.

Darlene Robinson was waiting for Drew in the gym after he had showered and dressed, telling himself he'd ice when he got home, first thing.

When he walked through the opening in the bleachers at the locker-room end of the court, Callie was there, with some of her teammates.

"Hey," he said, hoping she wouldn't chill him out because her friends were there.

"Great game," she said. "And by the way? I accept."

"Accept what?"

"Your apology."

Drew didn't need to do the math: she'd just said more words to him than she had since she walked out of the gym that day. More words *combined.*

And not just any words. The ones he wanted to hear.

Before he could respond, something else pretty amazing happened. Amazing to him, leastways: Callie told her friends she'd catch up with them later.

They left. She stayed.

Now Drew didn't know *what* to say.

In a quiet voice, Callie said, "You feeling okay?"

"I'm good."

"You weren't moving like you do," she said. "Like you can." The girl had watched the game with basketball eyes.

"Little nicked up is all," he said. "Caught a knee at practice the other day that was a little bit like catching a beating."

"*Thank* you," she said.

And smiled at him.

Drew smiled back, saying, "Nice to see my pain is working for you."

She laughed. "God got you."

"Payback," Drew said.

They both stood there. Drew could see his mom at half-court, still waiting.

Finally Callie said, "You doing anything?"

"No," he said. Fast.

"I've got my car," Callie said.

Drew knew she'd gotten her license about five minutes after she turned sixteen.

"Yeah?" Drew said.

"I was going to stop by the library," she said. "In town. I'm finishing this paper."

"Me too." Drew answered almost before she stopped talking, like he was jumping out on a pick.

"We could stop there and, like, get a burger after," she said.

It was amazing how his knee had suddenly stopped hurting. "Yeah, sure," he said. "But . . ."

"If you're busy—"

"No, no, nothing like that. I just . . ." He shrugged and smiled, and some air came out of him so loudly it made him laugh. "So you're not hating on me?"

Callie laughed again. "Well, as you may have noticed, I *was*. But then the more I thought about it, the more I thought, 'The boy couldn't help himself.' Being a guy, I mean. And then I started thinking on something else, that somebody who played the game as smart and clean as you do, at least *most* of the time, can't be *all* bad."

"I'm not."

With that, he went over and told him mom that he was going to the library. Something he sort of hoped would make *her* stop hating on him.

"The *library*?" she said. "You sick? Let me feel your forehead."

"I'm going with Callie," Drew said.

She looked past him now, nodded, like that explained everything. *"Oh,"* she said, making that one word seem as long as a term paper.

"Then we might get something to eat after."

"Oh," she said again, and now she smiled, something he hadn't seen her do since the whole Maserati deal.

"So don't worry about dinner for me," he said. "I'm good."

Was he ever.

THIRTY-SEVEN

Callie didn't drive a Maserati.

Her father had bought her a Kia when she got her license. Not the roomiest front seat in the world—Drew wanted to stretch out his legs, but when he tried to do that, he bumped his knee into the dash.

And winced.

"Hurts that bad?" Callie said, putting the car in gear.

"It just gets stiff after games."

"I could drop you at your house, if you want."

"What I want," he said, "is to go to the library and then go get something to eat."

He didn't add, "With you."

On the way into town, Callie asked him about what she called "Lee's accident." Drew just said that he felt bad because it was really his fault more than Lee's, that Lee would never have taken the car out without Drew saying it was, as he said now, *aight*.

"But he was still the one driving," Callie said. Her hands—beautiful hands, Drew couldn't help but notice—were at perfect driving-manual position on the wheel, ten minutes after ten.

Drew only knew that because Lee had told him one time. He hadn't cracked open his driver's manual yet. Just another book he hadn't opened. A guy on his way to the library.

Drew changed the subject as quickly as he could, got Callie talking about her own team, asking her how many games they had left and if anybody had a chance to stop them from going into their tournament undefeated for the season.

"We should be good to go," she said. Just a small smile this time, not even turning her head, eyes on the road. "Long as somebody on our team doesn't borrow somebody's car."

"You," he said, "are definitely not feeling *my* pain."

"Poor baby," she said.

They laughed together.

She parked in the lot behind the library, said that what she needed to do shouldn't take longer than an hour. If that.

"Do you have to work on your English paper for real," she said, "or are you just keeping me company before I get you fed?"

"For real," he said.

He wasn't totally sure he needed any more material on playground ballers than he already had. But there was one more book Mr. Shockey had suggested, called *Heaven Is a Playground.*

"Just go do your thing. Don't worry about me," he said. "I've got this one book I need to check. Might not even have to check it *out.*

I might just find myself a quiet piece of floor and stretch out my legs and read."

"Text you when I'm done," Callie said.

He watched her walk away, this cool girl, even breezing through a library in a way that made you watch her. Drew thinking, *I don't understand girls now, and I never will.*

He didn't try now, just went to a computer and punched in the title of the book, found out the author was named Rick Telander. Then Drew had to ask where to find it and what the code meant. He wouldn't have admitted this to Callie, but he had never been inside the library before.

And Agoura Hills, for a small town, had a big one, three levels, looking pretty much brand-new to Drew. It turned out *Heaven Is a Playground* was on the third level, all the way in the back. Drew made a couple of wrong turns getting there and twice found himself in the wrong stacks before finally managing to locate the book.

It was even quieter up there than it had been downstairs.

He hadn't brought a notebook, since he wasn't planning to be there, but he decided that if he found something he could use, he would walk himself back downstairs and get the first library card of his life.

On his way into the stacks, he'd seen this open area with chairs and a couch overlooking one of the town parks. But the chairs and couch were taken. So Drew decided the stacks were fine; there was a nice soft carpet on the floor. He'd noticed an empty spot near a window, bright light coming in, and decided to head there.

He made sure his cell was on vibrate, and powered up, not wanting to miss Callie's text if she finished early.

Came around a corner and stopped.

The man with the hotel room full of books sat surrounded by them now.

THIRTY-EIGHT

"Leave me alone." His voice was like some sad note from the jazz music Legend liked.

He didn't say "*please* leave me alone," but Drew heard it anyway in Legend's quiet library voice, like he was asking and not telling.

"I can't," Drew said. "You got to know that by now. If I was gonna let you be, I would have done it in the park that first night."

"I ran then."

"I didn't run after you," Drew said, "but I started following you just the same."

"All the way here," Legend said. "Funny . . . I didn't take you for the library type."

"This time I wasn't following, I just found you. Like it was meant to be."

"What's meant to be is what I am," Legend Sellers said. "And you can't change that, and neither can I."

"Bull," Drew said.

Sitting there, Legend looked older today. Smaller. And sadder. He made no move to get up or go anywhere, just put down the book he was reading. Drew saw it was called *Out of Sight*, which he thought was a movie with J-Lo and George Clooney.

Drew made a motion with his hand that asked if it was all right to sit down next to him.

"What am I gonna say, no?" Legend said. "You're more stubborn than I am, which might make you the most stubborn guy ever."

The older man watched Drew sit himself down, get his legs out in front of him, seeing the effort it took to stretch out the bad knee.

"You get that looked at?"

"It's getting better. I played today."

"Your team win?"

Not asking how Drew had done. How the team had done.

"Yeah."

They sat there for a minute, the quiet between them just part of the quiet all around until Drew finally said, "You promised."

"Promised what?"

"You wouldn't run."

"I did."

"You lied."

Legend said, "I wasn't lying when I said it. You can believe that or not. But that's what happens sometimes. What they call in books the law of unintended consequences. Stuff you say turns out to be the opposite of what you do, and that turns out to be the same as a lie. But you can't stop yourself. And that *is* the truth."

"Nobody made you run."

The man made a sound that was like a laugh that didn't make it all the way out of his throat. "I made me."

"Why?"

In a whisper, Legend said, "Because I'm afraid."

"Of what?" There was another long pause. Drew turned himself so he could watch the man's face.

Legend's eyes were closed.

"Afraid of stepping back into the light," he said.

"What about your job?" Drew said. "What about your place to live and your talk about getting a degree? Maybe even going on to college?"

"I wasn't ready," Legend said, eyes still closed. "Because I'm never gonna be ready to take that step, or the one after it, or the one after that. It's the same as in ball. When you're growin' up, there's finally a game you're not ready for."

Drew nodded his head, yeah, like he understood, even though he didn't—there'd never been that kind of game for him, even when he was the littlest and youngest one on the playgrounds back in the Bronx.

Legend said, "I can't make myself into something more. It's too late for that. This is who I am. Maybe who I was always gonna be."

Opening his eyes, putting those sad eyes on Drew now, hard.

"Liar," Drew said.

"Leave me alone, boy. Leave me *be*. This here, the bust-out you're looking at, I took a good look at him the last few days. This is me. The rest of it is just dreams. Just worry about your own."

"Too late."

"No!" His voice got louder. He dialed it right back down. "No. It's too late for me to go back to being Urban Sellers."

Now Drew was the one putting a loud voice on him. *"No!"* he said back to him. Imagining his voice carrying all the way down to the front desk, or to wherever Callie was.

"You're just a punk kid. Your whole life, you only cared about yourself, playing ball, and now you're gonna make things right for me? Who do you think you are?"

The answer came from Seth Gilbert, all the times he'd said this to Drew: "I'm your guy."

Legend actually laughed, but not in a mean way. "Are you, now?" he said. "And how do you know I won't run again?"

"You can try," Drew said. "But you're not as fast as me. Probably never were."

"You say."

"I *know,* old man."

And for the first time today, he saw some life in Legend, some little spark in his eyes.

"You're trash-talkin' me now . . . in a library?"

"Word," Drew said.

"All just words today," Legend said, "that neither one of us can back up."

Drew said, "If you didn't want to be found, you would've run farther than this. But you didn't."

Legend closed his eyes, looking tired again, and said, "You got no way of understanding this, but as you get older, your world gets bigger or it gets smaller." He let his breath out now, almost like he'd been holding it all in. "I didn't run farther on account of I got nowhere else to go."

"Where are you living?"

"Got myself a room at the Y."

"Never thought to look there."

"Shouldn't've bothered to look anywhere."

"Give up? You got to know that's not me. Tell me I *can't* do something? Now you have lost your mind."

"I may have underestimated you."

They just sat there, both of them comfortable with the quiet. Or maybe just comfortable being with each other.

"How's that paper of yours comin'?"

"Comin'."

"Doin' it on your own for once?"

"Couldn't find anybody smart to help me out with it. So, yeah."

"Look at you. Just another Hemingway."

They laughed at the same moment. Something else too loud for the library, even with the two of them stuck back here. This time they heard somebody shushing them. Drew looked up and smiled.

"So I see you made a library friend," Legend said.

Callie was standing there, hands on hips, smiling.

"I did," Drew said.

And without hesitating or asking for permission, Drew introduced her to Urban Sellers. By name. And her to him.

Legend didn't hesitate, either, stepped forward, took off his Lakers cap, put out his hand. "Pleased to meet you," he said. Even gave her a little bow.

Drew had stepped back to give them room. Or maybe just to take it all in.

As he did he noticed something: the last of the afternoon sun coming through the window, hitting Legend square.

Like he really had come back into the light.

THIRTY-NINE

Callie drove them all to the Y, about four blocks from the train station. Legend had collected his bag, which was mostly filled with the five or six books he hadn't put into storage.

Then they went back to the Conejo Valley Hotel.

The man behind the desk seemed about as interested in Legend's return as the fly buzzing around above his head. "You're back," he said, sliding a room key across to him.

"Miss me?"

"Oh, something terrible."

Drew asked if Legend wanted them to help move the boxes of books back in tonight. Legend said no, he was tired, he could manage tomorrow.

"Tomorrow you meet Mr. Shockey," Drew said. "World's greatest English teacher."

"You being such an expert on English, and teachers," Legend said. Turning back into his old self, right in front of Drew's eyes. "You told him about me?"

"Not your real name. And not *all* about you. I told him I couldn't tell everything about you in a paper. You got one of those lives that if you wrote it all, people would think it was made up."

"Sometimes I get to thinking maybe it was."

They were in the room now, Legend sitting on his bed.

"Nah, it's real," Callie said. "Like us being here with you is real. You got two point guards with you, not one. How can you lose?"

"Got real good at that over time."

Callie said, "Yeah, but I hate to lose."

Legend said, "As much as him?"

She put one of her best Callie smiles on him and said, "Not so sure about that. Someday I'll tell you about this game of H-O-R-S-E we played one time."

Drew said to Legend, "I have to know something. You gonna be here tomorrow when we come back to get you?"

Legend nodded.

"We're clear on that, right?"

"Clear," Legend said. He looked over at Callie then and said, "The young man will tell you. I took this fall a long time ago, thought it was the worst thing ever happened to me. But it turned out to be the easy part."

On the way back to the best burger place in Thousand Oaks, called P & L, Drew told her as much of the story as he could fit into the short ride, including the fall in the club.

"It's hard to see him as that guy," Callie said. "He seems so sweet."

"Sweet? *Legend?*" Drew shook his head. "Only because you were around."

"Nah," she said, "it's in him. I can always spot it when it's in somebody. She gave Drew a quick look, just with her eyes, and said, "It just takes more work with some people than others."

They went inside and ate like fools and then had banana splits for dessert, and when they were finished with the banana splits, they just sat and talked. So it was nearly eleven o'clock when they finally pulled up in front of Drew's house.

Even then, he didn't get out of the car right away.

Callie shut off the engine, like she wasn't ready to call it a night, either.

"You think he'll be there tomorrow like he said?"

"Yeah. I do."

"And you think he'll see things through once you get him with Mr. S?"

"Not a clue."

Now they sat there in silence until Callie said, "Well, a pretty interesting first date, all in all."

"Is that what this was?"

She leaned forward, before Drew had any idea what was going to happen next, and kissed him lightly on the cheek.

"Well, it sure was a lot better than H-O-R-S-E," she said.

When her car was out of sight, Drew ran for his house. Feeling as fast as he ever had.

In that moment, feeling no pain.

FORTY

After school, Drew and Callie got into her Kia and went to pick up Legend for his meeting with Mr. Shockey.

If Legend was waiting for them at the hotel.

If he'd kept his word this time and hadn't run off.

"You look more nervous than you'd be on the line with a couple of free throws to win the game," she said.

"I never get nervous there."

"Sor-ry," she said. But grinning as she did. "That True Robinson talking?"

"Nah, just me." He grinned back at her, feeling more comfortable with her all the time. Not *having* to be anybody but himself. "Just speaking the truth."

"He'll be waiting for us," she said.

"You sure?"

"I'm just going off the vibe I'm getting from the man. And I think he's tired of running."

Drew put his head back. "You know that TV commercial, where the younger guy turns around, and there's the older version of himself standing right next to him? That's what I think about sometimes when I'm with him."

"You're not anything like him," Callie said.

Like she was defending Drew *to* Drew.

Eyes on the road, Callie said, "He sounds like he was a total jerk when he was our age, on top of all the other issues he had. Not that you can't act like a jerk, telling me I was lookin' fine, girl. Or throwing one down at the end of a H-O-R-S-E game." She gave him a quick, sidelong glance. "Or being in a car you're not supposed to be in."

Driving that car, Drew thought. He'd wanted to tell her that because she was making him want to tell her everything, but he'd promised Lee.

And speaking of promises, there was Urban Sellers waiting for them out front. A backpack on him. Wearing what looked like the nicest pair of jeans he owned, a white shirt rolled up at the sleeves. No cap.

He'd even shaved.

Callie said, "Like he's waiting for the bus on his first day of school."

If Mr. Shockey had any idea who Legend was—or used to be—he didn't show it when they got to his office.

He just shook Legend's hand, said he admired what he

was doing, asked where he'd gone to high school. Legend told him where, and when, and that he'd been a ballplayer in his day.

"A great one," Drew said. "Off-the-grid great."

Mr. Shockey nodded, looking at Drew and then Legend.

"This is the player you're writing the paper about?" he said. "The playground legend?"

Urban Sellers said, "The paper *we're* writing."

"Interesting," Mr. Shockey said. "Never had a subject walk right off the page and into my office like this."

Callie was sitting on the edge of Mr. Shockey's desk. "Not sure you know just *how* interesting, Mr. S," she said.

"And now you're part of the story?"

"I'm just the wheel man," she said. "Or wheel girl."

Mr. Shockey focused his attention on Legend now. "You have a job?"

"Working for the town."

"You're willing to do the classroom work we'll need to do at night?"

"Don't have a choice if I want to do this right. And I do."

"Every night would be out of the question, with my schedule," Mr. Shockey said. "How about two two-and-a-half hour sessions per week?"

"Whatever it takes."

It was as if Drew and Callie weren't even there now, as if Mr. Shockey and Legend were having the kind of teacher-student conference Drew would have in this same room. When Drew would be the one in the chair Legend was in.

"Why are you doing this, really?" Mr. Shockey said. "There's still a lot I'll need to know, and I assume you can put your hands on your old transcripts somehow. You can do that, right?"

"My old coach can help me with the transcripts."

"Then back to my question: why?"

It was quiet in the office. Legend's big hands were folded in his lap. Backpack was on the floor next to him. Finally he said, "Because it's the right thing to do. Sometimes you can't plan it out, it's just there, and you react." He took a deep breath. "This is a way for me to start being the person I should have been. The one I hope I still have a chance to be. And that's the truth, sir."

He was answering Mr. Shockey's question, but Drew heard something else in his answer.

He's talking to me.

"You can spend your whole life hiding from the truth about yourself," Legend said, "but it will find you sooner or later. I learned that the hard way."

Callie waited for Drew after practice, the girls having gotten to go first, and passed the time by doing her homework in the Oakley library. Lee had his car privileges back—"My folks decided that taking my wheels away was like punishing themselves"—and had offered to give Drew a lift home, but Drew told him no, thanks, he had a ride.

"More mystery?" Lee said. "I thought we were past that."

"Callie."

It was just the two of them in the locker room; everybody else was gone.

"Reallllllllly," Lee said. He made the word sound like it went the length of the room. Maybe a whole basketball court.

Drew said, "Don't start busting on me, or I won't tell you stuff."

"Dude, I'm not busting on you. I'm *happy* for you. Don't know if I'd say the same for Callie, of course—"

"It's gonna be what it's gonna be."

"Deep," Lee said. "I never knew you were this deep." Then he made a motion with his hand, as if he were doing some math on an imaginary blackboard.

"What?" Drew said.

"Just trying to guesstimate how much gas money Callie is going to save me."

Lee left. Callie was waiting for Drew outside the locker room.

She said, "Before we go, you have to see something."

She led him out of the arena and into the main classroom building and up the stairs to the second floor, the hallway mostly dark.

One light came from the end of the hall.

Mr. Shockey's classroom.

Class was already in session.

He and Callie walked down there, trying not to make any noise. Saw Legend in a front seat, Mr. S sitting on his desk, facing him, legs dangling over the side, talking away.

Legend taking notes in his Mead Square Deal composition book.

"We have to get him a laptop," Drew whispered.

Callie put a finger to her lips.

They watched for another minute or so, and then left. Drew thinking that in that moment, he loved school more than he ever thought he would in his life.

FORTY-ONE

They had three regular-season games left, Coach telling them they had to treat them as if the tournament had started already, that they were all the same as knockout games if they wanted to win the regular-season title.

The first of the three was against their old friends, the Conejo Valley Christian Wildcats, the guys who'd upset them at the buzzer the first time they met, the night Drew didn't dive for that loose ball.

His knee was still sore, but not as sore as it had been. In a perfect world—when anyone would use that expression, Drew's mom would say, "Call me when you find one of those perfect worlds"—the Oakley Wolves would already have clinched the regular-season title.

Only they hadn't.

And one of the reasons was that Drew hadn't dived to the floor for that ball. In his mind, it was the same as if he'd lain down. Just given them the game.

But he evened the score at their little gym, even with Lee still parked on the end of the bench. It hadn't been the Wildcats' point guard who'd stopped Drew from going for the loose ball in that first game. Drew had done that all by himself.

Drew made him pay anyway. Not forcing it. Not doing anything on this night that was going to cost his team a single basket. But going after the kid the way he should have the first time, taking him down low and backing him in every chance he got, exploiting his natural advantage, first with his shot, then with passes when they were forced to double-team him, finding the open man, shot after shot.

Oakley was up twenty-three at halftime, and Drew knew already they could win by twice that if they wanted. But Coach finally took him out with nine minutes to go. Even with that, Drew still ended up with a triple double: Twenty-three points, seventeen assists, ten boards.

When it was over, the Wildcats' point guard, Gregg Sutter, came over and shook Drew's hand, shaking his head and grinning as he asked, "Was it something I said?"

"Nah," Drew said, "but I had to get you back for that shot you made."

"Figured it was something like that."

"See you guys in the tournament," Drew said.

"After tonight?" Sutter said. "I hope not."

In the locker room, Drew could see how relieved Lee was that they'd won without him, that his being on the bench hadn't cost his team. Even though Drew knew it was killing him, missing one of the handful of high school games he had left.

"Even Legend would have approved of your performance tonight," Lee said.

By now, Lee knew everything there was to know about Urban Legend Sellers. When Drew was finally able to tell him, he felt like he'd been let out of some kind of jail.

"Don't be so sure," Drew said. "He would've found something to rag on me about."

"Dubious," Lee said. "By the second half, I thought that guy Sutter was gonna have a restraining order taken out on you."

"You know what they say about payback."

Lee smiled, looking happy. "I'm almost positive it rhymes with rich," he said.

Drew knew he should have been happier himself on this night, getting his team a little closer to a championship, one that mattered so much to his teammates. And one that was becoming more important to Drew. Because he knew how important it was to Lee and the guys. Drew could see it tonight, every time he looked over at Lee. It was on his face, in his body language—as if he was trying to play the game from the bench.

But Drew was quiet on the bus ride back to school, staring out the window, until Lee finally knew enough to stop talking.

The same thing was nagging at Drew that had been nagging for days.

What, he asked himself, *now you have to go looking for ways to get yourself sideways, just when things are starting to go good for everybody?*

The team was winning. Things with Callie were so good they were stupid, especially when he remembered where he'd been with her only weeks before—nowhere.

Legend was with Mr. Shockey.

Drew—with Legend's input, the two of them turning his hotel room into a classroom a few times—had even finished his paper. *Their* paper—Legend had been right about that.

Both of them pulling A's on it.

First A of his life that Drew felt as if he'd actually earned.

So what was eating at him?

He knew.

Practice over the next day.

The night before the Oakley–Crespi game. Second-to-last game. Five days before the rematch against Park Prep on ESPN2.

Drew didn't like to get ahead of himself, but if they could beat Crespi and then do one of those wrestling smackdowns on Park Prep, they would give themselves a chance to win the league championship without ever leaving the Henry Gilbert Athletic Center.

In a perfect world.

He was going to try finding one of those.

Drew knocked on the half-open door to Coach's office. Coach was on his laptop. He looked at Drew over his reading glasses. "Hey," he said.

"Talk to you?"

"Sure," he said. "But what are you still doing here?"

"I wanted to wait until the guys were gone."

"Sounds serious."

"Guess you could say."

"Close the door," Coach said, "in case there are any stragglers."

Drew did. Sat down across from him.

Coach said, "How's Legend doing? Still can't get my mind around it, him being alive, you two being boys."

"He's doing good," Drew said. "He seems fixed on finding a way to get to college."

Coach said, "But we're not here to talk about him, are we?"

"No," Drew said.

He'd waited long enough. No use in waiting any longer.

"It was me driving Mr. Gilbert's car that night," he said. "It was me speeding. Me behind the wheel when the damage was done." Drew paused, took a deep breath, staring down at his practice sneaks. "I lied to you and everybody and got Lee to go along."

Drew paused again and went on. "It was all me. And I let you suspend Lee anyway."

The only sound in the room was Drew's breathing. Coach took off his reading glasses, folded them, put them next to his laptop. Closed the laptop. Folded his own hands and put them on top of it.

"You tell your mom yet?"

"I did," he said. "'Fore school this morning. She told me that the truth, even when it's hard, sets you free." He tried to smile. "Though it probably won't with you."

"No," Billy DiGregorio said. "Most certainly not with me." He moved some papers around, as if he needed something to do with his hands. Or he was collecting his thoughts.

He didn't say anything right away, so Drew kept going. "I told myself it was best for the team, me playing instead of him, justified it that way. Me playing gave *us* our best chance to win it all, hundred percent. But that was just . . . it was like this small truth wrapped up inside the lies I'd already told. And I finally figured out that I was the loser on that one, even if the team did keep winning."

"Loser how?"

"I was losing myself, I guess."

There was another long silence between them in the small room.

Until Coach managed a smile. "And they say Lee is the smart one," he said.

"Coach?"

"You're right," Coach said. "What you and Lee did was dead wrong. But you're right."

"Don't punish Lee any more than you did already," Drew said. "He never should have had to sit in the first place. He was just being my wingman. My friend."

"Lying for you," Coach said. "And with you."

"Yeah."

"Like I said, you're doing the right thing, telling me."

"Even though it could be the wrong thing for our team."

"Doing the right thing is never wrong."

"What if it costs us the championship?" Drew said.

"You're assuming I'm going to suspend you now?"

That got Drew's attention. "You're not?" he said to Coach.

Coach shook his head, not smiling now. "No, you're suspended," he said. "Because that's the right thing, too. Because if team rules don't apply to you, then I got no team. I'm just another guy in sports letting his star player do whatever he pleases."

"How long?" Drew said. "Am I going to be out, I mean."

"I'll think on that tonight when I get home," Coach said. "And when I announce it tomorrow, which I will, I'll just say that it's for a violation of team rules and leave it at that. If the reporters press me, I'll tell 'em that when they have a team, they can tell everybody everything. But that I don't talk."

"Coach," Drew said, "I'm sorry."

"Be sorry for what you did taking the car out, driving it without a license. But don't be sorry for what you did here tonight."

"But you came here to win this title."

"We'll win," he said. "Maybe we already did, you and me."

Coach asked if Drew needed a ride home. Drew said Lee was waiting for him in the parking lot.

One more stop Drew needed to make.

Seth Gilbert was still shouting.

"He's not suspending anybody!" he said. "Unless Mr. Billy DiGregorio is under the impression he hired himself!"

They were in his living room. Or one of his living rooms. Lee had dropped Drew off. Lee only lived a few minutes away and told Drew to text him when he was ready to be picked up.

Drew had said he didn't think he'd be long.

"Don't be so sure," Lee said. "That guy can talk the way Michael Phelps can swim."

Then Lee had wished him luck, saying Drew was going to need it.

He'd been right. Drew hadn't moved from the couch, watching Mr. Gilbert pace. Listening to him yell.

"Suspend *you*?" he said now, dialing it down a notch. "With the Park Prep game about to be on national TV? Where I put it, by the way? I . . . don't . . . think . . . so."

Drew said, "This isn't about Coach."

"No? Who's suspending you, then?" Mr. Gilbert said. "The Board of Ed?" He was red-faced, out of breath, like he'd been running sprints in this room, which was big enough for that. Chest heaving underneath a T-shirt that had the picture of a pit bull on it and read, "Alpha Dog."

Drew, trying to calm him down even though he knew he had no chance, said, "I'm the one who took the car."

"Forget the stupid car! You want the car? Take it. Take five more just like it."

"Mr. G, you're not hearing me. None of this happens if I don't drive the car and lie about it."

"Your buddy lied right along with you."

Now Drew shouted at him. First time ever. *"To take care of me! It's what everybody does! Takes care of* me*!"*

Now Drew was the one who felt like he was out of breath, just like that.

"It's about time I started taking care of myself," he said.

"No," Seth Gilbert said. "That's my job. *I* take care of you." Standing over Drew now, looking down at him. Like this was some kind of mismatch.

Doing what he did, talking down to people without even thinking, without hearing himself.

"When did you start thinking for yourself?" Mr. Gilbert said.

Drew slowly stood up, giving the man a chance to move back, to give him room. "Today," he said. "I started doing it today."

"You know what I mean," Mr. Gilbert said. Backing up in all ways.

"I know exactly what you mean, Mr. G," Drew said.

"How am I gonna look, you getting suspended before the biggest game of the year?"

Still not hearing himself, still making it all about him. Still thinking he was the big player here.

Drew wanted to tell him, *Figgeritout.* But Mr. Gilbert was still his mom's boss. One more time, he heard her inside his head, telling him the same old thing, mind his manners.

In a quiet voice he just said, "All due respect, Mr. G? This isn't about you. It's about me."

Then he was walking past him, toward the front door. He'd wait until he was outside to text Lee, because he needed to be outside, get himself some *air.*

When his hand was on the doorknob, he turned around.

"You're always calling me *the man,*" Drew said. "Maybe I finally figured out how to act like one."

FORTY-THREE

"He should be here by now," Drew said to Lee in the layup line.

Talking about Legend, who was still nowhere to be seen in the gym.

"He'll be here," Lee said. "But we're *already* here. With sort of a big game to play."

"Maybe he ran away again."

"That's crazy talk," Lee said.

He repositioned Drew so he wasn't looking into the stands, so he was facing their basket.

"The game," Lee said.

The championship game.

Oakley versus Park Prep.

Park Prep's gym.

Coach had given Drew a two-game suspension. The Crespi game and the Park Prep game to end the regular season. Oakley had lost them both. Lost to Crespi by a basket. Lost to Park Prep by twenty in this gym, got hammered on ESPN2, national television, Lee saying afterward when they made themselves watch on TiVo that Drew had gotten more face time on TV watching the game than King Gadsen had gotten *playing* it.

Now they were back in the Park Prep gym, having won their first two tournament games at home, against Conejo Valley and Crespi. They were back for the best kind of game there was in sports:

The big game.

The kind of big game Drew had convinced himself—or let Mr. Gilbert convince him—wasn't really coming for him until he got to the pros.

But now here they were against Park Prep, against King Gadsen, for a game that mattered more to Drew than he ever thought it could.

He wanted this game as much for himself now as he did for Coach and Lee and the guys. He'd found out that Coach had been right all along, even if it had taken Drew such a long time to hear him—that if you didn't have a team, you had nothing.

Now, where is Legend?

Ten minutes to the tip. The Park Prep gym, not as big as the Henry Gilbert Athletic Center, but big enough, was insane with noise and excitement, not just because of the home crowd, but because a lot of Oakley fans were here, too.

Just not the fans Drew's eyes kept searching for in the stands.

His mom, Callie.

Legend.

Lee actually shoved him toward the basket now, and Drew took a bounce pass from Tyler, laying the ball in, running to the end of the line on the other side of the court.

He saw them then.

Saw his mom and Legend coming through the double doors at the other end of the gym. Callie right behind them.

And one more surprise guest walking with her: Coach Fred Holman.

Drew caught Callie's eyes. Pointed to his wrist, to an imaginary watch, like asking her where she'd been. She mouthed, *Traffic.* Then she was the one pointing.

Toward the court.

Telling him the same thing Lee had been telling him: the game.

Lee clapped Drew on the back now, seeing what he was seeing, that Drew's real cheering section had arrived.

"Now can we do this?" Lee said.

"True that," True Robinson said.

Didn't matter if this was a road game or not.

Drew felt more at home than he ever had.

FORTY-FOUR

King Gadsen kept trying to get Drew to engage, all the way through the pregame introductions, eyeballing him hard, nodding his head, talking to Drew, even though he knew Drew couldn't hear.

Then, when they were lined up for the tip, King on the other side from Drew because he was guarding Lee, King came over to him, like he wanted to be a good sport, shake Drew's hand.

Right.

"I *know* I know you from somewhere," he said.

Drew looked off.

"Wait," King said, "now I remember. You're that True-or-False Robinson guy can't get a game off me. Couldn't even get on the court last time, I'm remembering right."

"Have a good one," Drew said. Wanting to add, *if you can.*

"By the time this one's over tonight," King said, "you're gonna *wish* you were still suspended."

Drew looked past him, wondering what the holdup was, and saw the refs at the table talking to the guy doing the clock.

Now he couldn't help himself—he turned back to King.

"Ask you something?"

"Why not?" King said. "I'm gonna have all the answers, all night long."

Drew said, "Talking as much as you do . . . you ever run out of *spit*?"

Drew didn't hear his answer. He went over and bumped chests with Tyler.

The two-game rest had done his knee good. What Sellers liked to call the law of unintended consequences. This one a good consequence.

If he wasn't at full speed, he was close enough. That meant close enough to being his bad self.

Park got the tip. Ball went to King. First time down, right out of the blocks, he took Lee down to the low blocks, posted him up. So focused on that he didn't even notice Drew coming from his blind side, didn't hear his teammates yelling at him to look out as Drew knocked the ball away, beat everybody down court for a layup, floating to the iron.

Imagining himself flying in that moment.

Gave a quick look to where his mom and Callie and Legend were sitting. Saw Legend leaning forward. Like he was back in the game himself.

King came out firing. But Drew doubled on him every chance he could. Coach had decided that was the best way, not having one of Oakley's bigs come over to help, not worried about Park's point guard beating them tonight from the outside. Tonight or any night.

So Drew would get right up on King, as close as he could without making contact or drawing a foul, not just trying to make it harder for him to get his shot, doing something even more important than that: trying to annoy him.

With eight minutes to go in the half, it finally worked. Oakley was ahead by four, having just gone on a 10–0 run. Drew doubled down again, King missed, then shocked everybody by actually following his shot, going for his own rebound.

But Drew had him boxed in. Frustrated, not making everything he looked at tonight, behind in the game, King shoved Drew with two hands, into the basket support.

Hard.

Foul.

And technical foul.

It would have been a dream moment if Drew's knee hadn't hit the floor when he fell.

He tried to get up, but quickly sat back down. He was limping when Brandon pulled him up. Lee started to go for King before Tyler Brandt grabbed him, held him back. Then Coach was moving all the Oakley players back, and they were all around Drew, asking him if he was all right.

He smiled at Coach and his teammates.

"Oh, yeah," he said, "look at Number One, boarding up like that."

Lee wasn't buying it. "You sure you're okay?"

"I'm fine," he said.

He'd promised himself no more lies.

But this was the championship game. And good enough was fine.

They were tied at halftime.

King finally found his shot right before the half. Lee, who'd come out hot, had finally started missing. So had Ricky, who'd hit his first four shots when his man tried to help out on Lee.

When they got to the visitors' locker room, Drew asked Mr. Shockey for some ice, saying it was just a precaution, he didn't want his knee to stiffen up.

Another championship-game lie.

The knee was throbbing.

I really have turned into Legend, he thought, *because now I feel like I'm the one fell down a flight of steps.*

But with all that? He felt good. Sore knee and all. Looked at a stat sheet while Mr. Shockey got the ice pack, didn't look at his points—he'd seen from the scoreboard he had fourteen—but at his assists.

Nine already.

He'd missed one shot from the field, a mid-range jumper that was halfway down before it spun out somehow. King had twenty. But on twenty-two shots.

At the half.

Not a team game in the other locker room, just a one-man team.

"We just keep playing our game," Coach said.

He never had much to say at halftime when he thought they were playing well, so he didn't say much tonight.

"We're better than they are," he said. "We know it, they know it. Just keep in mind: it's not us against him, even if he thinks it is. It's still us against *them*." Then he said, "Every loose ball, every possession, every pass, every rebound. *Ours*. This is our moment. Ours. Not his."

Drew understood perfectly.

At last.

He passed even more in the second half, not able to get the elevation he needed to be sure of his jumper. Even now, dinged up this way, he had enough burst to beat their point guard off the dribble when he had to. He could still get to the basket and score or get fouled.

But that wasn't his primary focus tonight. He was here to pass the ball. Like the kid from Crotona Park in the Bronx who'd passed his way into the game with the bigger kids.

Three minutes left.

Drew beat his man, got to the hoop and King fouled him, knocking him to the floor again—nothing dirty or flagrant this time, just a good, hard foul so Drew couldn't get a shot off.

Drew made sure not to show anybody the slightest sign of a limp. Just picked himself up and knocked down the two frees. He wasn't hearing Mr. Gilbert anymore, telling him not to get himself hurt. Just the cheers from the Oakley corner of the gym.

He did catch Callie's eyes on his way back up the court, big eyes of hers on him.

You okay?

He nodded.

Oakley by two. King made a three, though, only his second of the game. Park by one.

Drew went back inside with the bigs, put up a teardrop shot before they expected him to, before he'd even left his feet, drained it. He still hadn't missed from the field in the second half.

Oakley back up by one.

"Lucky shot!" King yelled at him.

Now the voice inside Drew's head was Callie Mason's.

"Not if it goes in," he said.

Forty seconds left. King got fouled by Tyler Brandt on a drive, but only made one of his two free throws.

Oakley 74, Park Prep 74.

Billy DiGregorio called time.

Before they were all in the huddle, Coach put his arm around Drew, grinning. "Got a good play for me, Number One?"

"Yeah," Drew said. "Give me the ball."

"One score, one stop?"

"Let's get our one, let them worry about theirs."

Coach put his hands on Drew's shoulders now, turned him around. "This is why we both came here," he said.

"Hundred percent."

"Whatever it takes," Coach said.

The teams took the court.

Drew wasn't going to wait too long to make his move. He hated it when he was watching a game and a point guard, college or pro, would wait too long to get a team into its play. Too often, someone ended by throwing up the kind of forced shots Drew had thrown up in that first game against Park, what felt like a thousand years ago.

He came down, threw the ball to Lee on the wing, got it back. Saw his opening, made his move into the lane, just like he had in the first game.

One of their bigs and King sealed him off with a double-team, but Drew went up anyway, making them think he was doing it again. Forcing the last shot.

But he didn't shoot. As he came down, he threw a no-look pass to Lee on the left wing, seeing the other nine, just like Coach Calipari had said. Seeing the whole court.

For a second, it must have looked as if he'd thrown the ball into the stands. But Lee knew where the ball was going and where he was supposed to be. He caught it at his waist, no dribble, knocked down a three.

Fifteen seconds left.

Oakley 77, Park 74.

King Gadsen didn't hesitate. He took the inbounds pass and raced up the court, no fear—pulled up short of the arc and buried a three of his own. The boy could talk. Lord, could he talk. But he could also shoot the rock.

Game tied again, ten seconds left.

Coach waved his arm at Drew.

No time-out.

Play.

The game they had both come here to play.

With his eyes, Drew told Tyler to come out for a high pick-and-roll. Where it had always started with Drew, all the way back to New York City.

Tyler set the pick with six seconds to go.

Drew went to his left-hand dribble. He was in the paint now. King came over to double one last time.

But then King saw what Drew saw—Ricky Colson had beaten his man, was streaking to the basket from the left.

Somebody yelled, "Cutter!"

King turned and went to cover Ricky Colson at the same moment that Park's point guard got his feet tangled up with Drew's, tripping them both up.

Drew felt himself losing his balance, about to lose control of his dribble at the same time.

Starting to fall.

In traffic, crowded from his right by the point guard, out of time, knowing he was never going to get a whistle, that no ref was going to decide the game on a foul call.

But he could still see the other nine.

Could see Lee cutting to the basket from the other side.

Before he hit the floor, Drew got him the ball the only way he could.

By bouncing it off King's shoulder.

Whatever it takes.

The old New Heights bank-shot pass.

The ball caught King just right, caught Lee right in stride, his friend laid it in one tick before the horn sounded to beat Park Prep by a bucket and win the championship.

Callie was the fastest out of Drew's cheering section, by far, once Drew's teammates stopped pounding on him for a minute. She was on the floor about the same time King and his teammates were leaving it.

When she got to him, she stood with hands on hips, shaking her head.

"You're as bad here as you are playing H-O-R-S-E," she said.

"How do you figure?"

"Well," she said, "I'm sure you didn't call bank."

"Do you have to on a pass?" he said.

Drew was afraid she was going to hug him in front of everybody, imagined for a second that picture in the papers or on TV. Eyes on Drew now as much as they'd ever been. But instead the cool girl just put up her right palm for a cool high-five.

Drew's mom hugged him with all her might, until he had to beg her to let him go, telling her he didn't want a cracked rib to go with his banged-up knee.

Drew saw Seth Gilbert then, behind his mom. No surprise that he had to be down here in the action, too. But tonight, Drew imagined him on the sidelines.

Almost out of the picture.

"You couldn't make that pass when we were on television?" he said.

When *we* were on television.

Drew shrugged. "I already made that pass on TV."

Lee came back, got Drew from behind, lifted him off his feet, yelling at him, "Dude! You did it!"

"Put me down!" When he did, Drew said, "No, *we* did it. Even the best pass in the world can't catch itself."

Lee smiled. "The point guard does make a solid point," he said.

Then his other teammates were on him again, arms around each other, Drew and Lee and Tyler and Brandon and Ricky, doing this crazy made-up dance.

Somebody was saying over the public address system that the court had to be cleared for the trophy presentation, and people started heading back to their seats. Drew found himself standing alone with Legend at midcourt.

"Last time you tried to beat King," he said. "Tonight your team beat his team."

"We did."

Legend said, "I never figured it out in the day. How to be a team man."

"You still got time."

"Not so sure about that."

"You got all the time in the world," Drew said. "See, you and me, *we're* a team now."

Legend smiled. "Heard of bank shots before," he said. "A bank pass? Boy, what was *that*?"

Now Drew smiled.

"Legendary," he said.

FORTY-SIX

"This is the most nervous I've ever been in my life," Drew said, looking around the Henry Gilbert Athletic Center, not an empty seat to be seen or found anywhere.

"No kidding?" Lee said. "I would never have picked up on that."

"Hey," Drew said, "it's a big day for you, too."

"Bigger than Park Prep?"

Drew began to vigorously nod his head yes, but said, "Nah."

"Just remember," Lee said, "this *isn't* all about you, as difficult as that might be for you to comprehend."

"I'm good with that."

"For once," Lee said, "others get to be the star."

"Good with that, too."

"Good," Lee said. "Now, go take a seat in the stands."

Graduation Day at Oakley.

The ceremony was a couple of minutes away from starting. Drew did what he'd been told, went and took his seat across the basketball floor from where the stage had been set up. His mom was already in her seat, in a new dress she'd bought for the occasion, sitting next to Lee's parents.

And next to them was Coach Fred Holman.

He wasn't dressed up in a sports jacket and tie like the rest of the grown-ups in the gym. Just wearing the same sweater he'd been wearing the day Drew and Lee went to see him in Santa Monica.

Here to see Urban Legend Sellers finally graduate from high school, graduate along with Lee and the rest of the seniors at Oakley.

Mr. Shockey had given Legend the option of having a private ceremony on his office.

Legend had said, "No, I'll wear the uniform and take the walk." Legend had turned to Drew that day and said, "Do something great for myself in a gym again."

This morning Coach Fred Holman had picked up Legend at his hotel, driven him to Drew's house. Legend had put on his gown there, saying, "I'll wait to put the cap on till I have to."

Drew had said, "It'll look better on you than that Lakers cap you were wearing the night I found you."

They were alone in Drew's room.

Legend had surprised Drew then by hugging him.

"We found each other, boy," he'd said.

The ceremony seemed to take forever. Darlene Robinson had to poke her son a few times, just to keep him awake. With that, Drew still felt himself getting the nod during the song part, and during the speeches, his eyes started to close all over again. He even excused himself, saying he needed to go to the men's room, during the speeches.

But he was back in plenty of time to watch Lee Atkins and Urban Legend Sellers take their walks.

When it was time, Mr. Flachsbart called out the name "Urban Donald Sellers." And Drew couldn't help himself—he stood up across from the stage, put his hands together, cheered somebody else in this gym.

The rest of the graduating seniors stopped the ceremony for a moment, because they were cheering, too.

Legend slowed as Mr. Flachsbart shook his hand, then handed him his diploma. The other graduates were still cheering. Then—diploma in hand—Legend was walking toward the steps.

Drew noticed he wasn't limping at all.

But then, how could he be?

In that moment, Drew imagined that Legend really could fly.

TURN THE PAGE TO READ A PREVIEW OF . . .

QB 1

Jake Cullen is a freshman quarterback playing high school football in the high-pressure land of Friday Night Lights (Texas). He is also the brother of Wyatt Cullen, who quarterbacked his team to the Texas State Championship last season—not to mention the son of former NFL quarterback and local legend, Troy Cullen. To be a Cullen in Texas is to be royalty . . . and a quarterback. All of which leaves 14-year-old Jake in a Texas-sized shadow. Being a good teammate comes naturally to Jake; being a winner and a celebrity does not. He's just like every other boy—awkward around a pretty girl, in awe of his famous family, and desperate to simultaneously blend in and cast his own shadow.

Inspired by the real-life Manning family of quarterbacks (father Archie, Super Bowl–winning sons Peyton and Eli) and set amid the football-crazy culture of Texas, ***QB 1*** is a coming-of-age story perfect for the fan of ***MILLION-DOLLAR THROW*** and ***HEAT***.

01

IF YOU WERE A HIGH SCHOOL QUARTERBACK, A *TEXAS* HIGH school quarterback, this was the moment you imagined for yourself from the first time somebody said you had some arm on you.

This was football now, pure football, the way you drew it up, but not in some playbook.

In your dreams.

And in Texas, usually your dad had dreamt all the best ones first.

Two minutes left, ball in your hands, game in your hands, *season* in your hands. State championship on the line, the new 1AA championship for small schools like yours. One of those small-town, big-dream schools. Like you were the one in the book or the TV show and you were playing for Friday Night Lights High.

Only this was *your* school, the Granger High Cowboys, against Fort Carson, in Boone Stadium, the fancy new stadium at Texas State University.

Fort Carson ahead, 20–16. Cowboys' ball at their own twenty-yard line.

One time-out left.

Even if you were a high school senior, already had a college scholarship in your pocket to the University of Texas, even if you could see yourself in the pros someday, there was no way to know if it would ever be exactly like this for you—one shot like this with it all on the line.

Unless you were somebody like Eli Manning, and you got to do it twice, in the Super Bowl, the way Eli had done it twice to the Patriots. Eli: bringing his team from behind in the biggest football game there was, winning both of those Super Bowls in the last minute, something no one—not even Eli's big brother Peyton—had done in the history of the National Football League.

But the quarterback in Boone Stadium now wasn't a Manning. It was Wyatt Cullen. Son of Troy Cullen, who'd been the greatest quarterback to come out of this part of Texas—at least until his son Wyatt came along.

Around here, people lived out *their* dreams through their high school football stars. All the ones who'd grown up in Granger and knew they'd probably die there wanted to know why you'd ever want to be one of those Manning brothers when you could be a Cullen.

Now Wyatt: in his senior year, in the last high school game he was ever going to play, his last chance to be a total high school hero and win the state title in the last minute the way his dad had once.

Like Wyatt was born to do it, born for this kind of moment, with what felt like the whole town of Granger in the stands on their side of the field.

Some sportswriter would quote Wyatt later as saying he imagined every pickup in their town was parked outside Boone Stadium, like there had been some kind of caravan of pickups all the way from Granger to here, to the kind of big game that made a small town like Granger feel like the capital of the whole world.

First down pass for him, left side, the kind of deep-out-pattern throw you needed a big arm to make, the throw all the scouts wanted to see and had been seeing from Wyatt since he became Granger's starter as a freshman. This one was to Wyatt's favorite receiver, Calvin Morton, a sophomore with big speed and big hands, tall as a tight end at six five, but skinny as a fence post. Gain of twenty to Calvin right out of the rodeo chute, as Wyatt's dad liked to say.

Ball on the forty, just like that. Room for Wyatt to maneuver now. Room to *breathe*. Clock stopped when Calvin went out of bounds. Minute fifty remaining.

All day.

Everybody standing in Boone Stadium. All those familiar faces on the Granger side, Dad and Mom pretty much in the same spot they had for home games at Granger High, fifty-yard line, maybe ten rows up. All the other Friday nights and Saturday afternoons had built up to this one. Cheerleaders on the field in the big area between the wall of the stands and the Cowboys' bench, not doing much cheering right now, almost like they were frozen in place, all those pretty girls watching along with everybody else to see how the big game would come out.

Sarah Rayburn, the only freshman on the squad, she was *that* pretty, looking so scared and so nervous you were afraid she might be about to cry, even with that cheerleader smile of hers locked in place.

Wyatt went right back to Calvin on the next play. Fort Carson's pass rush made Wyatt work this time, flushing him out of the pocket, same kind of pressure they'd been putting on him all day. But Wyatt bought himself just enough time, scrambling to his right. Wyatt was as accurate on the run with that arm as if he had all day in the pocket and hit Calvin in stride at midfield.

Clock running.

Wyatt hurried everybody up to the new line of scrimmage, going with the second play he'd called in the huddle, a right sideline route to his tight end, Roy Gilley. Another strike, Roy shoved out of bounds by their strong safety.

One minute, one second left.

Next came the play they'd talk about for a long time in Granger, in the ice-cream parlors and barbecue joints where they all grew up, where the only thing they talked about all week in those places, and on the town's one radio station, was last week's game.

Wyatt Cullen, number 10, in that Cowboy blue that matched the blue of the Dallas Cowboys, surrounded this time, huge pressure now, one of the defensive linemen with a handful of blue jersey, trying to fight off a blocker and pull Wyatt down with his free hand.

The action actually seemed to stop in that moment, everybody saying afterward that they were sure Wyatt was getting sacked, guys on both teams saying they kept waiting for the ref to blow his whistle.

But he didn't.

Because Wyatt wasn't about to go down.

Instead he stumbled as he somehow freed himself of the guy's grasp and left the pocket, pulling free, *getting* free, running for his life to his left.

Half the Fort Carson defense still coming for him.

But Wyatt wasn't looking behind him, he was looking down the field. Having bought himself just enough time to do *that,* Wyatt was able to fling the ball while running, barely taking long enough to plant his right foot, heaving it half-sidearm as far as he could in the direction of Calvin Morton.

Letting it rip even though Calvin was double-covered by a corner and a safety. Wyatt told everybody later that he'd overcooked the sucker on purpose, that's why it looked like an overthrow as it started to fall out of the sky, Wyatt wanting Calvin to be the only one with a chance to go up and get it.

And there was Calvin, going up for that pass like this was the way he'd drawn it up in his own dreams.

The safety and the corner could both jump pretty good. Yet not like Calvin Morton, who went up and outfought both of them, bobbling the ball just slightly, somehow pinning it to the front of his right shoulder pad with his huge mitt of a left hand.

Landing hard on his back, helmet going sideways as he did, somehow maintaining control of the ball.

Now there was Wyatt racing down the field, maybe as fast as he'd ever moved on a football field, waving his teammates to run with him. Not wanting to burn that last time-out in his pocket, wanting everybody lined up as soon as the ref started the clock again, having stopped it because of the first down.

He spiked the ball as soon as it was snapped to him.

Twenty-eight seconds left.

Ball on the Fort Carson seventeen.

Wyatt figured he had all the time he needed, even if they didn't make another first down, that he could make four throws to the end zone, easy, if he had to.

But he needed only one.

Needed only one because Calvin made this sweet, tight inside move on the corner, like he was going to run a post, then just flat froze the guy and the safety giving inside help when he made an even better cut, at full speed, toward the left corner of the end zone.

Wyatt's pass, dead spiral, hit those big hands as softly as your head hitting your pillow, and it was 22–20, Granger.

Now it had become the high school moment, in Texas or anywhere else, they all dreamed about, going ahead in the last seconds of the big game like this.

Couldn't tell it by watching Wyatt Cullen, though. He was the coolest guy in Boone Stadium, pointing up to where his parents and his kid brother were, all of them losing their minds the way everybody around them was.

There was Sarah, the close-up of her face they use not only in the TV highlights, but also in the *Granger Dispatch,* looking about as happy as a high school girl ever could, eyes on Wyatt.

There was old Coach John McCoy, his Granger jacket halfway

zipped the way it always was, no matter how hot the Texas weather was, showing you the white shirt and the tie he always wore, had worn since he coached Troy Cullen in games like these. Coach getting some love from the TV cameras his own self, as they liked to say in Texas, calmly holding up one finger, not saying the Cowboys were already number one, not getting ahead of himself, just telling his boys to kick the point after.

Clay Smolders's kick was center cut. Now it was 23–20 for Granger.

Fort Carson managed to get off three desperation heaves. When the last one fell harmlessly to the ground at around the Granger forty, it was over.

Then Wyatt Cullen was in the air, above it all, carried around by the bigger guys on his team. Even looking cool up there, above the action now instead of in the middle of it. Smiling when the cameras closed on him, like he was exactly where he was supposed to be, like he knew all along that this was the way his day and his high school career were supposed to end.

His kid brother, Jake, froze the scene right there.

Hit the remote and froze his big brother on TiVo. Right there on the close-up, on Wyatt's smile. Like Wyatt really had known all along, since he first played catch with Troy Cullen in the pasture behind the barn, the first time Dad was the one telling him he had the arm.

Jake pointed the remote at the big screen, sat there in the quiet den, waiting for his buddies to come pick him up and head over to Mickey's Bar-B-Q, wondering all over again what the view was really like up there for Wyatt. What it was like to actually *be* Wyatt Cullen, even though he'd grown up in the same house with him, looked up to him his whole life.

Jake: wondering if he'd ever get anywhere near a moment like that at Granger High.

Or if he'd ever even be the first-string quarterback at Granger High, whether he was a Cullen or not.

TRAVEL TEAM

Danny may be the smallest kid on the basketball court, but no one has a bigger love of the game. When the local travel team cuts Danny because of his size, he's determined to show just how strong he can be. It turns out he's not the only kid who was cut for the wrong reasons. Now Danny is about to give all the castoffs a second chance and prove that you can't measure heart.

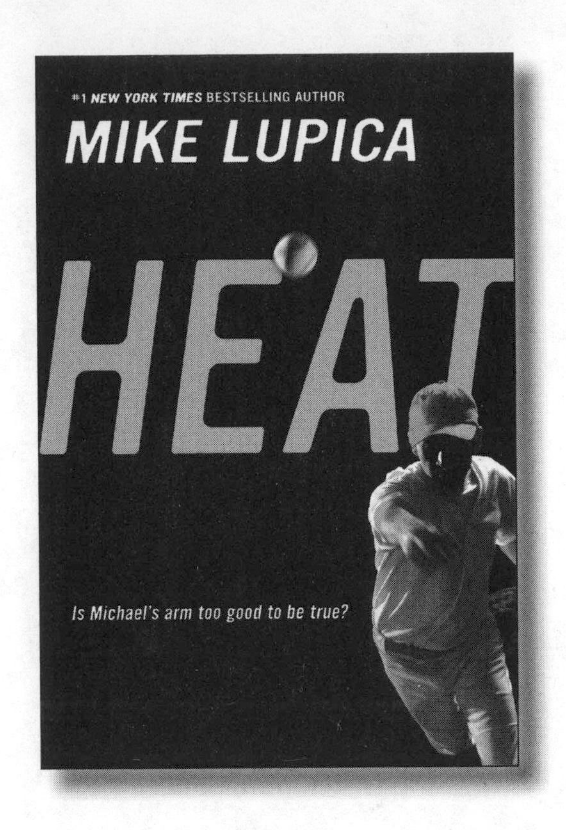

HEAT

Michael has a pitching arm that throws serious heat. But his firepower is nothing compared to the heat he faces in his day-to-day life. Newly orphaned after his father led the family's escape from Cuba, Michael carries on with only his seventeen-year-old brother. But then someone discovers Michael's talent, and his secret world is blown wide-open.

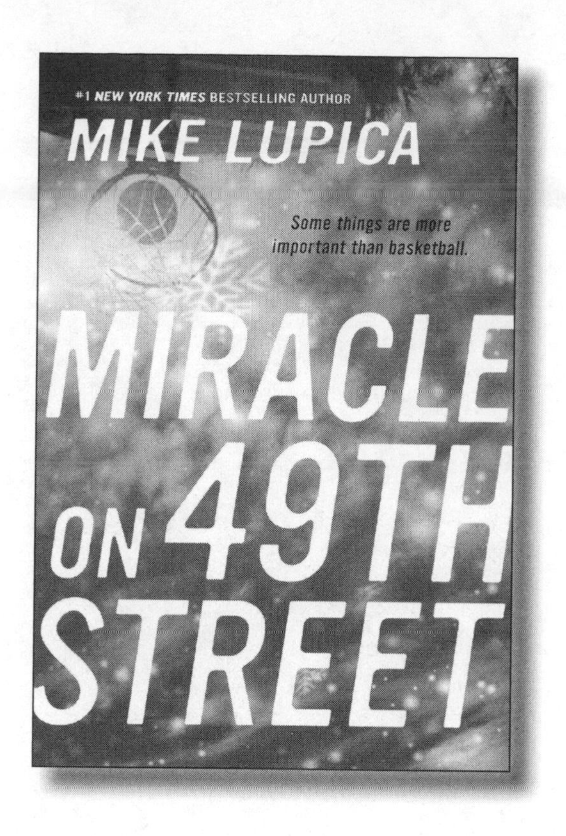

MIRACLE ON 49TH STREET

Josh Cameron is MVP of the championship Boston Celtics. When twelve-year-old Molly arrives in his life, claiming to be his daughter, she catches him off guard. But as Molly gets to know the real Josh, she starts to understand why her mother kept her from him for so long. Josh has room in his heart for only two things: basketball and himself.

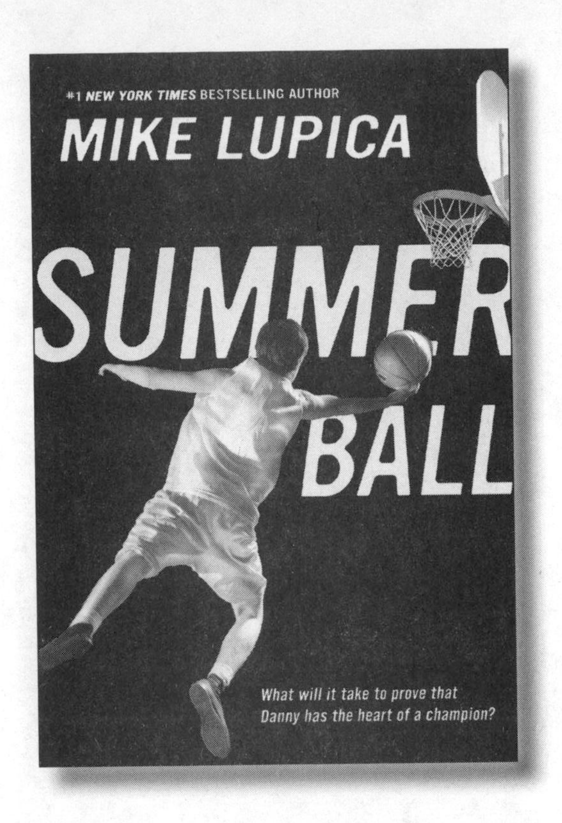

SUMMER BALL

Leading your travel team to the national championship may seem like a dream come true, but for Danny, being at the top just means the competition tries that much harder to knock him down. Now Danny's heading to basketball camp for the summer with all the country's best players in attendance. But old rivals and new battles leave Danny wondering if he really does have what it takes.

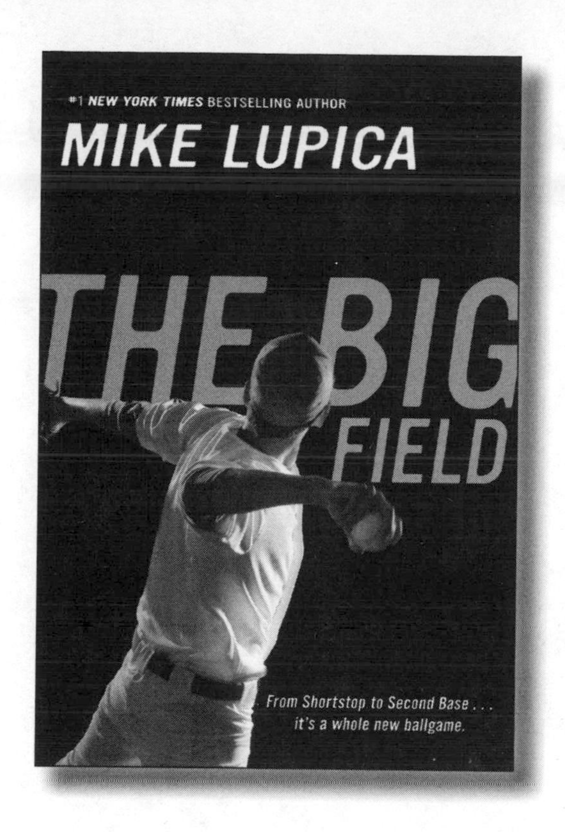

THE BIG FIELD

Playing shortstop is a way of life for Hutch—which is why having to play second base feels like a demotion. But Hutch is willing to stand aside if it's best for the team, even if it means playing in the shadow of Darryl, the best shortstop prospect since A-Rod. But with the league championship on the line, just how far is Hutch willing to bend to be a good teammate?

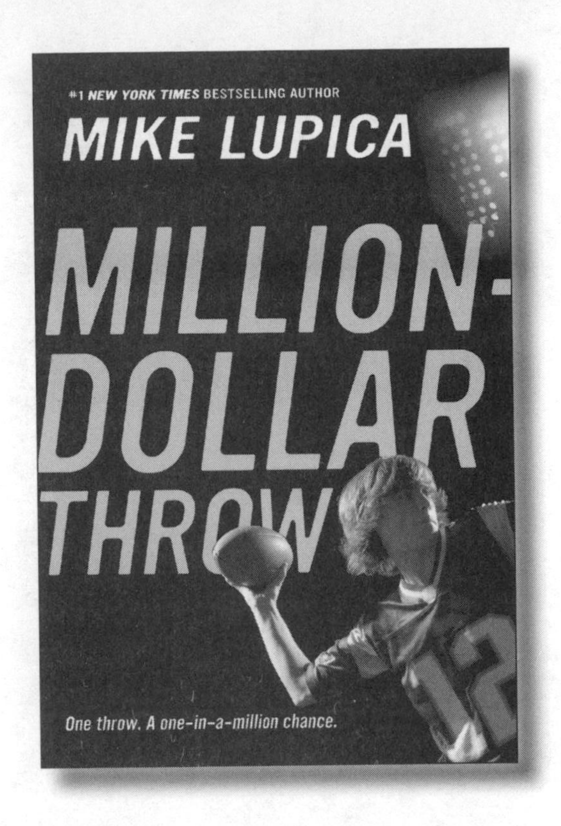

MILLION-DOLLAR THROW

Everyone calls Nate Brodie "Brady" because he's a quarterback, just like his idol, Tom Brady, and is almost as good. Now he's won a chance to win a million dollars by throwing one pass through a target at halftime of a pro game. The pressure is more than he can bear, and suddenly the golden boy is having trouble completing a pass . . . but can he make the one that really counts?

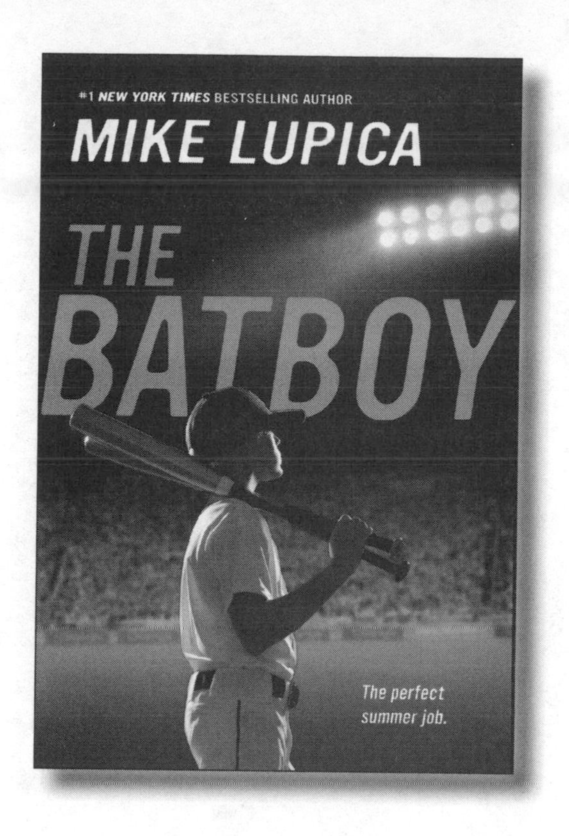

THE BATBOY

Brian is a batboy for his hometown major-league team and believes it's the perfect thing to bring him and his big-leaguer dad closer together. This is also the season that Brian's baseball hero, Hank Bishop, returns to the Tigers for the comeback of a lifetime. But when Hank Bishop starts to show his true colors, Brian learns that sometimes life throws you a curveball.

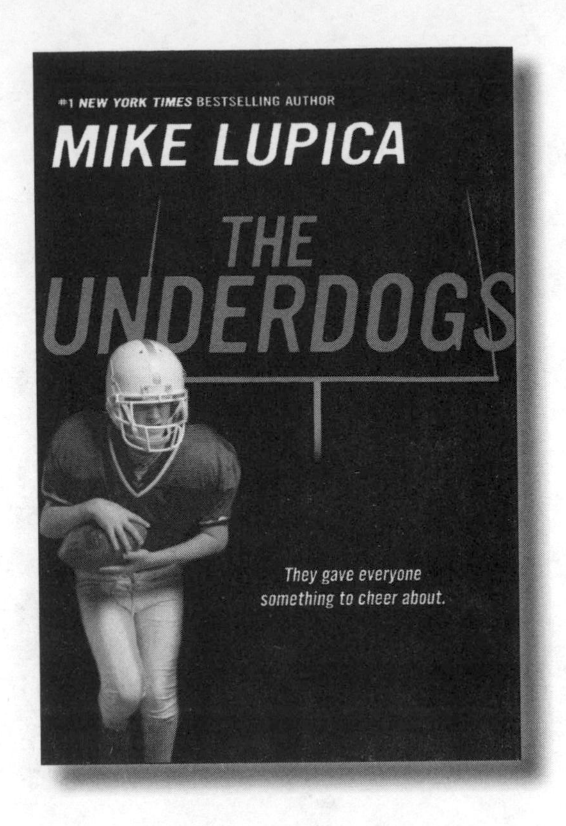

THE UNDERDOGS

Will is about the fastest thing on two legs in Forbes, Pennsylvania. On the football field, no one can stop him. But when his town experiences a financial crisis, putting many of its residents out of work, it's up to Will to lift the town's spirits by giving everyone something to cheer about.

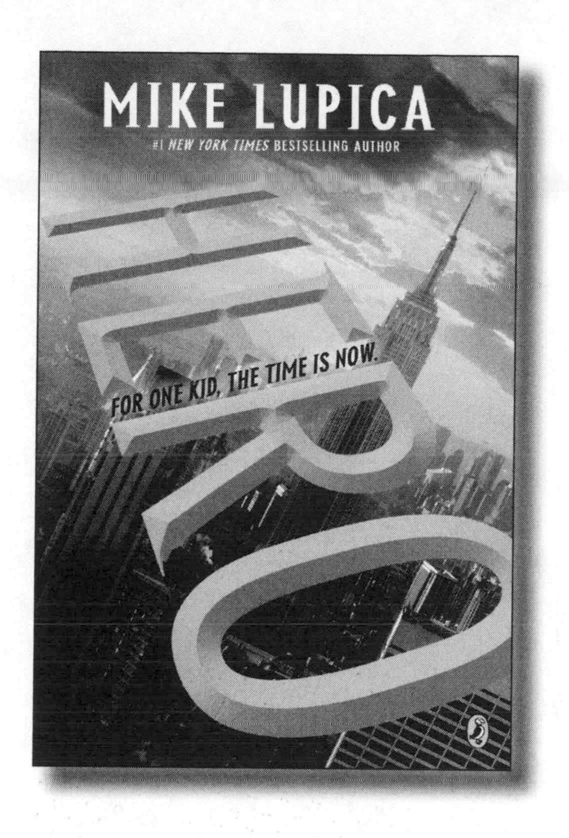

HERO

Zach thought he knew his dad—former football star, special adviser to the president. But then Zach's father's plane crashes under mysterious circumstances. Now Zach is left without a clue of who *he* really is: a fourteen-year-old superhero.